THE FOREIGNERS

THE FOREIGNERS
A Novel

Based on the Journey of Childhood Friends
Who Emigrated from Ethiopia

NEWAY ATNAFU

This is a work of fiction based on real-life scenarios. It is not intended for scholastic reference. Names, characters, events, places and incidents either are the product of the author's imagination or are used fictitiously, and any resemblance to actual persons, living or dead, businesses, companies, events, or locales is entirely coincidental.

Copyright © 2024 by Neway Atnafu

All rights reserved.

Self-published in the United States by Neway Atnafu. Philadelphia, Pennsylvania

Copyright fuels creativity, encourages diverse voices, promotes free speech and creates a vibrant culture. Thank you for buying an authorized edition of this book and for complying with copyright laws by not reproducing, scanning or distributing any part of it in any form without permission. You are supporting indie authors and self-publishing.

Library of Congress Control Number (LCCN) cataloging Data:

Name: Atnafu, Neway, Author.

Title: The Foreigners.

Library of Congress Control Number: 2024908912

ISBN-979-8-9901397-1-8 (Paperback)

ISBN-979-8-9901397-2-5 (Hardcover)

ISBN-979-8-9901397-0-1 (eBook)

Printed in the United States of America

To find out more about this book and the author visit TheForeignersByNewayAtnafu.com, and use the contact information in the website to plan for an author speaking event or for information on bulk purchases.

All internet addresses given in this book were correct at the time of going to press. The author and publisher regret any inconvenience caused if addresses have changed or sites have ceased to exist, but can accept no responsibility for any such changes.

Dedicated to everyone who was forced to leave home, betrayed by close ones, outcast by their communities and subjected to government discrimination; to those who stood against all odds, refused to be victims, challenged norms and designed their own path; and to the ones who made it to the better side, forgave the past, moved into a promising future and still managed to share their blessings with others who needed assistance.

CHAPTER 1

On a hot and humid afternoon, three teenagers in a small Ethiopian village called Kako sat under a Warka tree[1] to rest after a long walk. The teenagers had footslogged to Kako from their neighborhood in Jinka, a town seven miles west. Ever since completing high school, they made a habit of hiking through the surrounding mountains, chatting, debating, and sometimes, agitating each other.

Mannie started it. "So why did your parents call you Henok?"

Not that Mannie hadn't heard the story before, but he liked to get a rise out of his passionate and brilliant friend, Henok, and this was the best way.

"It was not my parents; my grandfather was the one who named me," answered Henok proudly.

"Isn't it from the Bible?" Mannie asked, knowing full well what the answer was.

"Well, that depends on which Bible you read," Henok replied, puffing up his chest.

"What do you mean?" Mannie pretended to need an explanation. Willie stayed silent. He, too, had heard this discussion before and these

---

[1] While the saying in the US is that "the story of every American city begins with a river," for Ethiopians, the story of every city begins with a Warka tree. Historically significant, the Warka tree is the center of every Ethiopian city. Pedestrians found shade from the often-burning sunlight, locals held public gatherings, and some traditions even worshiped the tree as the channel to the Almighty and offered sacrifices beneath.

kinds of conversations bored him.[2]

"If you are an Ethiopian Orthodox Christian, you will find the story in the Bible. But if you are an Evangelical, their version does not say much. Henok is in our Amharic language. The English translation is Enoch," replied Henok.

"Ohhh, really?" said Mannie with a smile on his face. He winked at Willie, who hid a laugh.

"Yes!" Henok was just warming up. "The Bible says Henok was the great-grandfather of Noah and one of only two people taken up to heaven without dying. Seven generations since Adam and before the Genesis Flood, the prophet Enoch wrote several scriptures known as *The Book of Enoch*. It said God gave Enoch visions that enabled him to travel to heaven and communicate with the holy ones. There, the sons of God showed him what was coming for the future generation. In the book, Enoch wrote stories about the fall of the watchers and the angels who fathered the Nephilim. He warned the world that the Messiah was approaching and that mankind had to be prepared, as 'the Lord comes with ten thousand of His saints to execute judgment upon all that are ungodly among them of all their ungodly deeds which they have ungodly committed, and of all their hard speeches which ungodly sinners have spoken against him.'"

"That sounds like crazy talk," the usually quiet Willie chimed in. He could no longer tolerate Henok passionately explaining this legend as if it had any validity.

"No, this is real. You can read the history yourself if you want. I have some reference books if you're interested." Henok wiped sweat off

---

[2] For the record, Willie distrusts historical facts, as he believes historians tell their own version of truth.

his brow.[3]

The friends had now left the shade of the Warka tree and kept walking, listening to Henok.

"Anyways," Henok continued, "today the Ethiopian Orthodox Church and Beta Israel, also known as Ethiopian Jews, are the only ones who accept *The Book of Enoch* as canonical scripture and an important reference of the apocalypse."

Willie didn't say anything, and Mannie shaded his eyes, watching the horizon. It made the walks go quicker when Henok told stories because they were always so engaging.

"You know, my grandfather was a good man. When I was a kid he used to tell me I was destined to do great things. He would say, 'I believe in you, Henok. One day you will lead my family's return to our homeland in Wollo.' I will not forget that!" Henok looked at his friends. "Don't you hate living in this town?"

Henok didn't seem to expect a response. Mannie was about to speak, but Henok didn't notice. He just kept talking. "I was born here; my father, too; it was my grandfather who migrated to this place during the war in northern Ethiopia. Yet the locals still treat us as if we are foreigners who do not belong here. Their initial excuse was that we don't speak any of the local languages, even though the town's official one is Amharic. And now, it doesn't matter if you speak their language, they identify you by name and exclude you from benefits. Do you know my cousin Abiyot?

---

[3] If you choose to believe Henok's words, here is the book's background story. Around AD 360 the Early Christian Church authorized the Bible to be constituted of only sixty-six scriptures. One of the books the church considered but decided to not include was *The Book of Enoch*. The church's scholars claimed to have found historical inconsistencies. Ethiopian religious scholars of the time protested the decision by their Jewish and Roman counterparts as racially motivated. The book was originally written in the ancient Ethiopian language of Ge'ez.

She was denied access to the state-sponsored trade school because her name indicated her ancestors weren't native to the region. She tried to argue that her mother was from a local tribe, but they rejected her, saying, 'your father's heritage defines your identity.' It is unbelievable!"

"Well, the people are not the problem, it's the government!" Willie argued, energized by the turn in conversation. "What kind of government creates a constitution that designates a region to the majority tribe, turning minorities into second-class citizens on land where they have lived for centuries?!"

"The Ethiopian government?" Mannie responded jokingly. He knew Henok was very passionate about this topic.

"Government, people, they are both the same to me!" Henok threw his hands up.[4] "Government is established by our people. This is what the majority want. They are more concerned about preserving their outdated culture, dying language and invisible identity than advancing access to education, economic expansion, and establishing a free and fair justice system." Henok took a deep breath.

"Whether they like it or not, change is inevitable. Society's way of life transforms with time. Prosperity demands the integration of resources and cultivating diversity in societal values and perspectives. I can't stand living in a society that doesn't believe better days are ahead of us, a society so determined to make the future look like the past. Something has to

---

[4] He's right. Ever since the new government came to power a few years ago, the country had been restructured into ethnic-based regional states. Each state was named after the majority tribe in that region. The political, civic and public sector institutions were required to be staffed primarily from the majority tribe. Minorities were largely excluded from key positions. It was the government's position that the quality of work was secondary to the people's right to self-rule. They believed self-governance would enable peace, which would then provide an opportunity for prosperity.

happen." Henok stared at the sky and started walking faster.⁵

#

Henok Desta Agegnehu was born and raised in Jinka, Ethiopia. He liked identifying himself by his full name; it gave him a sense of purpose and pride. His father, Ato Desta Agegnehu, was a tailor and his mother, Woizero Zeineb Dagne, was a housewife and part-time brewer.⁶

Henok's grandfather, Ato Agegnehu Yimer, was also a tailor, and founder of the family's tailoring shop. From him, Ato Desta learned tailoring skills and eventually inherited the family shop as his father battled with Parkinson's disease.

When Desta turned eighteen, his father sent him on his first journey to Wollo. Desta had never traveled anywhere outside the twenty-mile radius of Jinka. Yet he was not excited about this trip. He knew his father had plotted with his uncle in Wollo to find him a wife. Desta considered arranged marriage as a thing of the past and knew he was not ready for

---

⁵ Imagine being treated like a "foreigner" in your own country, the only place you'd ever known and the land that your grandfathers had called home. That was the case for those born from a minority tribe, who were mixed race and whose parents came from tribes outside of the newly established regional territories. The government had no desire to address their concerns. To make matters worse, the majority tribes were also demanding greater autonomy and removal of "foreigners" from their land.

⁶ Ato and Woizero are titles prefixing names in the Amharic language, the most widely spoken language in the country, and are the proper way to address adult men and women, respectively, similar to Mr and Mrs in English. Ethiopian naming structure is hierarchical; a person's given name is followed by the father's and then the grandfather's names. There is no family name in Ethiopian culture. The hierarchical naming system also serves to keep track of ancestry. For example, if two people want to marry, elders would count the individuals' ancestors to ensure there is no shared relative within seven generations. This helps avoid inter-family marriages which are considered abnormal in the Christian-dominated nation.

a serious commitment; he'd never even had a girlfriend. But all this did not matter; he had no choice; he could not reject his father's wishes.

The bus used to come to town only twice a week, every Tuesday and Friday, linking Jinka to Addis Ababa, Ethiopia's capital and normally taking two to three days. Desta boarded the Friday bus and waved goodbye to his hometown. The wind blew on the dirt road, suffocating the bus with dust. Potholes knocked the bus up and down, dropping luggage on passengers from the overhead compartment. Yet Desta never felt as alive as he did then.

The uninhabited mid-highland region presented fascinating views of nature. It seemed as if the only life in the area were those seated and standing in the overloaded bus. As they climbed the mountain, Desta looked out the window and wondered what would happen if the tires lost their grip and the bus slid down the edge to the deep gorge. How long would it take for help to arrive?

A shouting match suddenly interrupted his woolgathering. He noticed the bus had stopped moving halfway up the hill. The driver and his assistant were urging everyone to evacuate. They had to unload the bus so it could roll up the hump. Some people were complaining they had disabilities. Mothers were screaming, "I have a baby!" And others were claiming to be too old to walk up the hill.

Desta quickly jumped out of the car and pulled the driver away from the crowd to make a plan. They hatched a compromise to let those with restrictive conditions stay on board, while the men moved the luggage to the top of the hill. After an hour of hard work, the bus was able to move forward. Everyone was excited; the men marched behind the bus singing and dancing. They forgot for a moment that they were all tired and hungry.

From then on, their ride was relatively smooth. The driver told passengers that the dirt road would be over when they reached the city of Arba Minch.[7] By midnight, they arrived.[8] There was no electricity in Arba Minch past midnight. Darkness made the city look like a ghost town. The bus pulled into a pension. They had to get some sleep before resuming their journey in the morning. Desta agreed with his seatmate to share a room to save money.

The next morning at 6:30 a.m the headcount was complete, and the bus continued its push to Addis Ababa. A few miles from the city, Desta could not believe what he was seeing. It was water covering a huge area; he could not see the land on the other side. Until then, the Neri River in Jinka was the largest body of water he had ever known.

"This is Lake Abaya," said the passenger next to him.[9] "Those animals you see on the edge of the lake are called crocodiles."

Desta fell in love with the captivating view. The lake was surrounded by forests. He did not even see a single house at the shoreline. He felt jealous of those wild animals cherishing such beauty alone.

After Lake Abaya, Desta drifted off to sleep, only to be poked awake. It was a little girl trying to sell him roasted corn. The bus stopped and everyone but Desta left for lunch.

---

[7] A city famously known for its forty natural water springs, Arba Minch is located 150 miles north of Jinka.

[8] Think about it, the bus had to be traveling at less than 15 mph; they had been on the road all day!

[9] What this passenger did not say, but should have told Desta, was that this is one of the most important water resources in Ethiopia. The area's economy is dependent on fishing and irrigation. Adjacent to the lake there is Nech Sar National Park, home to many endangered wild animals and a popular tourist destination. The south, where they are now, is called Gamo. The northern part is home to the Wolayita people. The other side of the lake belongs to the Oromos.

"Mister, you're in Boditi," the girl told him when he asked. He looked at the corn and felt his mouth salivating. He gave the girl two quarters and received a corncob in return. The corn was roasted in a pot filled with salty water.

Desta took a bite and looked at the girl. "Wow! It's juicy!" he complimented, and gave her a thumbs-up.

"Thank you!" She smiled in response. She was confident of her cooking skills and was expecting this reaction. He watched her walk away in search of other customers.

Desta hopped off the bus to relax his muscles. Thirty minutes later, everyone returned and the bus continued to head north. In the evening, they finally arrived at the bus station in Addis Ababa. Desta disembarked holding a small plastic bag which he used to carry some clothes and sandals. He became overwhelmed by the crowd size at the station. Everyone seemed in a rush and rude! At the station there were more buses than cars he had seen in his entire life in Jinka. Desta hurried in search of the ticket office. He had to purchase another bus ticket to continue his journey north in the morning. It was getting dark and he worried the office could soon close.

There were several ticket offices as the station served over one hundred routes. Desta walked door to door, searching for the right one. When he finally found the office, he was shocked to see the waiting line. Then there were the passengers who jumped the queue and argued they were there first. After some nerve-racking encounters, he finally got his ticket and left the station.

Desta tried to remember hotel directions his father told him, but he could not think straight. He was distracted by the bright lights of

Merkato.[10] The pushing and shoving of pedestrians reminded him of what he used to visualize of Babylon during his Bible-study days. Every hotel he enquired at was unaffordable. He was tired and hungry. He took a seat in a corner of a hotel patio and ordered dinner and a pitcher of Tej.[11]

The more Desta thought about the journey, the angrier he got. *How did my father send me on the road knowing I was not carrying enough money?* Then he calmed down and said to himself, *maybe this is a test of my resilience before my father can trust me to handle business trips in the future.* Desta looked around and thought to himself, *so what's the plan?*

One of the prostitutes stood up from her seat on the other end of the patio and walked straight to his table. She met his gaze, smiled, and sat down next to him.

"Haayiii, I'm Ruth. What's your name?" She smiled at him. "You look troubled. Is everything okay?"

"Ahh…yes, yes. I'm just tired, that's all," he mumbled. "Desta. My name is Desta Agegnehu. I'm going to Wollo to meet my uncle and the rest of my extended family."

"That's nice! It must be exciting for you!" She tried to cheer him up. "Is this your first time coming to Addis Ababa?"

He nodded. They started talking as if they had known each other for a while. Desta told her that he was worried he would run out of money before reaching Wollo. He was also open about what would be waiting for him there: a wife-to-be! Yes, he would be marrying someone he had never seen before!

But Ruth was not surprised at all. She grew up in a small town as well. She ran away from her parents' home two years ago after finding out that

---

[10] One of the largest open marketplaces in the African continent.

[11] A popular Ethiopian honey-based homemade wine.

her father had agreed to give her away as a second wife to a man three times her age. She told Desta that the person who gave her a ride out of town introduced her to her current occupation. She described some of her good and bad experiences since the time she left her hometown.

Captivated by her beautiful smile and fascinating stories, Desta lost track of time. He then realized that he needed to go find a place for the night. But he didn't want to cut off the conversation. As if she could read his mind, she proposed, "Look, my roommate found a customer and she will stay out all night. Why don't you crash at my place?"

It was an evening he would never forget. Young Desta tasted the bad apple! He fell for Madeline's perfume! He indulged in his first romance! Desta was not sure what to feel. All his life he was reminded that intimacy before marriage was a sin and yet, here he was sleeping next to a prostitute. He didn't have any regrets, either. And why should he? As far as he was concerned, she was a beautiful and smart girl and he was happy to have met her. As Desta contemplated the events of the night, Ruth woke up and reminded him that if he was going to keep his seat on the bus, it was time to leave. They went to the bus station together, where she helped him find the correct bus for his destination.

"When will you return? Will you visit me when you get back?" she asked.

He grinned at her. "Of course. I promise. This isn't the end of our story. Trust me!"

"Okay, good!" She smiled and gave him a hug. Even though he sounded sincere, something told her that he was not coming back.

Desta tried to hide his emotions as he boarded the bus and waved goodbye. Ruth watched until the bus disappeared from sight.

#

It seemed as if the bus was scaling mountain upon mountain. They would finish climbing one plateau for a moment, and before they knew it, begin ascending another mountain. The passengers began babbling about the driver's handling of the vehicle. Everyone was worried that this bus seemed too old to deliver them safely to their destination. To make matters worse, a rumor was spreading that the vehicle had failed inspection the night before, but the agency decided to use it anyway because all the other buses were already booked. As the passengers were bickering about this and that, the bus slowed down near a small market.

The driver's assistant yelled, "You're in the town of Debre Birhan. You have a thirty-minute lunch break. We need to get back on the road fast, if we are to cross Tarmaber[12] before dusk!"

The lunch break went by fast, and the passengers loaded back onto the bus. For two more hours, they climbed mountains until Desta wondered if there were any mountains left in Ethiopia to climb.[13]

As the sun began to fade, the bus started to race down the hills. The altitude continued to drop and everyone became optimistic that they probably would not have to spend the night on the road. At around 8:00 p.m, they arrived in a town called Shewa Robit. The bus driver proposed spending the night there, as it would be unsafe to continue riding in the dark. There were no street lights at the time, at least in this

---

[12] A mountainous area well known for making drivers' lives very difficult.

[13] Geology enthusiasts will find this part of the journey fascinating. They are at an altitude of over 10,000 feet above sea level, in the area at the central junction of the Great Rift Valley. It divides Ethiopia from north to south, creating adjacent but separate mountain ranges. Scientists believe that the rift continues to develop at a rate of 6-7 mm per year, splitting Africa into three distinct plates.

part of the country.

But the passengers revolted, refusing to get off the bus. They insisted there was only one place they would be sleeping tonight and that would be in their home. They urged the driver to keep moving. Since Desta could not afford to pay for a hotel, he collected tips from the passengers and gave the driver an incentive to keep moving. After a brutal five more hours on the road, they finally arrived at their destination.

"Ladies and gentlemen!" announced the assistant driver. "We are finally in the city of Kombolcha! The heartland of Wollo! The city of brotherly love!"

The crowd cheered. The door opened and everyone picked up their luggage and disappeared into the darkness. But Desta was not thrilled as he still had a long walk to get to his uncle's home and there was no way he would be able to do that at this hour. The place was very dark; Desta could not even see the road. Tired and lonely, he spent the evening lying at the corner of a fence near the bus stop.

"Cock-a-doodle-do! Cock-a-doodle-do!" The crowing of the neighborhood roosters woke him up. Desta quickly got off the ground and wiped the dust from his pants. He looked around and saw churchgoers dressed in white; they were rushing to arrive before the morning prayer started.

Desta hurried toward one of them and cleared his throat. "Ehhh.... uhuhuhu." Desta realized he was being mistaken for a homeless man, so quickly got to his point. "Excuse me ma'am, can you please guide me?"

"Who are you? Where are you from? Where are you going?" The old lady bombarded him with questions.

"My name is Desta; Desta Agegnehu Yimer. I grew up in the south, but my father was from around here. I am here to meet my relatives.

My uncle's name is Abreham Yimer. Do you happen to know him?" He expected a quick response because he had heard that everybody knew everybody around here.

But the lady took a long pause and said, "Do you mean Ato Abreham Zeleke? Woizero Ejigayehu's husband? If so, their house is not too far from here."

"No, no. Ato Abreham Yimer." Desta realized the "everybody knows everybody" quote was probably just a saying. "I am told he is popular at the Ancharo Giyorgis church." He shared more details.

"Woowoo!" the lady replied. "Young man, you have got a long way to Ancharo. I never climbed those mountains, but I wish you good luck." She empathized with him. "Go straight down this road until you see a house whose doors are painted yellow and then turn left," she said while pointing the direction with her hand. "Then, turn to the left and that will get you on the main road. Turn right on the main road and go straight. You will come across a small stream and that should tell you it is the right direction. Keep going and you will arrive at a crossing where you will also see a small farmers' market. I know it is then left, but from there on you will have to ask people." She wished him well and went on her way.

Desta thanked her and strode in the direction she pointed him. Whenever he came across a pedestrian, he asked for directions to check that he was still on the right course. He walked about eight miles out of town to the highlands in the southeastern direction. Finally, he arrived in front of farmland that, based on the directions he received, belonged to Ato Abreham Yimer.

There were three separate houses on the farm, built from wood and mud; the roofs were some form of grass. The small house in the back had an open door; he guessed that would be the kitchen. The second house to the left of the kitchen looked like a barn where the goats and chickens were kept. The big house in the front had nice doors and windows. He could tell it was the main residence. Desta walked closer and knocked on the door.

A man opened it.

"Are you Uncle Abreham?" Desta asked excitedly.

Ato Abreham was expecting Desta. He quickly realized who this tall and handsome young man was; Desta had the look of his father. The two hugged and kissed each other on their cheeks. A woman, Abreham's wife, Kedija, and her three children were standing behind, eagerly waiting for their turn. More and more hugs and kisses for Desta. He never experienced so much love. They all surrounded him, asking questions over questions. So many big smiles, he could almost count everyone's teeth.

A few moments later the family gathered around a circular dining table. Desta was seated between Abreham and Kedija, and his three cousins filled the rest of the seats. Lunch was semisolid camel's milk with hot pepper spread on top and served on Injera.[14]

This was an adventure for Desta as he had never seen a camel, let alone eaten its milk! Abreham passed the first bite to his wife, fed Desta a mouthful and then his children.[15] They all continued to feed each other. Looking at the traffic line of hands, it seemed as if nobody was feeding themselves.

When lunch was over, Kedija came back from the kitchen holding

---

[14] A traditional Ethiopian bread that looks like an extra-large pancake.

[15] It is an Ethiopian tradition for friends and family to feed from each other's hands, which is known as Gursha.

cups and a jar of Tella.[16] Sipping the unfiltered beer, the men went on talking about everything they could think of.[17]

#

Desta fell in love with the culture of Wollo. He regretted some of his actions as a kid in Jinka, where he used to distance himself from his parents' heritage to fit into the local lifestyle. Everyone he interacted with was genuine and polite.

One night, one of the girls from the neighborhood insisted that she would wash his feet. He'd never had anyone offer that before. He remembered how much he used to dislike it as a kid when he had to wash his father's feet before bedtime. So he refused. But the girl stressed that she would not return home until he let her. Puzzled and shocked, Desta received a traditional pedicure and the girl was able to return home with a smile on her face. It turned out that to treat guests by washing their feet was considered the ultimate show of respect in the local custom and a good deed that would earn credits from God.

Three weeks went by very quickly for Desta. He was introduced to many relatives and made some new friends as well. But eventually, the time came to address the main reason that brought him to Wollo. The time for an adult talk arrived.

Early one morning, Abreham was reading Wudasie Mariam, a Christian book that praises the Virgin Mary. Desta overheard his uncle's rehearsal and followed the voice outside.

---

[16] A traditional Ethiopian beer made at home from a type of grain called Sorghum.

[17] At the time, Ethiopia did not have an age limit on alcohol consumption. It was up to parents to decide what was best for their children.

"You woke up early today! Good! Come over here son; have a seat." His uncle closed the book. Over the last few days, Desta had been coming home late. He had been busy attending dinner invitations from distant relatives and his father's old friends.

"Ahhh, it's very cold out here," Desta complained.

"You will get used to it. In fact, today is not so bad." Abreham smiled. "I have exciting news."

Desta could tell where the discussion was heading. His uncle had been giving hints.

"Really?" replied Desta, trying to hide his true feelings.

"Yes, really." Abreham looked eager. "You see, I found you an excellent girl! She will make a great wife! She is very beautiful! And she studied until elementary school before she had to drop out to assist her mother in the house. I have heard nothing but great stories about her. I know her father very well too; we have attended the same church since they moved to the area five years ago. Trust me, she will make you a strong man! Our Ancharo women are dedicated to their family."

Desta was still surprised to learn that tribal divisions did not exist only in Jinka, they were everywhere. If it wasn't for ignorance during his childhood, he could have learned about the culture of Wollo from his parents. He didn't even know Wollo was a big area with many different tribes living in cities, towns, and villages. He always imagined it as one large place where everyone lived in peace and unity.

As a child, his friends called him "Wolloyew!" And now that he was in Wollo, he learned he was from a specific tribe within Wollo. He was an "Ancharo"!

When departing Jinka, Desta already accepted the idea of returning with a wife. But he preferred having a say in picking his future soulmate.

"Uncle, may I get to meet her and see what we have in common?" Desta requested politely.

"What do you mean by 'what we have in common'? How can you have anything in common with a person you have never met? You, this generation of men! You are destroying our tradition with this nonsense about dating a person to get to know them before becoming involved in any serious engagement. All that is doing is spreading fornication and adultery!" Abreham snarled. "Listen to me carefully, son. This Western civilization and individual freedom crap is the act of atheists to deceive God's people. We live in a community. A strong community is built upon principles and societal values that bond its people. We have our own values and cultural norms. Copying others' traditions with the perception of 'modernization' will destroy the fabrics that unite us as a nation." Uncle Abreham blustered, waving his hands to emphasize his thoughts.

Desta would have liked to challenge such generalization and misconception, but he needed to show respect to his uncle. He was an elder, after all. But one thing became clear to him: he better keep secret Ruth and the fascinating night that he had spent with her…maybe even forever! Meanwhile, his uncle kept moaning about their great culture and how civilization was threatening its existence.

Desta tried to redirect the conversation. "So what is her name?"

But Uncle Abreham was not finished. "Good relationships are built on faith. If you accept her to be your wife and she accepts you to be her husband, then the marriage will be holy." So he sidestepped the question and continued his preaching. "That is when you begin to build common interests. You will shape her thoughts to fit into yours. God will bless you with children. She will be your rock that you use to build your destiny. You should pray to God's blessing, instead of asking these nonsense questions."

"I hear you, uncle. So what's next?" Desta finally gave up.[18] Why fight a battle impossible to win?

"That's a good question, son." Abreham relaxed. He knew Desta would come to his senses and follow the tradition. "We will send elders to convince her parents of the marriage proposal. The elders will need to arrive with presents. We will prepare a young cow as a gift to the family. Most likely, the parents will not accept the proposal in the first meeting. An appointment for a second gathering will be made. As the parents contemplate the proposal, our elders will return offering a mule as an additional present. I know her father is an avid rider. So that should then seal the deal." Abreham clearly laid out the process.

"Zeineb. Her name is Zeineb. She is fifteen years old.[19] She will turn sixteen in two months. She fetches water from the stream down the hill every Wednesday and Saturday evening. I'll make arrangements so you can watch her secretly. You do not want to interact with her. If

---

[18] Within the short period that he had spent in Wollo, Desta learned that the culture here was a lot stricter than his hometown. It forbade a man from directly approaching a woman romantically. The honorable way was to negotiate with the parents through mediators. Establishing pre-marital romance could spell trouble, especially for the woman who would be labeled as bringing shame to her family. This outdated tradition had been changing across Ethiopia. But Wollo was one of the places where progress was slow. The society's pride in their identity and history enabled naysayers to easily garner public support against "foreign" philosophies.

[19] There was no age restriction on romantic relationships at the time. Most communities used to allow underage marriages, and in some it was the norm for parents to arrange engagements for their children when they were very young. Once the kids grew up to an appropriate age, whether they wanted to be with each other or not, they would be wedded to one another for the rest of their lives. Of course most of these traditions have evolved over time as societal values transformed and Western modernization expanded across the country.

any word reaches her parents about you dishonoring her, there will be no wedding."

"Thanks uncle! I won't let you down!" Desta appreciated his uncle's goodwill gesture.[20]

Young Desta understood that he was not sent to break their tradition.[21] In fact, his father wanted him to bring the tradition to the next generation in Jinka. Desta was determined to honor his father's wishes. But he was also making his own plans for the family that he would build with Zeineb. For now, he had other things to worry about: what does she look like? Who would be his best man? Would he ever get a chance to see Ruth again?

#

Four weeks later, Desta and Zeineb got married in a traditional Ethiopian Orthodox Church ceremony on a Saturday morning.

---

[20] Historically, the people of Wollo had lived under ultra-orthodox Christianity. Wollos trace their roots from the biblical King Solomon and the Queen of Sheba. Their region was home to some of the greatest Ethiopian dynasties, such as the Zagwe dynasty which ruled large parts of the East African territory from ~900 to 1270 AD. It was established by descendants of a Solomonic dynasty known as The Kingdom of Aksum that ruled over territories on both sides of the Red Sea. The last king of the Zagwe was overthrown by Yekuno Amlak, who reformed the Solomonic dynasty that lasted up to the mid-20th century. Today, some remnants of the Zagwe still exist in Wollo including the rock-hewn monolithic churches of Lalibela, a UNESCO World Heritage Site.

[21] Islamic tradition also has had a significant influence on the culture and lifestyle of Wollo. Historians say that the religion entered northern Ethiopia during its very inception when the Prophet Muhammad directed a group of his followers to seek refuge in the Christian nation to avoid persecution in the homeland in Mecca. As the religion continued to spread, Wollo became its principal center for religious study and cultural propagation, where today about half the population are Muslim.

When the church ceremony was completed, the bride returned to her parents' home. There were wedding parties at both houses. A few hours later, the bridegroom, accompanied by his entourage of friends and family, headed to Zeineb's home singing and dancing. The men chanted:

> *We have come on time, this house's mom and dad;*
> *Please open the door, it's cold outside.*
> *Our son Desta, honest and proud;*
> *Blessed be God, Zeineb is in good hand.*
> *Give us our queen, we can't wait no more;*
> *Our hive's empty, hollow without her.*
> *We're grateful you brought her this far;*
> *She's got a new man, he'll take it from here.*

As the men flocked in, the bridesmaids raised their voices. With competing songs from the two sides, it sounded like a screaming match. Following the tradition, the bride sat in the middle of the house surrounded by her bridesmaids. Since the marriage had already taken place at the church, the parents had already given away their daughter. The bridegroom arrived to claim his queen. But the ladies would not allow an easy passage. The men would have to roll their shoulders dancing the traditional Ethiopian "Eskista." Then they would have to push through the wall of ladies to reach their prize. As Desta finally held Zeineb's hand and led her out of the house, the songs got louder. The bridesmaids accompanied her, singing:

Our dear bride, don't feel sad, don't feel sad;
Turn by turn, everyone gets married.
Mr bridegroom, you should be proud, you should be proud;
We deliver you this beautiful bride.
Our dear Zeineb, sweet like honey, sweet like honey;
Love is the train, marriage is destiny.
Desta of Jinka, please keep her safe, make sure she's happy;
You're now her shelter, she's your duty.

For the next three days, Ato Abreham's home was the town's party center. Young men and women of the neighborhood sang and danced. Being surrounded by friends and family reduced the level of discomfort the young couple would have felt as they got to know each other for the first time. The following Saturday, the couple visited Zeineb's parents for dinner. She initially felt awkward noticing her parents treating her as an adult visitor. No more "Go help your mother!" or "Pick up the dishes!"

Her brothers and sisters were looking at her differently as well.

When dinner was over, she took her siblings to the back and made a pact. "I will visit you as much as I can. Please take care of our mother. Please write to me as much as possible; I will do the same. I love you all so much!" She cleaned tears from her eyes as she returned to her seat.

Desta tried to comfort her as they bid farewell to the family and left.

A few weeks later, the newly wedded sixteen-year-old and her eighteen-year-old husband were on an early-morning bus to Addis Ababa. They sat silently together, each not knowing what to say to the other. On her first trip out of town, now married to a young man she barely knew, Zeineb let tears pour down her face as she realized that she might never see her parents again. Desta held her hand tighter, as if saying she was not alone.

Zeineb tilted her head on Desta's shoulder and took a deep breath. This was her life now. She knew it was up to her to make the most of it. All of a sudden, Zeineb's face started to glow as she envisioned the beautiful family that she would build. Based on what Desta told her about Jinka, she had no doubt that she would have a great life. She was beginning to enjoy his presence and felt confident that he would make a good husband.

Zeineb quickly adapted to life in Jinka. She also had help from fellow Wolloyes who quickly became one of the strongest and most successful immigrant communities in the town. Desta continued to work at the tailoring business with his father. Zeineb started a side business catering Tella and Tej at the local market.

About a year after leaving Wollo, Desta and Zeineb welcomed a baby boy. They called him Henok. Henok was a handsome baby boy with a beautiful smile. Zeineb was very happy because her son closely resembled her father. The family welcomed their second child a couple of years later. They called him Mekit. Despite the wonderful family that God had blessed her with, Zeineb sometimes still felt homesick. She missed her little brothers and sisters and could not wait to return to Ancharo with her kids to visit her family. She strongly believed in the tradition that children need to receive blessings from their grandparents.

CHAPTER 2

Willie and Henok were lifelong friends. Their homes were across the street from each other. Henok's mother, Zeineb, used to tell them that they were born at the town's clinic on the same day. Willie had just been born there when Zeineb began labor. That made Willie the older of the two by about half a day, which was very upsetting news for Henok. Growing up, they used to fight each other a lot; age difference was the main source of their conflict.

Zeineb always tried to be a fair mediator. Willie's mother passed away when he was five years old leaving behind him and his two-year-old sister Frehiwot. His father never wanted to talk about the story surrounding their mother's death. But Willie had heard the rumor that she was killed in a car accident while traveling from Jinka to Arba Minch on a minibus.[22]

Willie's full name was Awlachew Dechasa, his father's was Ato Dechasa Gupta and his mother's was Woizero Tiruwerk Bekabih.

---

[22] Willie's mother used to work in logistics for the township and regularly traveled for business. One unfortunate afternoon, the minibus carrying her and twenty-seven others was on the way to Arba Minch. Halfway there, in a desert land known as Woyto, the minibus was attempting to cross a dangerous, dry sandy channel known for flash floods during rainy seasons. Drivers sometimes assumed the sandy channels were dry and attempted to sprint across, only to discover water under the sand was sinking the tires. As they dug to free the tires, flash flooding would turn the dry channel into a violent river, with heavy rain from nearby mountains quickly able to create a river over 10 feet deep. With no time for escape, the flood would wash out anything in its way. The rumor was that the minibus was a victim of a flash flood, with everyone inside drowning including Willie's mom.

Dechasa and Tiruwerk were both born in a very small town in an area known as Shewa, in central Ethiopia. When they reached high school, news of their romance became the talk of coffee shops across the town. At the time tensions had peaked between the area's rival ethnic Oromo and Amhara people, after a rebel group from the Oromo tribe burned down about a dozen homes of Amhara residents. Dechasa was from the Oromo tribe, but Tiruwerk's parents were Amharas. Dechasa's parents threatened to disown him unless he stopped the romance with Tiruwerk. And her parents also rejected the relationship; they threatened to send her to a monastery where she would become a nun. But the lovebirds escaped from town and disappeared with the intention of never returning home again.

Dechasa and Tiruwerk traveled to Jinka and rented a room. He got a job as a store clerk and she started work as a server in a restaurant. Their jobs were hard labor and low paying. But they were happy to be free from judgment. They were just two strangers to their new neighbors. Sometime later, Tiruwerk found a good job at the township's Logistics Department. With help from Tiruwerk's connections at work, the couple were also approved to receive public housing. Their new home was across the street from their new neighbors Desta and Zeineb. The two families became close. Desta helped Dechasa in opening his own store, while Zeineb became the godmother of Frehiwot. Willie and Henok spent most of their time playing together.

The passing of Tiruwerk shook the foundations of the family. Dechasa became an alcoholic and emotionally distant from his children. He made it a habit of staying out late, leaving the burden of childcare to housemaids. Heartbroken by the loss of his mother and disappointed by his father's behavior, Willie's personality also changed. He became quiet and reserved. Frehiwot was still too young to grasp the impact of events at home. She loved her brother very much. One evening, after the maid tucked them in their beds and left the room, Frehiwot whispered to her brother. Willie was just staring into the darkness; usually he could not sleep until he heard his father's footsteps entering the home.

"Willie?" Frehiwot whispered.

"Hi Friye, aren't you asleep?" He was the only one to use that nickname; everybody else called her Fre.

"I miss Mommy!" Fre cried.

"Me too, Friye!" Willie tried to control his emotions.

Her voice went lighter as she asked, "Will she ever come back again?"

Tears suddenly filled Willie's eyes. He wept as he replied, "No, she won't."

She stayed quiet for a little bit. Then she broke the silence again and said, "Willie, I'm scared!"

"Do you want to come sleep here with me?" he asked his baby sister.

Without saying a word, Fre went and snuggled under his blanket. He hugged his sister tight and kissed the back of her head. At that moment, Willie understood that he needed to become strong and look after his little sister. Fre quickly descended into a deep sleep. A few moments later, Willie heard footsteps entering the house. The footsteps made their way into the children's bedroom; then stilled in the darkness, his father listening to make sure they were asleep. Willie pretended and began to snore. Then he heard footsteps moving away and into the master bedroom. As he gathered his thoughts and tried to monitor his father's activities, Willie also fell into a deep sleep.

Henok sympathized with Willie and Fre. Henok's younger brother Mekit was a year older than Fre. The four children loved playing soccer on the street as the closest soccer field in town was a few miles away. But they had to be careful of vehicles; some drivers would not slow down even for children. One time Mekit barely escaped from being hit by a car; the driver did not even bother to stop and check if he was okay. But the kids were used to it, seeing it as an adventure and a hot story to talk about for the rest of the day.

One day when first graders Henok and Willie returned from school, Mekit and Fre were waiting for them on the street. They had breaking news to share. Zeineb was in labor at the clinic. As soon as the students dropped their school bags at home, they wanted to go to the clinic. But the adults refused to allow them.

The next morning Desta told his kids that their mother had twins. He told them to get ready to go meet their new sisters.[23] Excited by the news, the boys went running to tell their friends. "We are having baby sisters! Two babies!"

Then they ran back to their father, Willie and Fre following right behind them. As they walked to the clinic, they bombarded Desta with questions. This probably was the first time the kids were excited to visit the clinic. There was a nauseating odor there, but the children were too busy welcoming the new additions to care. The new babies were named Feker and Selam.

#

---

[23] Twins were not common at the time. The clinic did not even have the tools to tell if a mother was having multiple babies. So Desta's family had no idea that they were in for a treat. Even the midwife nurses did not realize immediately there was a second baby.

Henok and Willie were among the top students in their classes. They studied together at home. They always wanted to be in the same class; but that never happened until they reached seventh grade, when they were included in a special class.[24]

All the students in the special class were very smart. They studied very hard and the grades were very competitive. By the end of the first semester, both Henok and Willie scored higher average grades than they ever did before. Unfortunately, the two friends also found themselves ranked at an all-time personal low in their class, with Henok in 8th place and Willie in 10th.

Henok was visually disturbed watching the ranking on his scorecard. He dropped his head down on the desk and sobbed silently. But Willie was chill; he saw it coming. He tried to calm his friend down and reflect on the facts. The reality was that those students who ranked above them had also outscored them in previous years; it was just that they were in different classes. Now that all the smartest students were competing against each other in the same class, the gap between them became obvious. Willie advised Henok to look at the bright side and reminded him of their personal-best grades. But Henok could not stop crying. As they walked home, he cried all the way.[25]

Zeineb was on her way to do grocery shopping when she spotted

---

[24] At completion of grade six, students had to take a region-wide examination which was intended to gauge their competencies and their abilities to cope with middle school. Students who failed the exams would be required to repeat sixth grade, even if they had good grades on their school's scorecards. Students who scored among the highest would be assigned to what was called "Special Class." The rest of the seventh-grade classes were organized randomly. Henok and Willie scored among the highest, and thus entered the special class.

[25] It was not like Henok to cry. Some students cried all the time, but Henok was not accustomed to these grades.

Henok and Willie returning from school. She rushed forward and said, "What happened Heniye? What happened?"

But he had no response. He looked into his mother's eyes and continued to whimper. Zeineb hugged her son and patted his head. She turned to his friend and asked worriedly, "Willie, why is he crying?"

"He's upset because he ranked eighth in class. That's all!" replied Willie as he lifted his two hands in exasperation.

Zeineb compassionately held her son's face with her hands and said, "Ohhh my boy! I am so sorry! I know this must be upsetting for you!"

Henok nodded his head while cleaning tears from his face and tried to say something. But all that came out of his mouth was "y…e…s Mamaye!" in a broken voice.

Zeineb encouraged her son to use his anger as strength and said, "Don't worry Heniye, you will get them next time! This is only the first semester!" She then held his hand and said, "Now come with me to the market and I'll buy you sugar cane."

She invited Willie to join them. But he respectfully declined and said, "Thank you, Emama Zeineb. But I must go to Friye. She's home alone."

Henok never liked going to the market, especially with his mother.[26]

---

[26] The grocery market was an open field where mostly farmers and some small-scale merchants sold their products directly to consumers. The market was surrounded by retail stores for clothing, jewelry and other imported items such as rice, pasta and canned food. There were also nearby restaurants and bars. The market had no shelves or tables to organize the fruits, vegetables and grains. All products were set up on the ground; some farmers used plastic or fabric sheets to protect their grains from getting dirty. There were no refrigerators to store eggs, milks and other dairy products. There were also no cages holding the chickens, goats and sheep which were brought to be sold. At the time, most residents prepared their own meat at home because there were not enough butcher stores to serve the masses. And there were also no chairs in the market for all those farmers who traveled tens of miles from their villages on foot. A few hundred to a thousand customers shopped in this market at any given day.

She took her time looking around for a good deal on prices, choosing clean and unrotten products, and making friends with the farmers for future networking. Then there was all the talk with everyone she knew; they exchanged reviews of their experiences and referred each other to quality products. Henok also never felt comfortable with his mom in a place surrounded by naked people.

The villagers traditionally opposed wearing clothes. The ladies were naked above their waist and the men only wrapped a scarf around their genitals. Henok would never forget how he felt last time at the market. His mother squatted and started to check the potatoes on the ground. When the seller, a villager, kneeled to negotiate prices, his long wagon got exposed from between his hips. Zeineb didn't seem to be bothered and continued to negotiate. Henok, on the other hand, was very embarrassed and a little upset. But he also knew there was nothing he could do.

On top of all that, he did not appreciate the loud noises in the market as everyone bargained prices. Then there was the pushing and shoving of the crowd, the perfumes of the females, the odors of rotten butters and the smell from animal feces.[27]

His happiest moments had always been when they reached the fruits section. He loved chewing sugar cane. His favorite fruits were mango, papaya and passion fruit. He also enjoyed eating the fresh-from-the-tree pineapple, banana, peach and berries. His mother had to manage the weight of the load that they would have to carry on their walk back

---

[27] Most products were transported to town on the back of donkeys, mules and horses. The farmers would park the animals on the streets around the market. One of the funniest events in the neighborhood was watching aggressive male donkeys and horses as they broke from their leashes and tried to mate with their female counterparts.

home. But Henok wished she would just pack all the fruits and leave everything else.[28]

#

During the second semester of the school year the relationship between Henok and Willie began to crack. Henok became obsessed with his grades and class ranking. He started to compare his test results with his classmates. He grew angry and irrational whenever he scored lower on exams.

In the class seating arrangement, Henok was paired with another student named Anteneh Ashagre. Anteneh was a fast talker with an impulsive personality. He added fuel to Henok's anger by exaggerating every incident. But Henok was pleased to have a friend who would listen to his frustrations without attempting to correct him.

In the meantime, Willie's seatmate was Seble Gebeyehu. Seble was very beautiful and one of the smartest students in the class. She was extremely reserved and usually spent most of her time with her best friend, Yalem Kebede. As Willie became frustrated with Henok's competitiveness, he started to spend break times with Seble and Yalem. They played puzzles

---

[28] In addition to its scenic atmosphere, the shopping market presented adventurous events. Farmers who finished selling their crops would fill nearby restaurants and bars. Cassette stores would play loud songs on outdoor speakers to attract customers. Drunk people would fight on the streets; nobody would try to break them up until the police arrived. There were over ten local tribes around the town including Ari, Male, Bena, Mursi, Hamer, etc. Most of them were involved in different farming sectors including pastoralists, beekeepers, gardeners, crop producers and more. So the products they would bring to the market were also different. As the public gatherings offered troublemakers a chance to spread rumors, the evenings would become chaotic from tribal conflicts. The market was basically the economic and entertainment center of the town.

together and challenged each other with math and spelling questions.

The three students also created their own little book club and started reading together. The first book they read was an Amharic fiction titled *Adefris*. The book uncovered generational gaps and cultural barriers of the early 20th century; the main characters Adefris and Tsion regularly clashed against traditional, political and religious norms as they attempted to form the future they envisioned for themselves. Willie, Seble and Yalem took turns reading a section out loud while the others listened. They picked specific stories from the book and passionately debated which character was right or wrong. This fun and interactive activity strengthened the bond between the three students.

At the end of the school year, Henok was saddened to find out that his ranking remained the same. His mother worried about her son's moodiness and urged his father to do something about it. So Desta enrolled Henok in a summer Bible-study program to help him change his focus. The Bible study teacher's name was Merigeta Estezia.[29] He appreciated Henok's competitive personality and encouraged him to speak his mind. Henok became a popular student in the program. He quickly grasped the teachings and was not afraid to profess these to other students.

Willie's summer plans were more ordinary. He spent a lot of time around home. He helped Fre and Mekit study English and math. Whenever he could, he also tried to assist his father at the store. But Dechasa did not want his son to get involved in the business, encouraging him to do other things instead. With Henok spending more and more

---

[29] Merigeta is a surname in the Ethiopian Orthodox Church; it is given to religious scholars who are also skilled in gospel songs. Henok did not think that Merigeta Estezia's voice was that good, but of course he did not say this aloud.

of his time at church, Willie started to hang out with a neighborhood kid named Kedir Ebrahim.

Kedir was raised by his grandmother. His mother moved to the city of Atlanta in the United States when Kedir was a child. Kedir had never heard of his father. But he always felt the luckiest kid in the neighborhood because his mother used to send him toys and action figures from the US. At the time there were no toy stores in his town.

Other kids had to build their own toys. They used wires and cardboard to make cars, mud and wood to create action figures, and soccer balls using worn out socks and trashed plastic bags. But Kedir was the special kid in the neighborhood with flashy attire. He was the only one to own sneakers. He even had a Dominique Wilkins jersey.[30] He recently got a new bike.

One morning Willie saw Kedir standing on the side of the street with his bike. He walked closer and said, "Hi Kediro."[31]

"Hi," Kedir responded while holding the bike.

"Why aren't you riding?" Willie asked.

With hesitation, Kedir said, "I don't know how to."

Willie had also not ridden a bike, so they agreed to try together. They pushed the bike to a nearby sloped street. First Willie hopped on the seat and Kedir pushed the bike down the hill. As the bike burst forward, accelerating down the hill, Willie tightened his grips on the handlebars and tried to maintain his balance. Unfortunately, as the bike approached the bottom of the hill, he could not steer the wheels to stay on track. Willie's hands froze and he could not keep his balance. He crashed into the side ditch. He fell onto the ground and rolled like a ball.

---

[30] At the time, not many people in town even knew about basketball.

[31] Kedir's nickname, used only by close friends and relatives.

Willie quickly pulled himself up. His entire body was covered with dust. He felt irritation all over and he was bleeding on his right foot and arm. But Willie was not discouraged. In fact he could feel his adrenaline pumping and something from inside saying "that was fun, keep trying!" So he brushed the dust off his clothes, muddied his injured body with dust to stop the bleeding, picked up the bike and started pushing up the hill.

The next turn was Kedir's. But after watching what happened to his friend, Kedir wasn't sure if he had the appetite to try.

But Willie encouraged him. "Come on Kediro! You can do this! Look, if you get scared, all you have to do is pull the brake and slow down."

With hesitation, Kedir sat on the bike. Willie pushed it from behind and the bike started to spiral down the hill again, this time carrying Kediro. As the bike descended, Kedir was swamped with fear. He began to scream, calling his grandmother's name, "Abiyiyee! Abiyiyee!"

Midway down the hill he pulled the brakes on both the front and rear wheels. As the bike was forced to make a sudden stop, the force threw Kedir forward. He fell badly on the ground and rolled down the hill like a soccer ball! As Kediro cried out, neighbors rushed to help him.

Hearing her grandson's voice while she was washing dishes in her backyard, Kedir's grandmother ran out of the house. She hustled down the hill while yelling, "Who did this to my child?! Wollahi, I'm coming for you!"

Sensing trouble on the horizon, Willie vanished from sight!

Willie and Kedir did not speak to each other for a few days. Kedir's grandmother complained to Dechasa and blamed the incident on Willie. She ordered Kedir to never play with him again. But a week later, the kids forgot about it and they started biking together again.

#

Summer was over and the kids returned to eighth grade, the most important year. They'd take a standard exam at the end of it. Their qualification to pass into high school would be dependent on the exam results. Going to high school was considered a major achievement at the time. Jinka had the only high school in the area. As the number of students grew rapidly, the high school was running out of space, so the pass rate was adjusted based on the school's capacity. If Henok was able to pass the examination, he would become the first generation in his entire family tree to reach high school. That meant a lot to him! He was determined to make it happen.

Willie was happy to be back in school too. He had not seen Seble or Yalem all summer long. He was full of smiles as he greeted his classmates. Yalem gave him a big hug. But Seble looked shy and greeted him with her eyes and teeth instead. The girls were chewing gum. Seble gave him one. While chewing their gum, they exchanged their summer whereabouts. With everyone in the class engaged in group conversations, the noise in the room felt like the British parliament's debate session.

Anteneh was the usual troubled kid. He told Henok many stories about his summer encounters. In one story he witnessed thieves abducting a little kid from his neighborhood.

He said, "I saw one of the thieves running away while carrying the kid on his shoulder and I shouted 'Thief! Thief!' I could tell the thieves were from the Bena tribe."

"What? Why would they abduct a child?" Henok asked.

Anteneh leaned forward, lowering his voice to a dramatic whisper. "I later heard that the lord of the tribe had died two days prior. Their tradition requires a child to be sacrificed and the dead lord's coffin to be painted with their blood, otherwise the ghosts will destroy cattle and murder the lord's heir. But nobody in the village volunteered to sacrifice their sons. Thus, the villagers decided to steal a boy from the town and make him the sacrificial lamb." Anteneh waited to see his friend's reaction.

"That's terrible. Did anyone stop them?" Henok was in disbelief.

"Everyone in our neighborhood came out of their houses holding swords, machetes, knives and sticks. We chased the thieves in the direction of their village. I was in the front giving the marchers directions because I saw which way the thieves had gone." Anteneh took a long breath. "But I got tired of running and could not keep up at the front. Halfway to the village, the marchers caught up with the thieves. The thieves dropped the kid and ran away. I tried to keep pushing forward, then I watched the marchers returning. In the middle of the crowd was the kid's father carrying his son on his head. We returned home singing and chanting."

Henok could not tell if Anteneh was making up the story or if it was real.

Before Henok could confront his classmate, Anteneh folded a paper, made an origami helicopter and said, "Watch Heni!" He targeted one of the girls seated on the other end of the room.

Henok tried to stop him. "Don't do it Antu! She will report you to the principal!"

Anteneh smiled and said, "She is shy. She doesn't have the guts to report me." Then he threw the flier in her direction. But it did not reach the target. It fell on another kid named Kibrom Fiseha, a tall and beefy kid who was known for his bad temper.

Kibrom stood up holding the flier and shouted, "Who threw this on me?"

The room became suddenly quiet. None of the students spoke a word. But they all led him with their eyes toward Henok and Anteneh.

"You!" Kibrom jumped over chairs and ran in their direction.

"It wasn't me! It wasn't me!" Henok tried to wash off the sin from his hands.

"Don't be scared, dude! What's he gonna do?" A defiant Anteneh gripped his fingers tight and prepared to fight.

As soon as Kibrom got within hand's reach, he started throwing punches at both Anteneh and Henok.

Anteneh dodged the attack, but Henok got struck on his face and fell backward on a chair. Then he got up quickly and kicked Kibrom's behind with his left foot.

Anteneh punched Kibrom in the face.

Kibrom grabbed Anteneh's shirt and pulled him closer.

"Watch out for a head kick!" Henok tried to warn Anteneh, but it was too late!

Kibrom dropped Anteneh with a monstrous headbutt.

Then Henok jumped and climbed on Kibrom's back. As the two wrestled to take down each other, Anteneh was still on the ground looking like a drunk old man.

As if they were watching WrestleMania, none of the other students attempted to interfere. With the noise getting louder, students from nearby classes began to pour in to watch the show. The teachers finally arrived and broke up the fight.

"Show's over!" It was the school principal. "Everyone out! Right now!" he ordered.

Everyone feared Principal Ashebir more than their own parents. His punishments were known to be barbaric. Principal Ashebir held Henok's right ear with his left hand, Kibrom's left ear with his right hand and ordered Anteneh to lead the way to his office. He then kicked Anteneh from behind with his right foot and told him to walk faster. He dragged the other two by their ears all the way to his office.

Typically Principal Ashebir would punish such a misconduct by whooping the children with his famous stick until his hands got tired. But today he was in a good mood. He gave them an ultimatum. "For the next five days you will water the school's flowers by fetching the water from the river down the hill. Or you will be banned from school for two weeks. It's your choice!" Then he sat back in his chair and waited for their response.

Kibrom got very scared. He didn't want his father to find out. Ato Fiseha had warned him saying, "If I get called to the principal's office because of you, I will kick your butt so hard that it will carry you from here to Adi Kuala. Abune Aragawin, I'm not kidding!" Kibrom did not want to find out if his father meant what he said; he also had no interest in visiting his father's ancestral land in northern Ethiopia.

Henok, too, was worried about the effect a two-week ban would have on his grades; he also did not want to disappoint his parents.

But Anteneh didn't seem worried about the consequences at home.[32] His biggest concern about being banned was that, with all the kids being in school, he would have nobody to play with. Well, nobody except for his mom.

So the three boys came to an agreement. They would become the school's gardeners for five days.

---

[32] Anteneh was raised by a single mother who was overprotective of her only child. In fact, if she heard the punishments that her son received, she would get into a confrontation with the principal. But then, Anteneh's ban would likely get extended.

#

As the school year came to the finish line, there was a lot of excitement. The students were looking forward to participating in the regional examination. It had been a special year. They envisioned becoming high schoolers soon. But they knew they needed to complete their classes before they could sit the exams. They also knew that they had to study hard and get good scores to pass.

Outside of school, it had also been a very difficult year. The political situation was getting really bad. People were no longer feeling safe and secure. The country had been in civil war for many years. But this time it felt different. Rebel fighters captured border towns with Kenya and were pushing towards Jinka. The military mobilized additional soldiers to go on a counteroffensive against the rebels.

The country's communist government had been at war with opposition and separatist movements from all sides. The war had been taking place mostly in northern Ethiopia where separatists were fighting to secure the secession of the Eritrean state from Ethiopia.[33]

The government's oppression was felt in all corners. Ato Fiseha, Kibrom's father, was regularly targeted by government forces who accused him of supporting separatists by organizing secret fundraising. He was arrested on multiple occasions based on mere suspicion.

The students didn't talk about it, but they knew what was happening. They'd heard of the government murdering people indiscriminately, men and women, young and old, guilty and innocent. The government harshly

---

[33] There were also strong opposition armies in the north, west and east of the country who had been fighting the central government. The Marxist-Leninist-inspired communist government had been known to be among the most cruel administrations of any society in history.

punished anyone accused of participating in anti-government activities.[34]

Henok once overheard his mother talking to a neighbor whose husband was missing. He was known in local coffee shops for being an outspoken critic of the government. The neighbor had been struggling to raise their two children as the family was dependent on his income.[35] The neighbor couldn't report it to the police, fearing retaliation. She could only weep on Zeineb's shoulder.

Willie's father had found a body in a ditch the week before. He'd left it there and told Willie and Fre to never get close to any dead body they might come across. It felt wrong to Willie. He just prayed he would not find a body.

In the meantime, the government continued to fight the armed rebellions on all sides. Public support for the government had dwindled as the brutality continued.[36]

As the war intensified, poverty plagued the nation.

One night, Willie and Fre refused to eat the dinner served at home. They complained it had been only a few days since they had had Injera.

---

[34] The government established a special operation agency who were tasked in infiltrating opposition and individuals who were considered enemies of the state. This agency was given full authority without accountability to the level that would make J. Edgar Hoover jealous.

[35] Hundreds of thousands of Ethiopian families were unaware of the whereabouts of their loved ones who had been taken away by government forces. Close to a million people were estimated murdered under this vicious operation. Many people died in detention camps. The families rarely got the bodies back for proper burial.

[36] As the government started to lose ground and faced a shortage of manpower, they started military conscription. The government used its communist party members as community informants. Not knowing who was a party member and who was not, neighbors distrusted each other. As the men were forced to serve in the army, women had to raise their children alone. Without father figures in the picture, kids developed bad habits.

They said they were tired of eating kurkufa, a type of dumplings made from corn flour and collard greens. The maid explained that the budget Dechasa allocated was no longer adequate and that she needed to be creative with groceries. The kids understood as they had already heard their father moaning about business being slow.

With the government being too busy in the military operations and underprepared for the changing environmental conditions, the country had also suffered from severe drought.[37]

Zeineb volunteered at a shelter for people who fled their villages in search of food and medicine. These villagers explained how their cattle died of hunger as the plants on their fields dried out. Henok once followed his mother to assist in the shelters. He was horrified by the scene of malnourished children crying because they could not find any milk in their mother's breasts.[38]

But the situation in recent months felt different. One evening after school, Willie was playing cards with Fre. Henok came running and barged into the house without knocking. During coffee, he overheard adults discussing concerning news, and he was eager to share the breaking news with his friends.

"What's the matter Heni?" Fre asked him nervously.

"You guys didn't hear?" Henok's heart was pounding. "The president

---

[37] Millions of Ethiopians had suffered from hunger and starvation. Journalists reported photos and videos of malnourished children and the bodies of dead animals. People begging for a sip of water had outraged the global audience. But the country's government attempted to hide the situation. They also resisted global assistance. International charities had to smuggle food aid to the public through unconventional routes. Millions of Ethiopians became refugees in their own and neighboring countries.

[38] People had been living under these horrible realities for several years. It became a normal lifestyle in some parts of the country.

fled the country!"

"What?" shouted Willie.

"He took all his family and friends with him. I also heard the country is broke now. He left with all the cash and gold reserves the government had. Everybody is worried. Nobody saw it coming!" Henok replied.[39]

Willie seemed outraged. "This is unbelievable! This guy has been singing 'We will fight until we are down to a man!' Now he abandons his soldiers at the battlefield and hides like a squirrel! I always hated him!" Willie's ears looked red as his anger accelerated. "I am outraged by this betrayal! He didn't even have the courage to face justice for his atrocious acts? What a traitor!"

Henok expanded on what he learned at the coffee gathering. "My father said there will be chaos across the country. It's not clear how all these rebels with conflicting interests will be able to form a government. He is worried that some of the rebels are worse than the communist dictator."

The kids continued their conversation until Dechasa's footsteps were heard. Dechasa told them that he had to close the store early because riots were brewing on the streets. As everyone sat down, the maid started serving dinner. They invited Henok to stay. But he insisted that he had already eaten and left without saying good night.

The next morning, the looting continued across town. Parents had to accompany their children to school due to safety concerns, but the school remained open for the calendar year. Despite the violence on the

---

[39] This dictator had escaped several assassination attempts before. Nobody thought he would accept defeat. Everyone expected his final hours to end like Tony Montana's in the movie *Scarface*.

streets, the brave teachers were determined to carry out their duties.[40]

After a daunting couple of months, the eighth graders finally completed the regional exams. As expected, all students in the special class passed. They were very happy. They were going to high school. Well, that was if there was going to be one next year.

---

[40] The teachers, as well as all other government employees, had to work without pay for a while as the treasury had shut operation during the turmoil.

CHAPTER 3

The great thing about childhood is that kids cherish everything that happens around them. Except for those life-altering incidents that leave stains on their brains, they will remember the ups and downs and the struggles in between as adventurous phenomena. But those feelings change as they reach their teens. They care more about what's happening around them. They question societal norms and want to influence the direction the future is taking them. When their parents make decisions that affect everyone in the family, they want to be involved. They begin to search their soul for identity, seek out their passions, and plan what they want to do with their lives.

For Henok, the year[41] started on the wrong foot. One day he walked into the town's only post office to check for mail.[42] The names of people with new mail were listed on a board. As he skimmed through the list, he saw his father's name. He told the mailman that he was Desta's son and received the mail. On his way back home he was tempted to open it. He was curious about what was in the letter. But he did not want to get in trouble. So he took it to his father.

"You have a letter." Henok stretched his hand out to pass the letter to his father.

"What letter? Who is it from?" Desta asked. He was preoccupied

---

[41] The first month of the year in the Ethiopian calendar is September rather than January, the first month in the Gregorian calendar.

[42] The post office does not deliver to people's homes in Ethiopia.

telling stories to Feker and Selam while his wife was serving food.

"It's from a person named Ruhama Abdulaziz from Babile. Do you know her?" Just then, Henok felt like maybe this was something he should have handled in private.

"I don't know anyone called Ruhama. And I have no idea if Babile is the name of a place or a tree. Open it and read what it says."

Henok wanted to explain what he could remember about Babile from his geography classes, but he did not see the point.[43]

"Dear Desta," Henok started reading aloud. "I hope you are well and alive. I have sent you letters in the past, but I never received a response. I am guessing they probably never reached you. I have asked around and confirmed that you still live in Jinka. You may not remember, but you told me, during our last encounter, that it was not going to be the end of our story. Well, you are correct. We made a bond that connects us forever. His name is Ismael."

Zeineb yelled, "Stop it!" She grabbed the letter from Henok's hands and ordered the children to go to their bedroom. "What is this, Desta?" she screamed at Henok's father.

Desta looked nervous. He shook his head in denial.

Zeineb continued, reading aloud, "When I found out that I was pregnant, I returned home from Addis Ababa. I am now, well we are, living with my parents in Babile."

Desta's appearance suddenly changed, his ears looked red as if they were on fire. He whispered to himself. "Ruth? Was Ruhama her real name?"

Zeineb could not control her anger. She tore the paper into two and started to cry. She looked at her husband and said, "You have broken

---

[43] Babile is a small town in eastern Ethiopia, located near the historic city of Harar.

my heart! I can never forgive you for this! You embarrassed me in front of my children!" She continued sobbing.[44]

Desta did not know what to say. He wanted to explain that this was something that happened before they were married. But what good would that do?

Desta was also in shock, as he had no idea that Ruth was having his child. He had told no one about Ruth and their one-night stand. Desta was heartbroken to see Zeineb like this. He had no good excuse to make her feel better. So he decided to do the only thing that made sense at that moment. He remained seated, with his head supported by his fists, and kept quiet.

In the following days and nights, their home looked like a haunted house. Desta hid himself at the shop sewing school uniforms and avoided looking his wife in the eye.

Zeineb didn't speak to her husband. She was still enraged. She had been getting angry at every little thing. She even started to mistreat her children.

The children understood their mother was under a lot of pressure. They tried to be as helpful as they could. But they knew this was going to take time. Concerned with their mother's sadness, they had not had a chance to listen to their own feelings. This was as shocking to them as it had been to their parents.

As time went by, Henok struggled to accept it. He just found out that he had another brother, from another mother. The worst part was that this brother of his might be older than him. That would make

---

[44] Zeineb would never in a million years have guessed Desta would betray her like that. He had been nothing but a good husband, and an even better father. She had grown to love him. But this? She felt like he stabbed her in the back.

Ismael the firstborn child. And this was upsetting news for Henok who grew up with the burden of being the oldest son in the family. Now, he would have to settle for second place. He wished his grandfather was still around so he could seek guidance.[45]

Henok remembered his grandfather's words. Tears started to fall from his eyes. His grandfather used to dream about moving the family to Wollo. Ato Agegnehu used to tell fond memories about his homeland. Once Ato Agegnehu realized that his days on this earth were counting down, he shared his thoughts with Henok. He told his grandson that there was no place like Wollo. Henok loved his grandfather and listened to his advice carefully. He promised to himself that he would grow into a man that his grandfather would be proud of. Then he remembered something and smiled. As far as his grandfather was concerned, Henok was still the firstborn son.

#

The year did not start any better for Willie. He got into a scuffle with his father. It was something he never thought he was capable of, disrespecting his father like that. But he felt no guilt or regret. As far as he was concerned, Dechasa brought it on himself. The father-son relationship had never been the same ever since Tiruwerk died in the car accident. Willie had too many grudges against his father.

What happened on the night of the scuffle was just the tip of the iceberg. It was a moment of awakening for both men; one that reminded Dechasa that his son was not a child anymore. It was also a revelation for Willie of what he was capable of. In the middle of the conflict was Fre.

---

[45] Ato Agegnehu Yimer died about a year ago.

Dechasa had been dealing with amebiasis disease.[46] Dechasa claimed vegetable oil was one of the ingredients that triggered his pain. He had instructed his family not to serve him food cooked with vegetable oil; he ordered them to use butter instead. Butter was very expensive at the time. The family's budget would not allow them to use it regularly. So they had been making two separate meals; one with butter for Dechasa and the second with oil for the rest of the family.

On the night of the scuffle, the housemaid traveled to visit her parents in a nearby village, so Fre cooked dinner for the family. She used vegetable oil on their meal.[47] A few minutes after dinner, Dechasa was forced to run into the bathroom. He returned about thirty minutes later. His face looked pale and he walked funny.

The kids, for they were just kids, could not hold their laughter and started giggling. Annoyed and a little embarrassed, their father felt like Fre intentionally tried to hurt him. He screamed at her and slapped her in the face. Grabbing her hair he dragged her to the living room. He pulled down his famous beating stick from its hanging place and started to beat his daughter.

Willie felt his hands shaking and his blood boiling. He sprinted to the living room and shoved his father very hard. Dechasa banged into the wall. Then Dechasa attempted to hit him with the stick. But Willie grabbed his father's hand in the air. Dechasa tried to free his hand and failed, shockingly. He just stood still and watched his son. But Willie released his father's hand and picked up Fre from the ground.

---

[46] An intestinal infection that causes severe diarrhea and intestinal pain. Many people used to suffer from this disease then. The pain is usually triggered by consumption of certain food types.

[47] Fre was never convinced of her father's claims.

Willie's eyes filled with tears when he saw his sister's scared eyes. He hugged her tightly and said, "I am sorry, Friye! I am so sorry! I have failed you!" He stared straight into his father's eyes and he added, "This will never happen again. I promise!"

There is a moment in every man's life that reveals his true identity. This was it for Willie. Standing up to his father's abuse was the ultimate commitment of his guardianship to his little sister. He had tolerated his father for a long time and kept many secrets. Willie had heard stories about how his father gambled away his money playing cards and billiards.

On one occasion, from what Willie was told, his father ran out of money playing billiards. Everyone urged him to quit and leave, but he insisted that he could win back his money. He bet his wedding ring, lost the game, then got into a fight as a last resort to recoup his loss. The young fella who won the bet did not hesitate to give the old man a memorable lesson. Willie believed the story because he remembered the time Dechasa came home with a broken nose and empty pocket.

Willie also remembered his nightmares in which his father used to sneak into their former maid's room. He would come home late at night as if he was waiting for the kids to sleep. He would enter the kids' bedroom and confirm that they were asleep. He would then go to his bedroom. Moments later, footsteps would be heard as he sneaked into the maid's room. Creaking of a bed, a woman's moaning and a man's husky voice would be heard from the other side of the house. Willie used to hold his ears hoping the noise would go away. A couple of minutes later, he could hear footsteps returning to his father's bedroom.

Willie wished these nightmares were dreams; sometimes he pretended they were. But he knew that he was not asleep. After a while, Dechasa and the maid started arguing in public. They never explained the issue, but Willie could guess it had something to do with their nightlife. Then one day when the kids returned from school, they were greeted by a new maid. Their father said he had to hire a new one because the previous maid had returned to her village. Willie wanted to say many things, ask lots of questions, but he held his tongue and walked away to his room.

Willie's grudge to his father had an even deeper root. Growing up, he had heard people talking behind his back. The rumor in the neighborhood was that Dechasa and Tiruwerk used to fight a lot in the days and months prior to her accidental death.

Tiruwerk's frequent business travels were the focus of the disagreements. He wanted her to quit her job and stay home. He was convinced that she was having an affair. She rejected his allegation as baseless. She in turn accused him of jealousy and being intimidated by her career success. On the morning of that cursed trip to Arba Minch, Dechasa did not even help her load her luggage on the minibus.

On the next day when the news arrived that the minibus was hit by a flash flood and that there were no survivors, Dechasa blamed himself harshly. He regretted that he did not tell his wife how much he loved her. He felt guilty that the last moments of their relationship were filled with such animosity.

Even though he never expressed his thoughts to anybody, Willie had always felt that their father had failed their mother while she was still alive, and also failed his children as a father ever since. The night of their scuffle clearly demonstrated some of that anger.

The morning after the scuffle and over the following days, Dechasa looked remorseful. He started returning home early. He became nicer to Fre. He even invited Willie to help him at the shop. The siblings' only hope was that this new personality was here to stay and not a momentary reaction to the incident.

#

As time passed, Willie and Henok cherished their experiences in high school. They had also made some new friends. One of the new additions to their special class was a guy named Amanuel Lemeta. He had moved from an area called Hamer, after completing middle school there, because his nearest high school was the one in Jinka. Amanuel preferred to go by the nickname Mannie.

Mannie lived in a hostel that was operated by an NGO who sponsored students from poor families and underdeveloped communities. At his new school, Mannie quickly established friendships with Henok and Anteneh. Mannie grew up in a community that had its own traditional beliefs. Henok taught him about Christianity.

Mannie asked, "What is the big deal; why should I follow Christ?"

Henok was happy to explain. "You see my friend, this world needs to be cleansed and Jesus is the janitor. Look around you. Our people live in darkness. They are filled with hate for one another. Everyone thinks they can do whatever they want. Faith teaches us to be humble. Without faith, this arrogance and hate we carry in our heart, and our selfishness will continue to haunt us," Henok preached. Ever since he met Merigeta Estezia, Henok had been passionate about religion. "We need to welcome Jesus to our lives. God sent his only son to give us light. Jesus shows us the righteous way of life. He tells us that 'truly happy people are those who want to please God and do as he asks.' Jesus wants us to love each other and show kindness even to people who do us wrong. The Bible says that if we become humble and open our hearts to let Jesus in, then we live a peaceful life."

Mannie did not see anything to lose. He asked, "So how can I become a Christian?"

Henok grinned with excitement as he answered. "Nothing really. You just need to be willing to change your way of life. We will get you baptized as a sign that you are born again as a Christian."

Henok also introduced Mannie to Merigeta Estezia.

As Henok and Mannie spent after-school hours in Bible study, Willie became invested in a new mission. There was a new girl in the class who just moved to town from a nearby one called Tolta. Her name was Delilah Wodajo. Delilah had long hair and big and beautiful eyes.

Ever since Willie had seen Delilah, he knew that he was in love. But he could not talk to her. Every time she walked past him, his hands shivered and his forehead beaded with sweat. So he tried that good old trick—he begged Seble and Yalem to befriend her.

"Come on guys, don't you see how she looks lonely? She could use good friends like you two. Can you please invite her to hang out with us?" He tried to hide his true feelings.

Yalem was very good at reading people. She looked at him staring at Delilah and laughed out loud.

Willie nervously asked, "What? What?"

Yalem continued to giggle and sarcastically said, "Poor Willie, you're in love!"

"No I'm not! Shut up!" Willie shouted angrily.

"Okay! Okay!" Yalem calmly said and stayed quiet for a moment. Then she noticed that his attention was still distracted. Yalem felt like she had to say something. "Seble, can you please tell this guy to talk to her? Look at him. His body is with us, but his soul is over there."

The usually shy Seble chimed in, "Yeah Willie, don't be scared. Just tell her that you like her."

"Are you kidding? You too? And for the record, I'm not scared." Willie lifted his chin.

"Ohhh ya?" Yalem challenged him. Then she called out, "Hi Delilah, this is Willie. He is a great guy! He has something to tell you." Then she turned to him and said, "Go ahead, tell her!"

Delilah smiled and said, "Hi Willie!" Then she kept looking at him, waiting for a response.

But Willie froze. He wanted to say something, but he could not open his mouth. Then he used all his energy and shouted, "She's just kidding! I have nothing to say!"

Looking a little disappointed, Delilah turned her head from him. Willie felt relief as she walked away. He also felt too embarrassed to look his friends in the eye.

"I have to go to the bathroom!" He told his friends and also walked away. Over the next few days and weeks, he became the topic of conversation. Everybody knew that he was in love.

One afternoon during gym class, Kibrom approached Willie and said, "Hi dude! I think you could use my help. I mean, with your Delilah problem."

Willie waved him away. "I don't want to talk about it. I don't need your help."

"Trust me, you do!" Kibrom got closer. He sat his left arm on Willie's right shoulder and whispered. "Look, you clearly don't have the experience. Girls can smell your fear from far away. If they don't think you're cool to be with, they wouldn't even touch you with a stick. Now you have already established good credit because of your friendship with

Seble and Yalem. Girls love some competition. You have to build on that credit before you lose it."

Willie admitted Kibrom had a point. Then the two began to discuss strategies. They decided that they would write a letter that he would give to Delilah. After several days selecting some fancy words and interesting proverbs, they finally completed it. They wrapped the letter in an envelope together with a beautiful picture of a flower that Willie painted for her. Then they sprayed it with perfume.

Willie and Kibrom plotted a delivery plan. The two discussed the where, when and how he would give the envelope to Delilah. With the plan in place, Willie prepared for the last step.

On a Friday afternoon during lunch break, Willie finally approached Delilah. He asked her if she could follow him to the back because he had something to tell her. She agreed and went with him.

The plan was to confess he had a strong feeling for her like he'd never felt before, and explain that he would need more privacy to discuss it in detail. Then he was supposed to pull out the envelope from his back pocket and say he would like her to read it, before politely requesting a meeting after school to talk more. He would then tell her that he would wait for her response, and head back to his desk.

As Willie and Delilah stood in the back of the building facing each other, he looked into her eyes. As if punched in the face, he suddenly forgot the plan!

Delilah waited patiently for him to say something. Willie could see that she was feeling nervous as well. The stress made him look like he was carrying a heavy weight. He mumbled and said to her, "This is not a good place to talk. Can we meet later, after school?"

Delilah's face turned red. "No, I'm not interested." She replied with a disappointed voice. She stood still and waited for his next move.

Willie did not hesitate. "Okay!" he replied and hurried towards his seat without even delivering the envelope. He felt like a failure. As he walked away, he recognized that he had made the wrong move. He realized that this case was probably closed. But he tried to convince himself saying, "Why all this pressure? It's not worth it!" As he sat down at his desk, he could feel the pressure slowly easing from his back.

After this unfortunate encounter, Willie avoided looking Delilah in the eye. He was not even sure if he would ever again try to date anyone.

#

In tenth grade, the special class welcomed a new English teacher who had just arrived in Jinka. His name was Molla Awtaru, a recent graduate from Addis Ababa University. He was tall, lightweight, with afro hair and glasses. Molla's charismatic personality and nurturing approach quickly garnered the attention of his students. His unorthodox teaching style inspired the classroom. One day Molla showed up in class holding a globe. He asked the students to select a country that interested them and write five facts that they could find on the map. Everyone had to stand up and read their notes. Then Molla served as a mediator and opened the floor for a discussion about what they learned from each other.

Another time, the class was organized into groups of five. Each group was tasked with building a case for why their group was the best. They were instructed to emphasize their strengths without demeaning other groups and to avoid negativity. They were only allowed to communicate in English.[48]

---

[48] In high school, education is provided in English. But teachers and students interact in Amharic. As a result, everyone was bad at speaking and listening in English.

The students were excited about the challenge. Everyone wanted their cool stories to be heard first. When they completed making their cases, two groups debated while the others served as judges. The winners moved to the next round of the debate. The final winning group was awarded the nickname "The Niches."

The students loved the new dynamics in their class. Molla quickly became popular in the school. The girls had a crush on him, and the boys wanted to be like him. As his influence reached beyond the boundaries of the classroom, Molla and a group of enthusiastic students including Henok, Mannie and Yalem created an after-school program called English Social Study (ESS).[49]

The ESS members were noticeable in the school. They mixed English words when speaking Amharic. They walked everywhere in groups. They listened to English music.[50] They even started a new fashion trend—growing an afro, wearing jeans which were tight on their hips and extra-wide near their feet, carrying books on their left arms, and holding pencils on their right ears. The ESS membership and popularity grew rapidly in the school. But critics also started to get louder.

One of the strongest critics of ESS was Merigeta Estezia. Henok and Mannie devoted time to their new roles in the ESS organizing committee, affecting their participation in Bible study. They were not the only dropouts from Bible study. Merigeta Estezia complained to Desta that

---

[49] The ESS program promoted speaking English in social gatherings, conducted essay-writing challenges and hosted group poem-reading sessions, with students from different classes and grades joining. Parents expressed appreciation and the program was complimented for offering teenagers an inspiring and positive atmosphere. The school received donations to keep the program going. Although it initially used classrooms, as the program became more popular it was awarded its own space for office use as well as large gatherings.

[50] Mostly Reggae and Rock and Roll.

his son was heading in the wrong direction. He also personally urged Henok and Mannie to return to the church. But they insisted that, other than attending Sunday Mass, they were too busy with schoolwork to do Bible study anymore.

ESS was also accused of spreading bad behaviors and challenging mainstream norms. Some members of the group engaged in romantic relationships, which concerned parents. They had hoped the program would help their daughters to stay away from boys.

Political leaders contacted the school to ensure the group would not turn into a movement. Rumors also started to swirl around town that Molla had been sleeping with his students.

The biggest blow to the program occurred when twelve students, including Yalem and her boyfriend Yonathan, went missing. Worried parents and police searched everywhere in town and the surrounding mountains. They contacted every vehicle that had left town at that time. But no success.

Police determined the only connection between all twelve students, besides that they were in the same high school, was that they were active members of ESS. The investigators interviewed Molla and other members of the program.

They uncovered that there had been talks between some members about fleeing the country. The students were heard talking about Western nations who granted temporary protection to Ethiopian refugees as the country continued to struggle with political turmoil and warring factions.

Investigators also found that some individuals had been communicating with smugglers who could provide safe passage to neighboring Kenya. The police concluded that they had fled out of the country through unidentified routes with the help of smugglers.

The town was shaken by the news. Walking from Jinka to Kenya through the desert was unimaginable. What if they died from dehydration? How could they survive the dangerous snakes and other wild animals? What if the smugglers kidnapped them? How did they become so selfish that they would put their parents in such a daunting position? Where did they find the money to pay for smugglers? Who else knew of their plans and how did they contact the smugglers? There were too many questions, but no one could give answers. Families of the missing students mourned as if their kids had passed away.

Four weeks since the kids disappeared, some parents received phone calls informing them that they were in Kenya. But the callers hung up before answering any questions or providing more details. This created even more chaos for the families. The public rumors and speculations did not help either. Another month passed without any further development.

But one rainy morning, Yalem's father answered a call and it was a familiar voice on the other end. "Yalemiye? Is that you? Are you alive? Dear lord!" Ato Kebede started to cry.

The rest of the family shouted in the background. "Is that Yalem? What is she saying? How is she doing?"

Kebede turned around and gave a look to the family; everyone settled a little bit.

"Babaye, I am so sorry!" Yalem responded. She cried like a baby who was missing her parents. "I did not mean to cause any pain."

"Don't worry about us!" Kebede interrupted her. "All we care about is your safety! Please tell us where you are. We can come and get you."

She continued to cry as if she was saying goodbye. "I am in a refugee camp somewhere in Kenya. I don't even know where exactly. There is no town nearby. The camp is located in an isolated place in the desert.

There are lots of Ethiopian and Somalian refugees. They registered us on the waiting lists for many countries around the world. We were told that the selection will be random and each country has a limited quota. Which means some of us may have to wait here much longer."

"Did you say we? Are you all together?" Her father interrupted her again.

Yalem told him the names of seven of her friends who were with her at the camp. She did not want to say what happened to the other four, but Kebede understood from her tone that they did not make it alive.

Yalem begged her father and mother to pray for her. She asked for their forgiveness and hung up the phone. The family was full of mixed emotions. They quickly reached out to the other families with the news.

The town was outraged by the passing of the four students. Molla and his ESS program became scapegoats for the incident, resulting in threatening messages for both him and the school. To avoid any further escalation, Molla was transferred to Addis Ababa and secretly escorted out of town. Less than two years after its establishment, the ESS program was forced to shut down.

Yalem continued to call her parents every Monday morning. But her last call came one Sunday evening. She told her father that she and Kaleb, another student who had fled with her, were set to board an airplane that was heading to Calgary, Canada.

She also told them that her boyfriend Yonathan and two others were taken to Melbourne, Australia the day before. Although she tried to switch spots with one of their friends to stick with Yonathan, the system did not allow this. She explained the remaining three were placed on a waiting list for a potential immigration to Oslo, Norway.

Yalem promised to call as soon as she arrived in Canada. The family prayed together. Her father and mother blessed her with their words. And the phone hung up one last time. The family wished their daughter would find her dream in the wonderland. But sadness quickly filled their home as they realized that they might never hear from her again, or at least not for a very long time.

#

Disappointed by the closure of ESS and the departure of their English teacher Molla, the students shifted their attention to preparing for the upcoming year's Ethiopian School Leaving Certificate Examination (ESLCE).[51]

Henok, Mannie, Anteneh and another classmate named Fetene Belay formed a team and used Anteneh's bedroom as their study room. It had a small desk with a single chair. Lying on the ground in the corner of the room was an old twin-sized mattress made from sacks of cotton.

The team's study sessions were very intense. Henok sprawled on Anteneh's bed, while Mannie and Anteneh sat on the floor, their legs stretched out, and Fetene sat at Anteneh's messy desk. They worked in silence most of the time, the only sound pages turning. But whenever one of them had a question, they'd break the silence, and someone would answer. And then they'd go back to scratching notes and flipping pages. Sometimes there'd be a debate over an answer, but they'd come to a satisfying conclusion before silence returned. They worked well into the night, until Henok realized that he was falling asleep with his cheek

---

[51] ESLCE was the nationwide grade twelve leaving examination and a certificate to be presented for admission into the country's higher education institutions. The results of this national examination were used to select students for various levels of further education including bachelorette, diploma and vocational studies.

on a textbook, and Fetene had slumped over the desk snoring.

On the other hand, Willie, Kedir and Seble studied together at Willie's home. With Fre barging in and out frequently, there was very little privacy. But they stayed focused on their books. Kedir brought special reference books which were not available even in the town's bookstores. The team established a schedule to ensure everyone had equal access to the references. There was no messing around; they barely exchanged words. Seble's parents gave a strict curfew of 9:00 p.m. The study sessions ended when Dechasa's footsteps were heard entering the room, which meant it was past 8:30 p.m. After dinner and when everyone fell asleep, Willie usually would wake up to study more.

Team Henok and Team Willie got together every Sunday at the town's only public library to exchange knowledge and resources. They also used the time to challenge each other with practice questions on all subjects. As the exam dates approached, the nature of the relationship between the two teams transformed into a friendly rivalry. Henok especially became obsessed with proving that he could do better than Willie. Willie never understood Henok's obsession, so he tried to ignore it.

The life of the two teams became study and yet more study, and nothing else in between; no soccer, no playing, no church and especially no dating. They told each other that their future depended on their ESLCE scores, and everything else would wait for them until after the exam.

After several months of hard work in preparation, the exam date finally arrived. Its first day was nerve-wracking; everyone was in intense mode. All exam rooms were monitored by independent proctors who were sent directly from the country's Ministry of Education.

To make matters worse, Willie almost lost his life about an hour before the exam. He went to Neri River on his way to school to take a bath and cool himself down before the main event. Unfortunately, due to heavy rain upstream, the water level reached a height he'd never witnessed before. Willie decided to boost his confidence by swimming across the river and back, and head to the exam with victory.

He jumped into the river and started to push forward, but the river carried Willie downstream. He used all his energy to try to swim to the river's edge, but the force of discharge was too powerful. His arms tired, his feet couldn't generate enough lift, and he began to drown as he inhaled water.

Then he felt something touching him—he floundered and held it tight. It was a tree branch from the riverside, and it saved Willie's life as he dragged himself to the edge. Willie sat down and cried. After putting in all the hard work, he almost died before taking on the biggest day of his life. Then he quickly got up and ran to the exam room.

When the exam was over, Henok and Willie organized a short trip to a nearby town called Gazer.[52] When the group arrived, there was heavy rain and the ground was badly muddied. They decided to get lunch at a Kurit House.[53]

After lunch, they wanted to walk around town. As if the sky was leaking water, the rain did not stop and movement was impossible on the muddy ground. So the group ordered coffee and stayed at the restaurant. The rain finally stopped, but the mud would not make walking very pleasant. Even vehicles struggled to move. The group was forced to leave town without any sightseeing.

---

[52] Located in a mountainous area, Gazer is a small vibrant town famous for its coffee production.

[53] A restaurant that has an in-house butcher and serves raw-meat dishes. Kurit Houses are one of the most popular restaurants in Ethiopian cities.

It would take two to three months for the ESLCE score to be posted. Students who achieved a score adequate for study in higher education would also have to wait another two to three months to find out their destination institutions. But that was not an issue for Team Henok and Team Willie; they were too busy making up for lost time by doing whatever they wanted to. They spent lots of time playing ping-pong, foosball, soccer and hiking across town and into the mountains.

But when it came to dating, these nerds had no luck.

CHAPTER 4

It was the most horrific and terrorizing evil of that time. A nation that had longed for peace and normality finally achieved some level of stability, but before citizens could rest and enjoy it, a new enemy called HIV/AIDS invaded the entire country. Little was known about this virus then and there was no treatment. There were also very few testing facilities. Many people had died without even knowing what killed them.[54]

The prospect of potentially getting infected by HIV/AIDS was a major factor in any family's decision making. Many children lost both parents and many parents also lost their precious children to this foreign invader.[55]

---

[54] Ethiopia was among the worst hit countries in the world, with millions infected and thousands of deaths every year. Prostitution is legal in Ethiopia and widely accepted. Almost every bar employs sex workers to attract customers. The industry plays a major role in the country's mainstream economy and is deeply ingrained in the public's culture and lifestyle. Unfortunately, the virus spread was alarmingly high in the industry. The pay-for-sex practice clearly played a major role in the rapid expansion of the HIV/AIDS epidemic in Ethiopia.

[55] Government and NGOs tirelessly worked to educate sex workers, provide protective measures and support testing and treatment. News media outlets also played a major role in informing the public about the cause, precaution and treatment options. One of the most popular slogans posted on car windshields, electric poles and building walls was "BE CAREFUL FROM AIDS" on a single sticker in the three main languages (Amharic, Oromo and Tigrinya). Another popular slogan was "ABSTINENCE / BE FAITHFUL / USE CONDOM" which was also known as the ABC Strategy. Schools and community centers also worked tirelessly to bring awareness.

Seble's parents did not want to be part of these statistics. They enforced strict guides on Seble to ensure that she was not tempted into dating the wrong person. Their worry grew higher as she was getting ready to study in one of the colleges or universities in the country. She was such a great student that there was no doubt that she would score above the minimum threshold.

But her parents had a different plan in mind. They had received a marriage proposal for their daughter from an Ethiopian-American man who lived in Washington DC. The family evaluated all their options and concluded that the marriage would be the best move for their daughter.

Seble was outraged when she first heard about the proposal. Her lifelong dream was to study hard and become the first college graduate in her family. But her parents insisted that the marriage was a great opportunity for her and the rest of the family. Seble realized that she really had no say in the matter; her parents were fully convinced.

Before Seble even had a chance to discuss it with her friends, the family flew her out of town to Addis Ababa where she met her husband-to-be and a small private wedding was held. A few weeks later, she boarded a flight to Washington DC with a husband who still felt like a stranger. She left her loved ones behind and ventured into a strange world.

When the news reached the other students, Willie was deeply saddened. He felt betrayed that his best friend departed without saying goodbye.

Willie also understood that, if it wasn't due to family pressure, Seble would not have chosen to marry someone before completing a degree. He wished her a better life in the USA.

On a beautiful morning Willie was sitting on the front porch of his home looking across the horizon as if he was searching for something, when Henok approached and silently sat down in the chair next to him.

"What's the matter with you?" Willie asked his friend.

"You know, I really loved her." Henok looked like he wanted to cry.

"Love? Whom?" Willie got confused.

"Her, you know. After hearing the news, I cried all night long. I'm still not feeling myself." Henok expressed his feelings for the first time.

Willie was surprised to hear that. He'd never seen Henok talk to Seble, or even look at her. "Wait, what? How come you never told me about this? Why didn't you say anything to her?"

Henok stared at the rising sun. "To be honest, I never told you out of jealousy," Henok said remorsefully. "I always thought she was interested in being with you. I couldn't ask her out because I was scared that she might reject me."

"I am sorry you had to go through this alone. You and I are more than friends; we're like brothers. I should have been there for you." Willie patted his friend's shoulder and then remembered something. "Wait a minute! Was that why you had been such a jerk to me lately?"

Henok smiled guiltily and apologized. "I'm sorry about that."

The two friends continued their heartfelt exchange till darkness surrounded the area.

Over the following days and weeks, Henok and Willie tried to recover from their heartbreak by shifting their attention to the remaining girls in town. As if they had a pool of willing volunteers, they spent their time picking and choosing, and created a list of ideal girlfriends for each other.

Meanwhile, Mannie got caught up in a traumatizing experience. He recently started dating a beautiful girl, but she informed him that she didn't feel a connection and ended it prematurely. The two had shared a romantic evening which did not elevate beyond kissing. The following morning Mannie noticed cuts on his lips. Later, when he met Henok and Willie, they also noticed his swollen lips and cracked some jokes at him. Then Mannie heard a rumor that was extremely worrisome. He did not know what to do.

So he consulted with Henok. "Heni, I am very troubled."

"What's wrong dude?" Henok peered at his friend.

"Do you know Hewan, Tiblet's sister? The daughter of Lema, the police officer who lives near the Red Cross Office?" Mannie muttered.

"Yeah, I know Lema." Henok knew Lema had two daughters, one who was tall and talkative, and the little one who was beautiful and disciplined. "Which daughter are we talking about?"

"The quiet one, Hewan. I just heard that Tagel the taxi driver used to smash her." Mannie started to explain.

But Henok interrupted him. "Are you serious? No way! She is on my fantasy list!"

"What list are you talking about?" Mannie got confused. "Anyway, that's beside the point. Let me finish my story." Mannie hesitated a little bit and continued, "Did you know Tagel also used to sleep with Emebet, the owner of Emy's Juice Bar? Her husband died last year; everyone believed it was AIDS that killed him, and she's also rumored to be a carrier."

Henok replied. "Yes, I heard the rumors about Emy. I would not be surprised if Tagel is HIV positive; he is a player. But are you sure about his relationship with Hewan? And why are we talking about them?"

"I'm not sure, I just recently heard it myself. Do you remember my swollen lips from the other day? It happened when Hewan and I kissed," Mannie explained.

"Are you kidding me? You and Hewan? This story keeps getting better! Then what happened?" Henok thought for a moment and looked into his friend's eyes and said, "Ahhh, now I get it. You're worried that if Emy and her dead husband were HIV positive, then Emy could have passed it to Tagel who then might have transmitted it to Hewan, with whom you shared a moment, and now you're worried if you got infected."

"Exactly!" Mannie jumped off his seat and walked around the house. "My head is spinning! I feel like I'm going crazy, man! What if I'm positive?"

"Relax man!" Henok tried to calm him down. "Do you know how many ifs there are in your case? There is likely nothing to worry about!" Henok was tempted to use his own concern to show Mannie that he was not the only one scared. Ever since Henok bumped into a street pole and got scratched by a sharp object, he had been doubting his health status.[56] But he decided to keep his concern to himself for now. His hope was that he would soon be accepted into a university at Addis Ababa and he would be able to get tested.

#

The ESLCE scores were finally announced. Jinka High School registered historic numbers as eleven of its students scored a "Distinction" or "Great Distinction". The percentage of students who qualified to enroll in higher institutions was still in single figures, despite

---

[56] The horrors of HIV/AIDS continued across the country, despite admirable work by government and NGOs in expanding healthcare, increasing test facilities, improving access to protective measures and introducing new treatment drugs. New infection rates eventually began to drop. But Henok and Mannie had to be prepared to bring their vigilance to college.

various efforts by the government to expand access to education.[57]

Team Henok and Team Willie led their high school scores. All of them secured a guaranteed admission into one of the country's best universities, except for Anteneh, whose score shockingly was only enough for a vocational study. Henok and Seble had the highest scores in the school averaging "Great Distinction" rating.

Desta and Dechasa organized a big party to celebrate this major milestone. Willie made sure that Seble's parents mailed her certificate to the United States and hoped that she would find a way to continue her studies.

Henok was disheartened that Anteneh didn't make the cut. He spent lots of time trying to console his friend.

But Anteneh seemed defiant; he insisted that this was not the end. He joked about the situation. "When life gives you lemons, you make lemonade. But when life takes away your friends and leaves you lonely, prepare to go at it alone."

Henok smiled and tried to hold off his laugh. "So you're planning to do something. That's great. What are you thinking?"

Anteneh tried to look strong as he discussed his plans. "I will work with my uncle on his truck. Then I will study and take the exam again next year. I'm not going to a vocational school!"

Henok could feel the anger and disappointment boiling inside his

---

[57] The new administration made it a key goal to transform Ethiopia from one of the most illiterate countries in the African continent to one of the best educated. New school construction projects erupted. With the number of students increasing rapidly, a shortage of teachers, lack of transportation, access to clean water and risks to workers' safety were among the biggest obstacles. The government had to diffuse the rising public discourse. Communities, who were used to isolated lives in remote areas, felt like they were being invaded, so they mistrusted the government's motives and objectives.

friend. He understood that Anteneh was far from okay. He hoped that time would heal his friend's wounded heart.

Meanwhile, Willie finally worked up the courage to talk to Delilah. She was among the eleven students from their high school who were destined to study in a university.[58]

It took a lot of work for Willie to convince Delilah to give him another chance. When she finally agreed to be his girlfriend, Willie could not believe it! He wanted to announce their romance to everyone. But she told him that they needed to keep it private.

Delilah also made it a prerequisite to get tested for HIV before considering intercourse. Willie would do anything to be with her. So he agreed to her demands. They secretly got tested at the town's first testing center. They were both free from the virus.

Willie cherished his romance with Delilah. As they waited to hear their assigned universities, his only dream was to be admitted to the same one as her. He dreamed about the two of them graduating with medical or pharmacy degrees, returning home to Jinka, getting married, making babies and growing old together. He prayed to God and promised that he would never ask for anything else again.

When the students received their university admission letters, Willie broke down in tears as he found out that Delilah was admitted to Jimma University while he was destined for Arba Minch University. He was worried that it was likely they would not be able to see each other until the end of the school year because of the distance between the two cities

---

[58] There were only seven government-run universities at the time in Ethiopia, and getting accepted to one was a mark of great accomplishment. The government was striving to improve access to higher education. But for now, Ethiopian students had to make do with the existing seven universities and compete to study in them.

and the lack of transportation.⁵⁹

Joining Delilah in the journey to Jimma was Fetene. Willie beseeched Fetene to look after Delilah and help her as needed.

Henok and Mannie were the happiest of all as they were both enrolled into Addis Ababa University. They quickly started fantasizing about the beautiful life they would have in the nation's capital and how they would shine in the bright lights of Sheger.⁶⁰

They hatched a plan to quickly adapt to what they perceived as the sophisticated lifestyle in Addis Ababa. They agreed to never mention Jinka and refer to Arba Minch as their hometown. Though they had never seen Arba Minch, they just assumed it had to be a cooler city than Jinka. They acknowledged that their dressing and hairstyles needed work as well. They also discussed being cautious about revealing their true accent in case other students made fun of them.

The loner Kedir was accepted to Mekelle University which was the farthest of all the universities in the country.⁶¹ His grandmother was devastated by the news. But she could not find another option; at the time there were no viable private universities nearby. She was afraid he would feel lonely and offered to relocate with him. But Kedir insisted that he had to overcome the challenge alone, like any other student would. So they agreed that she would travel with him initially and return to Jinka after a few days of helping him become used to the new environment.

---

⁵⁹ On a good journey, it would take two full days by bus to travel from Arba Minch to Jimma. The two cities had little interaction; most residents in each had never been to the other.

⁶⁰ One of the many nicknames of Addis Ababa.

⁶¹ Situated at the opposite end of Ethiopia, Jinka being in the south and Mekelle in the north, with at least five days by bus between the two.

CHAPTER 5

As Henok, Willie, Mannie and their friends prepared to depart for their assigned universities, they understood that they were among the luckiest students in the entire country.[62] Even though their hard work delivered them the opportunity, they felt privileged to be among less than 10 percent of high school graduates across the country who were granted a place in one of these universities.

It was an even greater accomplishment, considering these students were born and raised in such a remote area like Jinka.[63] They were celebrated in their hometown. They noticed younger kids looking up to them like they were some sort of role models. It would not be out

---

[62] University was a place only for the few and the braves. Even finishing high school was a big deal at that time. In addition to the lack of educational facilities, a lot of families were not cooperative about sending their kids to school. Since most families were uneducated, they did not see the value in education. They thought their children were better off staying at home. At home the boys would be trained how to run family businesses, whereas the girls helped out their mothers with housework. The society was fairly new to the brick-and-wall western education system.

[63] The first elementary school that was ever established in Addis Ababa was less than one hundred years old. Thanks mostly to one of the worst kings the region had ever seen, who was later dethroned by the communist junta and forced to take the Solomonic dynasty with him down to the ground, the vast majority of the nation's population did not see a school in existence for another fifty years or so. The country's new government, which took over after destroying the communist dictatorship, was determined to change that reality. To put it in perspective, there was no institution on Ethiopia's soil that produced a PhD graduate prior to the arrival of this new government.

of order for them to expect a warm reception at the universities. After all, they were special.

However, Willie did not find life at Arba Minch University as expected. For starters, he was pick-pocketed by a thief at the bus station and lost his wallet. If it wasn't for Fre who had split his money, keeping some in his wallet and hiding the rest in his luggage, he did not even know how he would have survived in the new place.

He took a taxi and arrived at the main gate of the university, but was confused to find the place looking like an open market. New students were running around asking for directions. Senior students competed to assist new girls who had just arrived. Various student religious associations recruited the newcomers for membership. But nowhere to be found were official representatives of the university. Willie realized he was on his own.

Willie bustled through the crowd and headed straight into a tall building. There were a lot of students surrounding one of the side windows, through which he saw a man handing out something. The students pushed and shoved each other to get closer to the window. Some were shouting to capture the man's attention. Those who were waving money had a better chance of getting noticed.

One freshman approached Willie and said, "Hi, my name is Hagos. I'm from Shire. Where are you from?"

Willie shook Hagos's outstretched hand and said, "I am Awlachew. But you can call me Willie. I am from Jinka." Then Willie pointed to the window and asked, "Do you know what is happening there?"

"That is the proctor's office for campus housing." Hagos told Willie. "Everyone is worried about a shortage of dormitories. There are three different room sizes which can accommodate six, twelve or twenty people.

As you can imagine, nobody wants to live with twenty roommates. Also, I heard that only two of the dormitory buildings have functioning showers and bathrooms. Dormitory assignment is on a first-come-first-served basis. That is why these guys are bribing the proctor; to get their names registered for the better rooms."

Willie looked surprised to hear that all this fuss was about dormitory assignment. He had no issue if he lived with six or twenty students. He grew up in Jinka; he felt like this place could not be any worse. Then he returned his attention to Hagos and asked, "Why aren't you in the line for registration?"

"I already have a place," Hagos replied. "My brother Nati is a third-year mechanical engineering student here. He saved me a vacant bed in his dormitory."

"Really? I am jealous of you, man." Willie smiled for the first time since he arrived at the university. "Look, I don't have a preference for a dormitory, they can randomly assign me to any of the rooms. But I would like to learn more about the campus. Would you care to join me and walk around to see what we can learn?"

Hagos nodded his head in agreement and followed Willie. As they walked around different buildings on campus, the two young men also learned more about each other—where they came from, their ESLCE scores, their encounters since arriving at Arba Minch and their expectations from campus life.

#

Willie and Hagos spent the rest of the week completing the enrollment process, obtaining library cards and registering for courses. They were extremely frustrated by the lack of guidance and over-bureaucratic administrative services. Fortunately, with help from Nati and his friends, they finally completed their tasks and prepared to start classes.

The next week, class began on Monday morning with Physics 101. Willie was very excited about starting his study. Physics was always his favorite subject; he scored A on his ESLCE physics exam. He expected nothing but a great start.

The classroom suddenly got quiet when a tall, bearded man walked in. He went straight to the blackboard and wrote, "WELCOME TO PHYSICS 101!"

Everyone clapped with excitement.

Willie didn't see anything extraordinary about the teacher. He wore glasses that looked older than his age. He talked using a condescending tone and walked as if the classroom was too small for his bloated stomach. The color of his lips and teeth indicated that this teacher probably liked smoking cigarettes and chewing khat more than studying physics.

The teacher mumbled about stuff the students had never heard of. Oh, he also instructed them to not call him teacher as he was just their lecturer. The lecture was about the velocity of objects using the X, Y, Z coordinates in three-dimensional space (3D). He used fancy words they had never heard of and went on and on about adding numbers in vector space. All the students could think of was "this space again!"

He provided examples about how to calculate the relative velocity of a rocket with respect to another moving object in space using the three coordinates. The students were completely lost and confused. In high school they were taught about the X, Y planes, but now this lecturer was discussing a third plane of reference.

The lecturer observed the classroom and gave a sympathetic look. "Listen, I get it." He cleared his throat and spoke in a low tone. "I'm sure each of you had some of the best scores in high school. And you probably think you are some of the smartest people in the world. But I need to be honest. Only half of you in this class will make it to sophomore, and the other half will either repeat this course or be cut from the roster by the end of this year. So the smartest thing you can do for yourself is to find out which half you will be in."

With that remark, he picked up his books and left the classroom. Some students started to cry. Others trash-talked about the so-called lecturer.

The remaining students rushed out of the classroom and to the library to find the relevant textbook. Unfortunately, they were told the only copy in the library had been checked out by the lecturer. It meant they would need to rely on their class notes and other reference books. Frustrated and disappointed, they returned to their dormitory.

Willie's dormitory was in an area known as "Monkeysville." This was a new residential complex about half a mile into the woods surrounding the main campus. By the time the students occupied the dormitories, the buildings were only partially completed. There was no shower, toilet or water inside. They had to walk to the main campus to use restrooms.

There were also no street lights in the area. Walking at night to and from the main campus was frightening as there were desert snakes who were most active after sunset. To make matters worse, the waiting line at the restrooms was very long; sometimes it took over an hour for their turn. The students had to fetch drinking water from a nearby underground water pump and store it near their beds.[64]

Perhaps the biggest disappointment was the food service. There was only one cafeteria for the entire student community, which served bread and tea for breakfast every day. The bread was as hard as a rock and it tasted like chalk. The tea reminded Willie of a hot drink made from the leaves of a coffee tree that he had while on a visit to a small tribal village known as Boshkero, near Jinka.

The cafeteria served vegetarian meals for lunch every Wednesday and Friday, typically fasting days for Ethiopian Orthodox Christians. Pasta with tomato sauce was served for dinner then.[65] The vegetarian food was so distasteful even beggars would not come to the campus on Wednesdays and Fridays to collect leftover food.

Lunch and dinner for the rest of the week was either curried or hot-peppered beef stew on injera. The hostesses made students choose only one type of the stew, unless the students deserved their good grace. The best flavor of the stew floated at the top of the gigantic pot, but the sediment at the bottom tasted like salted mud. Students lined up for hours before the cafeteria opened to get their meal while the stew still had its flavor. The hostesses knew the situation. Sometimes when they were in a bad mood, they would stir the stew until the students begged them to stop.

After a long and persistent battle, Muslim students finally convinced

---

[64] Sometimes monkeys from the surrounding jungle would challenge the students for a turn at the pump. Located near two of the largest water bodies in the country, Lake Abaya and Lake Chamo, Arba Minch is usually warm and humid. As a result, drinking water was a major source of conflict in Monkeysville, especially at night. Thirsty students used to steal water from their roommates. Some students used to sleep holding their water bottles.

[65] Foods like pasta, macaroni and rice were considered distasteful at the time by the Injera-loving Ethiopian society.

the cafeteria to change their menu.[66] The shift in schedule created an opportunity for some students who preferred the other religion's food to the vegetarian lunch or pasta dinner options. Although he was not proud of it and would not admit it in public, Willie made a pact with his Muslim roommate, Hasen Mustefa, and the two shared each other's meals on Tuesdays, Wednesdays, Fridays and Saturdays.

The great thing about life is that tough times pass; those who sustained under difficult situations will live to see the bright days ahead of them. When Willie felt stressed out from classwork or when he felt like he could no longer bear the difficult living conditions on campus, he remembered what he used to do as a child when he was scared of darkness. He used to close his eyes, pretend he was dead and fall into a deep sleep—when he woke up, it was always a shining morning and the ghosts were gone. So he used a similar trick on campus; he slept in the day and he slept at night hoping that it would get better soon.

When at last it was time for the final exams of the first semester, the students were in disbelief of the exam schedules. They had no time between exams for preparation. Some students called out sick during some of the exams, hoping that they would be admitted to sit for a makeup exam at a later time. Others had to suck it up and take it.

English was the first exam in the morning followed by mathematics. Willie and his roommates completed the morning session and returned to their dormitory to take a nap and get some rest before the afternoon physics exam.

---

[66] Since Friday is an important day in their religion, the vegetarian/pasta days were switched to Tuesday and Saturday for Muslims. Even though they live relatively in peace with each other, Christians do not eat meat products prepared in Islamic tradition and vice versa. Thus, the cafeteria served separate dishes for Muslim students.

Unhappy students made the dormitory feel like a funeral home. Some cried about not having enough time to answer even half of the math questions. Others were more worried about the upcoming exam.

The room suddenly got quiet when they heard an unusual voice from the bed in the corner. The roommates shifted their attention towards the voice. It was a student named Yared Efersa. Yared was always the quietest student in the room. Unless it was to communicate an important matter, he always kept his thoughts to himself.

But this time, Yared poured out his heart. "I can't go back to Asosa empty handed. I can't fail. Ever since our father was killed fighting in the civil war, my mother had to wash clothes for other people to raise me and my younger sisters. She always hoped that I would one day change our future. She will be heartbroken if I fail now. Guys, I really don't know what to do."

The roommates consoled Yared. They shared with him their own struggles to show he was not alone.

Hasen tried humor to change the mood in the room, "Look Yared; look at me. My eyes turned red from lack of sleep, I lost 15 lbs from sweating, and I am eating a kaffir's meat. Do you know why? I will tell you why! Because if I get suspended from college, my father promised me that he will kick my butt so hard that I will fly to the sky and never return."

Yared smiled a little. Everyone tapped Yared's shoulder and told him that he was going to be fine. Then they all left for lunch before heading back to the exam room.

Prior to the exam, the attendance record showed one person absent. Yared was missing. Hasen offered to go find him, but the physics lecturer did not want to wait any longer and the exam started.

There were only five subjective questions on the exam sheet.

Inside each question there were multiple analytical questions that were interdependent. So a wrong calculation at any step would result in wrong answers for the remaining sets of questions. Everyone was convinced that they were going to fail this course. They gave it their best shot anyway and left.

When they reached Monkeysville, they were unable to enter their dormitory as the door was locked from inside. One of them went in the back, broke in through the window and opened the door. There they found Yared inside, motionless.

Yared's life had ended tragically in an apparent suicide by hanging. The roommates were all shocked and saddened.

But over the next two days they still had to complete the remaining exams. Then it was time to pack their bags for a two-week midterm break. The students returned home heavy-hearted and with an uncertain future.

#

Henok on the other hand was having the time of his life in Addis Ababa. There were only four students in his dormitory. The cafeteria food tasted very good; it was like eating in a restaurant every day. There were also plenty of restaurant options on and off campus, all in convenient locations.

And then there was fabulous equilibrium in the diversity of men versus women student population. The women, they were all beautiful and sophisticated. Plus the university offered a scenic atmosphere, located in the center of the city where the African Union is headquartered.[67]

---

[67] The country's national palace was within walking distance. Also nearby was the famous Sheraton Hotel, the only 5-star hotel in Ethiopia at the time. And that wasn't the only scenery Henok was taking in.

Henok had never seen multistory buildings before, as there were none in Jinka. But now, his dormitory was on the sixth floor, surrounded by other tall buildings.

Henok and Mannie were living in the Arat Kilo campus of the university, but in different buildings. They were both excited by the opportunity to live and study in such a vibrant city. They felt like people did not sleep in Addis Ababa.[68]

Henok and Mannie used taxis and toured every famous neighborhood in the city including Piassa, Merkato, Shiromeda, Sengatera, Biherawi, Kera, Bole, Kazanchis, Kotebe and many more. They visited churches, parks and museums during the day and partied at nightclubs until the sun started to rise. For the first time ever, they watched live theaters and big screen cinemas.

Henok was like a spy; he quickly learned the ins-and-outs of this vibrant city. He came up with some mind-boggling ideas. One time, he started a project to chase local high school girls and network. He would get up early in the morning, grab Mannie and the two jogged up and down between Minilik and Cathedral high schools. Henok had no problems yelling at the students to get their attention and engaging in conversations. He encouraged Mannie to do the same. In the afternoon when the students returned home, Henok and Mannie hovered around Nazareth and Etege Menen high schools. Henok was able to exchange information with several beautiful girls. But none of it materialized into a meaningful relationship. So Mannie gave him a nickname, The

---

[68] As the capital city for the nation's politics, economy, entertainment and every other valuable category, Addis Ababa hosts thousands of tourists, diplomats, traders and other passengers every day. So students from small towns were wide-eyed in wonder at Sheger's beauty.

Asymptote.[69]

After a while, Mannie realized that they were falling behind in their studies. He urged Henok to cut down gallivanting and concentrate on classwork. Henok started to get agitated. After all the obstacles they overcame in their childhood, Henok believed that they deserved to enjoy the blessings of this wawaland.

Henok could not tolerate Mannie's conservativeness and continued nagging. Their relationship started to crack. The gap between the two friends widened when Mannie started spending more time with a new girlfriend.

Bethlehem Dires, who went by Bethi, was a psychology major at the Sidist Kilo campus. Bethi was a proud daughter of the town Mer Awi, a suburb in the south side of the city of Bahir Dar. Mannie first met Bethi while they were both touring Anbessa-Gibi.[70]

Bethi had stood near the lion cage and taken a closer look at a lion that pretended to be sleeping. The lion had suddenly opened her eyes, turned towards Bethi and roared.

Bethi had screamed and jumped backward, where she fell into the arms of Mannie who calmed her down. "Don't worry, I won't let it eat you," he had joked as he helped her balance.

After the tour, Bethi and Mannie had gone to a nearby cafe, ordered Coca Cola and learned more about each other. From that time on they started to study together at the library. Bethi inspired Mannie to study harder. Mannie was completely captivated by her beauty and politeness.

Bethi was a leading member of the Sidist Kilo Chapter of Mahbere

---

[69] It was a blow for him not to achieve his goal even though he had created many opportunities.

[70] A historic zoo at the heart of the city famous for its lions.

Kidusan.[71] Thanks to Bethi's positive influence, Mannie returned to Bible study and started participating in the association.

While Mannie and Bethi's love story continued to be written, Henok developed a stronger bond with his roommates. Two of these, Sisay Wakjira and Getnet Belete, were from the eastern cities of Harar and Dire Dawa, respectively. They considered themselves freestylers who took life for whatever it was at that moment. Their love for chewing khat was so much that they used to hide it in their pocket and secretly chewed in classrooms. Sisay was especially addicted to khat; he would not get out of bed in the morning unless he stimulated his brain with it.

The other resident in the room was Tesfaye Berhane from the suburbs of Addis Ababa in a town called Akaki; but he preferred identifying himself as from the city. Preferring to be called Tesfu, he was raised by strict parents. As soon as he moved to the campus, Tesfu was eager for new adventures.

Driven by similar desires, the roommates became inseparable. They were frequent customers at the khat bars around the Aware neighborhood and spent weekends at nightclubs in the famous Doro Manekia neighborhood. They were also popular antagonists in their classrooms and across the campus. The friends experienced their first setback when they were confronted physically at an on-campus party.[72]

---

[71] Mahbere Kidusan was an association of students who followed the teachings of the Ethiopian Orthodox Tewahedo Church. The mission of the association was to cultivate leaders for the next generation by shaping students' mindset and lifestyle. The group members were expected to establish a daily ritual of morning prayers before class, do Bible study in the evening and participate in academic mentoring programs. The association created a new dynamic in the Orthodox Church which was traditionally resistant to change and culturally dominated by religious hardliners.

[72] Americans say, "what goes around, comes around!"

One evening Henok, Getnet (a.k.a. Get) and Tesfu, uninvited, crashed a party hosted by a right-wing student association that promoted greater autonomy for ethnic Oromo Ethiopians. The party was organized to commemorate "Oromo Day" which celebrated the culture and heritage of the Oromo people. There was plenty of food, drinks, music and dancing as well as storytelling and campaign speeches. The friends only attended the party to meet some girls. But they got bored when they found out the only language spoken there was Oromo. Every girl they talked to looked at them like they were some weirdos for talking in Amharic.

The keynote speaker was a famous activist who called for support to force the government into allowing a referendum for the Oromo people to decide if they preferred to secede from Ethiopia.[73]

The crowd got swamped with emotions as the speaker recounted racially motivated attacks that citizens of ethnic Oromo had endured over the last one hundred years. Tesfu interpreted the speech to his friends as much as he could. He knew enough of the language to get himself out of trouble; his mother used to talk to him and his siblings in it during his childhood. But Get could not take it anymore.

So he screamed, "Amharic please!"

His protest was so loud that the speaker had to pause. Henok and Tesfu tried to shush their friend. But it was too late! Punches were thrown at them from left and right. They fell to the ground. Feet stomped them from every direction. They cried out, but the crowd's noise drowned

---

[73] A few years prior, the Eritrean region held a referendum and gained independence. Ever since, there was tension in Oromia between Ethiopian nationalists and ethnic nationalists. The ethnic nationalists argued it was degrading for them to be identified by a country founded on the sufferings of their ancestors. The Ethiopian nationalists believed dwelling in the past would not change anything and argued that Oromos were beneficiaries from the reformed Ethiopia which concentrated the nation's power and wealth at the heart of the present-day Oromia region.

their voices. As angry people pounded on them, their bodies gave up and stopped moving. One of the organizers by the name of Dejene Gabisa dispersed the attackers. "Please don't kill them! We don't want any trouble!"

When they regained consciousness, they found themselves in hospital beds. Their faces were stitched and their arms and legs bandaged. Bruises hurt a lot. They could hardly move. The only person next to their beds was Dejene. He told them how they got to the hospital and said, "You guys are lucky to be alive! What were you thinking?"

They blamed alcohol for their rude behavior at the party and were sorry for disrespecting the girls and making fun of the speakers. They apologized to Dejene in case they had ruined the program. The lesson was learned for now. Their wounds would heal in time. As the year end approached fast, they just hoped that their grades would not get damaged as well.

#

Kediro felt like he was far and away from everything. He struggled to cope with life at Mekelle University.[74] He had no complaints about the locals; they were some of the most polite and hardworking people. He had no complaints about the quality of education either. The university's brand-new facilities also provided outstanding services. But for some intangible reason, there was something very difficult to cope with.

---

[74] Mekelle University was a relatively new academic institution at the time. Located in one of the hottest parts of the country and about five hundred miles away from the capital, the university garnered little excitement from students. The surrounding population was relatively homogeneous, which did not help either.

Kediro witnessed several students suffering from mental illness. It was not clear what was causing all the psychological effects. It could have been the hot temperature and the absence of air conditioning. Or maybe because of the political tension that existed as the region was the fiercest supporter of the central government who was considered divisive and abusive in other regions. It could also be that the students were too bored of the lifestyle in a community well known for its strict discipline and strong religious beliefs. Nobody could be certain about the exact reasons.

Ever since his arrival at the university, Kediro was not feeling normal. He felt stressed even while he was asleep. On some days, he was unable to sleep at all. He spent the nights walking around campus. He had never had alcohol in his life. He did not do any drugs either. But he certainly lost his path and he knew it. Every time he tried to study for exams, his anxiety increased as if he was allergic to reading. He regularly missed classes to minimize the headaches, but that did not work either. The worst part was that he was not alone. There were many students who were unable to keep focused on the task at hand. Some even ended up being addicted to alcohol and drugs by choosing the wrong course to alleviate their pain.

One evening, Kediro and two other classmates were studying when he realized that he had no recollection of the topic he was learning. He read it again and again. It was like his memory was overfull; it could not store the new information. He became nervous.

He told his friends, "Guys, I think I am losing my mind. I can't remember anything that I am reading."

They said they too were unable to concentrate, so they all agreed to take a walk. While on the road, they discussed why they were struggling so much mentally. They wanted to study and recover their reputation as outstanding students. But they could not pinpoint the void that was troubling their souls.

One of them suggested that they needed to get laid; maybe a woman's touch could heal the wound. Everyone was excited by the idea, but none of them had dates. So they decided to visit a popular nightclub known for its prostitute collection. They pooled all their money and worked out a spending plan for their limited budget. At the club, they each ordered Pepsi and invited the girls to sit with them.

The girls wanted to drink alcohol, which was out of their budget but they felt too embarrassed to say no. While the girls enjoyed their drinks, the men discussed Plan B. Instead of renting three rooms and paying for an entire night, they decided to go for "Short."[75] About an hour later, the three men committed their most sinister act yet in their young lives and left the club. But they did not feel any different, other than guilty and dirty.

"I'm not getting any satisfaction. I just feel like I betrayed Allah!" Kediro cried.

The next morning, he went to the public telephone and dialed a number.

His mother answered. "Hello?"

"Mama." Kediro suddenly was filled with uncontrollable emotion. He burst into tears and sobbed like a baby.

"Kedir, my son! Please calm down! Basseme Allah. What can I do? Do you want me to come?"

Kediro kept sobbing. "Mom, I don't know who I am anymore. I don't know how to fix it."

He told her some of his struggles. But he knew that last night's experience was off-limits.

---

[75] A term used to refer to one round of service.

After he hung up, Kediro went straight to his dormitory and packed his bag as his mother instructed him. The following morning, he was on the bus to Addis Ababa. He left the university, promising to himself that he was never going to return. He stayed with his mother's cousin in Addis Ababa until his mother processed the visa application. Two months later, Kediro was at the check-in area of the international airport.

He hugged his grandmother tightly and could not let go. He always knew that moving to Atlanta to live with his mother was a possibility. He just never thought that he was ever going to leave while his grandmother was alive. But with no easy access to education, staying in Ethiopia had become unfeasible. Kedir's grandmother kissed him all over his face, dabbed tears from his face and struggled to appear brave.[76]

# #

After completing the first year of their college study, the children of Jinka returned home.[77]

---

[76] That was her heartbeat standing in front of her, someone she had raised since diaper days. She would not know what she was going to do once he flew out of the country. But she was convinced that it was the best move for him. So she did not want to be seen broken up over his departure. After instructing him to call her as soon as he arrived in Atlanta she stepped back and watched until he disappeared from sight.

[77] It's always good to be home, especially when life gets tough: the brain stops generating solutions and the heart begs for love and affection. Childhood is the frame of reference for adulthood. Home is the hard drive that stores all good and bad memories. Adults strive to turn their childhood dreams into realities. Their life principles and motivations are largely the byproduct of circumstances that occurred at an early age. When returning home after being away for some time, there is this special feeling that one experiences. It is genuine belongingness and true love. Home is the best place for self-reflection, soul searching and to gauge progress over time.

Friends and families treated them like they were local celebrities. People on the streets stared in their direction. Some were too intimidated to greet them and would wait for them to start conversations. Former teachers visited their homes and asked about college life. Their parents asked for their opinions on important matters. Kids in their neighborhoods showed them respect. The best part was they no longer had to wash their own clothes; their younger siblings were happy to do it for them.

Henok, Willie and friends found homecoming to be a relaxing break from everything that was happening on campus. They were amused to watch how much Jinka had changed in just less than a year. Their neighborhood kids were all grown up. The town's population had increased significantly. Lots of people from local tribes had moved into the town. Entrepreneurs from different parts of the country had arrived with different business ideas. Large-scale agricultural investors had started coffee, cotton, corn, bamboo, honey and livestock projects. New cafes and barber shops opened at every road intersection.

But the most noticeable change of all was the transformation of women everywhere. Ladies were now going out and socializing. They were seen going in and out of restaurants alone or with their lady friends. It was no longer unusual to watch local girls drinking at the bars or dancing in nightclubs. The girls Henok and Willie would have considered too young to date already had boyfriends.

Henok decided to make the most out of his vacation. He still had his fantasy list of girls that he had wanted to date in high school. Using his popularity and the skills he learned at Addis Ababa, he got to work quickly. With help from other boys in the neighborhood, he got up every morning with a plan. They visited different neighborhoods and studied their objective's routines and any obstacles that they needed to overcome like fathers, big brothers or noisy dogs.

Henok started writing a diary to document his project's daily progress. Whenever the opportunity presented, they made moves. Some of the girls agreed to go out with him. But he realized that he had nowhere to take his dates. He was not ready to be seen in public with someone that he was not serious about. And no way the girls would agree to meet in a hotel room for a first date. So Henok and his friends searched for better options.

As Henok juggled his projects, Willie was unhappy as Delilah was yet to return. He had not talked to her all year. There was no cell phone at the time. He tried to make an appointment to reach her through the campus telephone operators, but that did not work out. But they had stayed in contact by mail. He wrote her letters every month. She wrote back during the first semester. Willie only received one letter from her in the second semester and he was not happy with the message.

Delilah seemed to think they could not maintain their long-distance relationship. Willie wrote back telling her their relationship was the opposite of a long-distance one; instead, their relationship was being tested by the temporary distance between them. He told her they were destined to be together forever, get married, have babies and grow old together. But she did not write back. Still, he was eagerly waiting for her arrival in Jinka. Unfortunately, there was a delay at Jimma University as class had to be postponed midyear due to conflicts between Oromo and Amhara students.

On a chilly evening, Henok and Anteneh showed up while Willie was sitting outside watching people go about their activities. The farmers were packing leftover products that they brought to sell at the market and dispersing out of town. Some were too drunk to lead their donkeys. Others seemed in a rush to get home before dark.

"You look like the shepherd who lost one of his sheep. Instead of sitting out here and moping, why don't you join us? You know there are plenty of beautiful sheep out there." Henok mocked his childhood friend.

"Why do you always have something to say?" Willie complained.

"It hurts my soul to see you suffering like this! You must be upset that your one half could not accept the other for what it is." Henok continued trolling him.

"If anything is hurting your soul, it must be the alcohol and khat. What do you even mean?" Willie could not recognize Henok anymore. He came back with bad habits. He did not even care what his parents would feel when he chewed khat in public. He partied regularly at local nightclubs. He became a notorious womanizer. Willie could not believe how much his friend had changed.

"Well, once again, your father's family continued to target your mother's family. And now, your girlfriend is a victim," Henok explained.

"Do not mention my mother!" Willie got enraged.

Henok quickly apologized. He knew he had crossed a line. He changed the direction of the discussion. "I didn't mean to go there. But it is sad what happened in Jimma. It's not just the students that were murdered; it's everyone else who has to live in fear."

"What can you do? This is a country whose citizens do not like each other. A nation built by force," Anteneh chimed in. "I wish something could be done."

"Willie, what is your position? How can we fix our problems?" Henok turned to his old friend.

"It doesn't matter. These people have lived in this land for thousands of years. They genuinely dislike each other. There is no way to fix it. They could not be united under one nation. Even if you divide the country into multiple places, our current problems would still happen in the new territories. Look at Eritrea. They thought independence would solve their problem. Now they are more divided than ever before." Willie shrugged. "If I had the power, I would morph the African continent into five new nations: North, South, West, East and Central African nations. Then I would make everyone in each nation speak only one language and abandon pre-existing cultural norms. But is that possible? No, it is not. So, there is no solution to fix our problems. We just have to exist and do the best we can for ourselves and our loved ones."

"I think you're just sad. You're just not making any sense. There are many things our government can do to solve our problems," Henok protested. "After watching the differences between Addis Ababa and the rest of the country, I am convinced that our country's resources are unfairly accumulated in Addis Ababa. Here is my proposed solution."

Henok looked to his friends for attention. "First, I think we need to build an interstate beltway from Jinka-to-Gambela-to-Gondar-to-Wikro-to-Asaita-to-Gode and back to Jinka. It is very important that we link the countryside without the need to go through Addis Ababa. Second, we need to make Addis Ababa a purely political capital. We need to move all the banking headquarters to Mekelle—that's where most of our millionaires are from, anyway. Dire Dawa should be our commerce capital; Ethiopian Airlines should build its main hub in the city—it's already central to the country's railway system; we also need to move the interstate bus transit system to the city. All import and export systems should be handled from Dire Dawa. Third, I would make Arba Minch the entertainment capital of the country. I would build the

Ethiopian Hollywood between lakes Abaya and Chamo; I would call it 'Betamwood'. Somewhere nearby, maybe in Konso, I would build the Las Vegas of Ethiopia. Last but not least, I would invest heavily to transform Bahir Dar into the Silicon Valley of Ethiopia."

Henok had to slow down as his throat dried and he started to cough. "I am not expecting the government to do this by themselves. But they could establish the master plan, invest in building the infrastructures, be the catalyst in other areas and provide investors with incentives like tax breaks and leasing of federal lands. I guarantee you that our problems can be solved using these approaches." It looked like Henok had spent a lot of time planning this while munching khat with his college buddies.

Anteneh interrupted as Henok's coughing got worse. "So basically you want Ethiopia to look a lot like America. Do you also propose that we adopt its constitution?" He mocked Henok's proposal.

"Now, who is not making sense?" Willie also laughed at him.

"You're all not making any sense." Fre sneaked up on them from behind. "All of your proposals require someone extremely powerful to execute them. Maybe you should think about electing a female leader. She can show you better ways to heal the wounds and love each other despite our differences." She wrapped up the conversation. "Come on into the house now. Dinner is ready."

"My best sister in the whole world! I would vote for you!" Willie complimented her and got off his seat. They all washed their hands and went inside for dinner.

#

Bethi introduced Mannie to her parents over the phone. They liked him. She also received permission from her parents to travel with him so she could meet his family. So Mannie returned to Hamer with his girlfriend. Bethi had read a fiction book while in high school that was based on the culture and lifestyle of the Hamer tribe. Her expectation from this trip was fairly modest.

From a distance, Mannie's two little sisters recognized him. They screamed, ran out of the house and jumped on his shoulders. His mother followed them from behind and greeted him with kisses on his cheeks. Mannie introduced Bethi to his mother and his two little sisters. The family spoke the local Hamer language, so he had to serve as a translator. But Bethi could tell that Mannie was not translating exactly what was coming out of his mother's tongue. She spoke loudly and angrily while staring at Bethi and using hand gestures. The girls were much nicer; they grabbed Bethi's hands and took her inside.

After a few days, Bethi could not cope with the living conditions. The drinking water came from a nearby river which the local community also used for cleaning themselves and their clothes. At bedtime, a rug made from ox skin would be rolled on the floor and everyone slept next to each other. There was no electricity. Out in the backyard, there was a big dugout hole with two wooden beams on top and about a foot between them; the hole was used as a restroom and garbage dumpster.

Bethi also struggled with food poisoning. Her arms developed a rash which was very itchy. Eventually, Mannie and Bethi decided to cut short their stay in Hamer and returned to Addis Ababa. As they traveled directly from Hamer to Arba Minch, Mannie did not get the chance to visit his friends in Jinka.

Meanwhile, Delilah and Fetene finally arrived in Jinka. In an effort to avoid any awkward encounters, Delilah immediately got on a minibus and left the town to visit her parents in Tolta. When Willie heard about her arrival and sudden departure without any contact, he felt nauseous and confused.

Fetene also kept his distance. When the two had the chance to meet, Fetene gave Willie a greeting that was colder than ice. Every time Willie tried to reach out for an explanation, Fetene made him feel like he was being too aggressive and insecure. Willie wanted to travel to Tolta to talk to Delilah, but Henok stopped him from making another mistake.

Henok told Willie, "Look man, I don't mean to be a smartass, but I think you need to read the writing on the wall. Obviously something is wrong as she is clearly avoiding you."

"But I think I can fix this. I just need to talk to her face to face." Willie expressed his hope. Even though he did not want to admit it, deep down he knew what this meant. He was a believer in love at first sight. Ever since he met Delilah, he knew she was the only one for him. But he started to understand that those feelings were not mutual. Relationships are a two-way road. No matter how committed one side is, if the other side is no longer feeling it, then that is enough reason for it to end.

Henok shook his head. "Look man, I think it's time for you to see beyond the horizon. If she returns to her senses, then let her come searching for you. But it's time to let her go."

"Okay. I know," Willie responded as he looked down at the ground. He understood that, for once, his friend was making sense.

Over the next couple of weeks, Henok tried to introduce Willie to different girls. But Willie refused to get involved, preferring to spend more of his time with Fre, Mekit, Feker and Selam. He took them out to juice bars and picnic areas. They cooked food together at home. They played cards in the backyard and soccer on the front road. Willie enjoyed his time with them. They helped him heal his broken heart. He wished he could stay in Jinka and play with them forever. But he had to pack his bags as the break came to an end.

CHAPTER 6

The living conditions at Arba Minch University reminded Willie how his ninth-grade history teacher explained to the class Darwin's theory of "the survival of the fittest" in relation to the evolution of the human species.[78]

At the university, the students were in a continuous struggle for survival. There were more students under academic probation or suspension than the number of graduates every year. Some faculty members took advantage of student girls in exchange for good grades. The faculty turnover rate was very high. Every time senior faculty members left for better income in the private sector or traveled overseas for graduate studies, the university replaced the vacant positions with the smartest students from the most recent graduates. New lecturers who were students a year ago used barbaric methods to get respect from their former friends. Because of the political situation in the country, the students were also racially divided. There was always some kind of student protest.

One day rumors spread across campus that some students had seen

---

[78] "The fit species use the unfit to survive transgenerational challenges," the teacher explained. "Imagine two people who were trapped inside a burning warehouse. The doors were locked. Then they saw an open window at a height neither could reach. The fit one convinced the unfit to help him reach the window. The fit stepped on the shoulders of the unfit, then on his head and was able to get out of the warehouse before it collapsed. But the unfit was unable to make it; his species ended under the collapsed building. After surviving the fire, the fit was forever grateful to his pal."

dead rats inside the cafeteria food. Before the truth was investigated, outraged students forced the cafeteria to shut down. Prior to this, there had been many complaints to the university board about the quality of food. The board had tried to reason with students explaining the budget constraints.

On this particular day, everyone's patience was already at its limit. The protest quickly turned to violence. Classes had to be postponed. As the security concerns escalated, the federal army was deployed. But the military presence only worsened the situation on the ground. Many students were arrested. In an attempt to force students to eat the cafeteria food, the soldiers shut down all access in and out of the university.

Most students from the Tigray region were known for their pro-government positions. So they pulled out of the protest when they sensed that it was turning into an anti-government revolt. They asked the cafeteria to serve them, and with the majority of students still protesting, the Tigrayans found the cafeteria food to be more delicious than ever. As they left the cafeteria licking their fingers, the hungry protesters turned against them.

As if the Oromo and Amhara students had finally found a common enemy, the Tigrayan students were targeted from every direction. They were portrayed as symbols of what was wrong in the country. Some soldiers and faculty members secretly assisted the protesters. It took two weeks for the government to control the situation.

The university announced that they had agreed compromises with the protest leaders that would improve the quality of service at the cafeteria. The lack of an alternate food delivery option was recognized and the university agreed to allow the student union to open an on-campus restaurant. The student union was also allowed to purchase its own satellite dish and broadcast live television at the cafeteria and new restaurant.

The protesters were delighted with what they had achieved. No more sneaking into the teacher's cafeteria to watch soccer games and risking deducted grades from a teacher who felt disrespected by their presence. The boys were excited by the prospect of watching the English Premier League and the Olympic track and field games. The girls were happy as they no longer had to wait until they returned home to watch *Tom & Jerry*.

Willie never understood why people had to fight for every good thing. He was happy to share any good thing that he had. If some people disliked having him around and pushed him out of their circle, he was not one to fight back. He was one of those who moved around and joined different circles willing to embrace him. Willie was barely hanging on to his academic status. But he loved the city of Arba Minch. Due to its proximity to his hometown, he always met people he knew in Jinka.

Through his father's connections, he also established good relationships in different neighborhoods of the city. He loved the mountainous neighborhood of Shecha which boasted having the most beautiful girls in town. Shecha girls generally never left their neighborhood—they literally had no interest in traveling to the other neighborhoods.

Although it could be a dangerous place, the Mebrat Hail neighborhood served the best fish soup, probably in the entire country. Thanks to the Arba Minch Textile Soccer Club, Willie could watch home games of the Ethiopian Premier League and take pictures with some popular national team players. There was nothing more entertaining for him than swimming in the natural pond of the Forty Springs and hiking in the surrounding scenic wild forest.

Like most Ethiopian cities of the time, Arba Minch was no stranger to violence either. One day Willie went to a movie room in the Sikela neighborhood. The paying customers packed the room because it was erotic movie night. The mostly male crowd protested that there was too much talking and too little action in the English movie; they wanted a different one.

In an instant reaction that he later came to regret, Willie said, "Come on guys. If you can be patient and listen to the conversation, I think you will find it to be very interesting."

Some people might have felt that he was condescending because most of them could not speak or listen to English. A big punch was dropped on his right cheek above his nose. Willie jumped off his seat and turned to the right. He helplessly watched while a second punch arrived in the same area on his face.

Willie couldn't see properly. He struggled to remain standing. Then he grabbed someone that he believed was the attacker and tried to fight back. But the crowd quickly interfered and separated them. The fight ended before he could even identify his attacker. As a self-conscious person and someone who understood the local custom, Willie blamed himself for being insensitive to the feelings of others. He then sat down and continued watching the movie.

Willie had also heard a rumor that university students had been targeted late at night in some neighborhoods. The students were easily identifiable from the way they dressed and their accents. There was a rumor that local gangs were attacking students at night and the victims had been heard screaming, "In God's name! Please don't take away my manhood! Ohhh God, please help me!"

Willie ignored the rumors and did not pay attention to what the screams meant. At least not until he found himself in a similar situation. One day he went out for dinner with his roommate, Fedlu Gezahegn. When dinner was over, they realized they were too late to catch the last taxi to the university. They waited on the side of the road, hoping they could find a ride or maybe it was their lucky day and one more taxi would come. But it wasn't their lucky day. They decided to rent a hotel room and crash there. But all hotel rooms in the area were sold out. As a last resort, they went to a nightclub in search of someone who could help them.

At the nightclub, Willie saw Anteneh and got very excited. Ever since Anteneh started working on his uncle's truck, he was a frequent traveler between Jinka and Arba Minch. Willie told Anteneh that they couldn't find a hotel room. Anteneh told him not to worry, that they were welcome to stay the night at his place. Willie and Fedlu were relieved to hear these words. But Anteneh continued partying, and they realized they had to wait. So they ordered beers and sat in a corner of the club. Anteneh was intoxicated. He finally came and told them it was time to go. They happily followed him out of the building.

But then they noticed they were not alone. There were three other men with Anteneh. Willie instantly recognized one. His name was Engida. He was a notorious gang leader with a reputation for attacking innocent people and even targeting police officers. Engida was a ruthless robber and former veteran who had lost one hand when fighting during the civil war. Willie was aware that these guys always carried knives in their pockets. He knew they were trapped and that he and Fedlu needed to stay calm. Once they walked far enough away from the main street into a dirt road, Anteneh told Willie and Fedlu that they would be staying with Engida and that he had to get back.

Willie knew that Anteneh had betrayed his trust and intentionally handed him over to dangerous people. But there was no time to be mad with Anteneh. He took the blame for finding himself in such a vulnerable situation. He had been in similar dangerous and embarrassing situations before. Willie's childhood was filled with nightmarish encounters; from a housemaid that used to put his hand in her lady garden to bad boys that used to drown him at Neri River. Willie always knew how to get himself out of sticky situations. He knew to trust his instincts and understood the wellbeing of Fedlu also depended on his next move.

Willie pretended everything was alright and thanked Anteneh who quickly disappeared. Willie was already working Engida, becoming friendly with him. He presented himself as a local kid with family roots in Engida's neighborhood. Willie and Engida led the way. A few steps behind, the two other men hugged Fedlu from left and right, and they seemed to be talking too close to his ears. Willie told Engida every great story that he knew about his neighborhood.

Willie told him how proud the neighborhood was when Engida returned from the war with his injuries; that everyone was honored to have a hero in the hood. Willie said that he even contributed to the welcome party that the neighborhood had hosted during Engida's arrival. Engida loved the compliments and enjoyed hearing about his heroism from someone who knew so much about him. Willie told a story about how he used to play ping-pong with Engida's little brother and said that he also knew the rest of Engida's family.

It was not all lies. Willie had friends in Engida's neighborhood and he had heard many stories about him. But he stretched the truth, hoping it would be his way out. Willie told Engida the name of his uncle who lived in the neighborhood. He also said that he and his cousins were regulars at a local fish soup restaurant. Willie could sense the shame and guilt that was surrounding Engida. As they approached their destination, Willie told Engida that his uncle would be mad at him if he were to stay the night somewhere else in the neighborhood. He insisted Engida take him and Fedlu to his uncle's home. Engida hesitated, but agreed.

As they walked past Engida's house, Willie could overhear the two other men grumbling about where Engida was taking them. Then they arrived in front of a fenced house. Willie quickly knocked on the fence door, calling the names of the people who lived inside. But nobody came to the rescue. Engida suggested maybe Willie and Fedlu were better off staying with him. Willie insisted that he was not going to sleep outside of his uncle's house.

Willie asked Engida to lift him up and he jumped over the fence. Then he opened the fence door from inside. He thanked Engida for taking care of him and promised to express his appreciation to Engida's brother as well. Then he told Fedlu to come inside. The two other men hesitantly let Fedlu enter the property. Willie quickly locked the door. As they walked away, Willie could hear the two other men moaning. He guessed they might be unhappy as they would have to submit to Engida whatever they had hoped to get out of Willie and Fedlu.

"Thank you! Thank you!" Fedlu hugged his friend. His body was still shaking. "These guys are evil. But I trusted you had a plan. So I stayed quiet and followed your lead." He told Willie the horrible things the two men were saying to him.

"Thank you for believing in me." Willie hugged Fedlu back. "If you had not been patient, my tricks would not have worked."

"I am really proud of you! You saved my life! These guys were up to no good and it was not like they gave me a choice." Fedlu breathed with relief.

The next morning, Willie and Fedlu ran into Anteneh at a nearby breakfast restaurant. Anteneh shamelessly said hello. Willie pretended there were no hard feelings and greeted him. Fedlu asked why Willie did not confront Anteneh. Willie told him that there was no need as they were safe now and that they had learned a big life lesson. But Anteneh would have to live with himself and continue to be a loser because of his bad behavior and poor decisions.

#

Mannie and Bethi continued to work hard in class and participate in Mahbere Kidusan's Bible-study program which was also known as "Gibi Gubaye." She introduced him to her spiritual father, Kesis HabteMariyam Bichena, who offered to hear Mannie's confession. Mannie did not think he needed to confess anything. But the priest insisted, "My son. I can see your soul was hurt. There is too much anger in your heart. You need to let go of the past and forgive the person that disappointed you."

"I can't, Father," Mannie admitted out loud for the first time. "My life is full of misery, Father. Anger is my motivation to work harder every day. It encourages me to prove to the world that I am better, stronger and more useful than who they perceive me to be. If I let go of my anger, if I forgive and forget, then there will be a huge void in my heart and that scares me."

Kesis HabteMariyam empathized with Mannie. "My son, I was born from a very poor family. I was sent to a monastery at a very young age. I had nobody to rely on when I first arrived in Addis Ababa. I have seen the angels and the Satans in this world. Trust me, love and kind deeds are the only treasures that you should keep in your heart. You are a good person. You do not need negative force to motivate you to make a positive impact on this world."

Mannie shook his head as the priest's advice made sense to him. He was a dean's list student in the most prestigious university in the country. He had a beautiful girlfriend who loved him a lot. He realized that he should have no room for negative energy in his life.

He prepared to confess. "Forgive me Father, for I have sinned. I have carried anger and disrespect towards my father and mother all my life. My father used to beat my mother all the time. One day I was playing outside with my baby sisters. I could hear my parents having a big fight. My sisters were too little to understand, so I kept them focused on playing. A few minutes later, my father came out of the house carrying a bag. He stopped for a second and looked at me and my sisters. That was the last time I saw my father. I don't know if he is dead or alive. But he took something away from me—my self-confidence. The fact that he never reached out made me feel like he was not proud of me. I have done well for myself, but I always feel empty because I believe my father never loved me."

"Son, from what you just told me, your father was not in a good state of mind. But you are not that child anymore. You are a successful adult surrounded by friends." Kesis HabteMariyam sensed that was not the whole story. "But why are you angry at your mother?"

"I was more disappointed than angry at her. I appreciate what she has been through. I mean, she is the only constant in my life." Mannie tried to choose his words. "But after my father left, my mother became bitter towards me and my sisters, especially me. Once she caught me eating baked potatoes in the kitchen. She felt that she needed to stop me before I turned into a thief. She punished me by forcing my head inside a blanket filled with pepper smoke. My entire body began to hurt from breathing the hot pepper. I cried out loud and begged her to stop. But she tightened her grip. I could not free myself. She kept me inside until I fainted. I can still feel that moment when I close my eyes. She also used to get mad at me for everything and beat me a lot. The more she beat me, the angrier she got. Like I reminded her of someone else." Mannie cleaned his eyes with his shirt and continued. "Sometime later, I learned that the major source of conflict between my parents was that my father was not convinced that my sisters were his daughters. I never told this to my sisters."

Mannie stayed silent for a moment. Then he looked up as if he remembered something. "You know, Father, my mother never appreciates what I do. She thinks I am wasting my time in school. She thinks I was better off raising cattle with my cousins. She tried to block me from joining the hostel. My uncle had to convince her that the NGO was a good place for me. Now when I return to my village and watch my sisters, my heart bleeds. She doesn't even allow them to go to school. She says she has already lost her son and she is not prepared to lose another child."

Mannie felt the weight being lifted off his shoulders.

"Listen to me carefully, my son. Holding a grudge was never good for anyone, let alone for someone who is already winning," Kesis HabteMariyam advised Mannie. "God's law orders us to respect our parents. There is no condition for them to deserve our respect. She might not show it, but I am sure your mother is very proud of you. Wherever he might be, I hope your father has found God."

"Amen!" Mannie prayed for God to bless the good things he had in life, to forgive all those who had done him wrong and give him strength to follow the path that Jesus had laid out.

"In the name of the Father, the Son and the Holy Spirit, I absolve you from all your sins," Kesis HabteMariyam announced. Mannie kissed the cross on the priest's hand and returned to Bethi, who had been waiting outside. He felt like a new man.

As soon as she saw him, without saying anything, Bethi hugged him and did not want to let go. Mannie also held her tight. "I love you!" Mannie announced. He realized he had never said that to anyone before. He was not even sure if he was capable of loving anyone.

Bethi could not believe she finally heard those words from him. "I love you too!" she cried.

"I love you! I love you! I love you!" Mannie was excited to be able to admit his feelings.

She was amused. "I love the new you! Promise me he is here to stay!"

"I promise!" He responded with a smile.

"Okay, dinner is on me!" She happily led the way to a restaurant.

#

After a short period of relative calmness, another conflict engulfed the northern border. Eritrean air forces attacked an elementary school in Mekelle killing at least fifty people, mostly children. A diplomatic dispute over border demarcation became another excuse for a new war. Henok was rattled by the images he saw on television. Bloodied children strewn all over the ground. He could not get it out of his mind. His outrage grew alongside the country's, as the government wavered on its response.[79]

Henok became a fierce activist for mobilizing fundraising campaigns across Ethiopian universities. He strongly advocated that the Ethiopian army should not just recover territories occupied by the Eritrean army, but annex the port of Assab and secure access to the Red Sea. His outspoken personality garnered him media attention. He was quoted in magazines. He appeared in radio and television programs warmongering and amplifying conspiracy theories against ethnic Eritrean residents.[80] Henok also reached out to Willie to coordinate support for the war at Arba Minch University.

"Hello old friend! How have you been?" Henok called his friend.

"What do you want, Heni? I heard you're now a bigshot, on TV, telling people all sorts of things!" Willie was mad to see his friend radicalizing the public. He was heartbroken after learning that Kibrom's entire family had been deported from Jinka to a place they had never seen, just because their parents maintained Eritrean citizenship. Willie thought of Kibrom's younger brother Haftom who struggled with severe epilepsy. He prayed that Haftom's frequent seizures would not turn deadly in the war-torn region. Willie also remembered Kibrom's little sister Asmeret; she was gorgeous and innocent. He wondered what her fate would be in that desert.

---

[79] Reminded by the sacrifices made for generations during the civil war, the government was reluctant to engage in a new war and sought alternate measures. Protesters nationwide called for immediate response. Caving to the mounting political turmoil, the Ethiopian air force launched a wave of airstrikes on Eritrea's capital and the two countries entered into a full-blown war. Thousands volunteered for military service. A nation long struggling with ethnic conflict finally came together when it was at war.

[80] Claiming security concerns, both countries expelled residents who maintained citizenship in the other.

"What is the matter with you? Our country is under attack by these monsters. We need to mobilize our young people and support our military. I need you to help me organize fundraising at your campus." Henok was focused and determined.

"Do you hear yourself? Since when did you become a supporter of this government? I would have expected you to be a peace lover," Willie snapped.

"I am pragmatic. We all need to work together when our country is under attack," Henok argued.[81] "This border dispute is bigger than you might think. When Eritrea became independent, it should not have been allowed to take all our ports. Ethiopia has a legitimate right in accordance with international laws to gain access to the sea. They started this war; we should end it by taking Assab."

"Don't you feel for the innocent victims of the war? How could Kibrom's family deserve to be expelled from their hometown?" Willie was gesturing, his arms waving, even though he knew Henok could not see him.

Henok's tone was dismissive. "There are legitimate security concerns. Some Eritreans were caught when plotting terrorist attacks inside our country. What happened to Kibrom and his family is unfortunate collateral damage. At least they were allowed to take their money with them. The Eritrean government is deporting Ethiopians without a single penny in their hand."

"As far as I am concerned, we are the same people but divided by leaders. The people shall resist the leaders from dragging us to another war," Willie insisted.

---

[81] He didn't support the governing party politically, but when it came to this issue, that didn't matter.

Henok disagreed. As he saw it, from the beginning, when Eritrea was confederated within Ethiopia following World War II, they were well positioned to work together for the common good. Ethiopia was an underdeveloped nation with huge potential and Eritreans were better educated. Instead of being open-minded about integration, they made their first mistake by starting a war that lasted thirty years.

Then, when the civil war ended, they could have been part of a national dialogue for unity and prosperity. They preferred their independence and that was their second strike, according to Henok.

He called out their third strike, "And now, they just started another war over a border dispute for some infertile land. That's it, they got their three strikes. Ethiopians should stop trying to relate with them." Henok became frustrated by the back and forth. "Look Willie, I am not here for a political debate. Are you going to help me or not?"

"I do not want any part of people killing each other for nothing. But I will send you the contact information for the student union leaders. You can coordinate with them." Willie forwarded him their contact information. Henok thanked him and the call ended.

As the war dragged on and diplomatic discussions produced little outcome, the political differences between nationalists and the governing party grew larger. The government, who had a reputation of retaliating against political dissent, became vulnerable to criticism. Political debates were broadcast on national television and radio. Inspired by the teachings of his university professor, Henok became one of the early members of a newly formed democratic party. His popularity as an outspoken activist helped him to get elected as Director for Addis Ababa University Chapter of the Democratic Party.

After graduating from Addis Ababa University in Political Science,

Henok accepted a teaching position at a high school in the city. Desta and Zeineb attended the graduation ceremony. One evening Henok and Desta went to a bar where Desta ordered a beer and invited Henok to order for himself. Out of respect, Henok asked for a Coke.

But Desta protested. "I know you drink alcohol. Besides, you're an adult now!" Desta proudly tapped his son on his shoulder and told the waitress, "Get him a beer!" Henok relaxed a bit. Then Desta quickly got into the main point of this special occasion. "Do you remember your brother? Ismael?"

Of course he remembered, how could he forget his older brother?!

"Yes! What about him?" Henok replied bitterly.

"He lives here in the city. He is a businessman now. He imports construction supplies from Dubai," Desta explained. "I think it is time for you to meet him. He always asks about you."

"I'm not interested!" Henok felt jealous that his father talked with pride about someone else. He also wanted to show his allegiance to his mother.

But his father insisted that he needed to introduce him before he returned to Jinka. Henok finally gave in and agreed to meet Ismael, as long as his mother didn't find out. The next morning, pretending to be going shopping, Desta and Henok took a taxi to the Megenagna neighborhood. From there, a connecting taxi brought them to a newly expanding neighborhood called Gerji. They walked for about five minutes and arrived in front of a tall, concrete-fenced building. Desta knocked on the door and a young lady, who could have been a housemaid, opened the door. She quickly recognized Desta, shook his hand and invited them to come in. Then a tall man came out of the house smiling.

"Assalam Alaikum baba." The man hugged Desta. He looked toward

Henok and said, "Hi, I am Ismael."

Henok already guessed that it was him. He basically looked like a taller and more handsome version of Henok. Flabbergasted by their apparent similarity and intimidated by the graceful appearance of Ismael, Henok did not see the stretched hand waiting for him. "Ohhh, I'm sorry. I am Henok. It's nice to meet you!" Henok shook Ismael's hand nervously.

"My God! You two look like twins!" Desta proudly hugged his two sons.

"Please come inside! Lunch is ready!" Ismael hugged Henok as they entered the house. Henok was impressed by Ismael's kindness and success. Considering everything Henok had heard about Ruth, he told himself that Ismael had to be a hard worker to live such a successful life.

After lunch, they talked about life, business, politics and the future. As the day began to dim, Desta and Henok remembered they needed to purchase some presents for Zeineb to make it look like they had been shopping. Henok told Ismael that he would keep in touch and left following his father.

The war eventually ended with Ethiopia being victorious on the ground, though the legal battle continued.[82] Post graduation, Henok continued to serve in various political positions in the party.

---

[82] A United Nations-led commission awarded some territory to each side. But the sides never settled. The blood of hundreds of thousands of people from both countries was shed in vain. Some Ethiopians were also not pleased that their government refrained from contesting for sea access at the commission's hearings. These controversies amplified calls for reform which allowed the democratic party extensive media coverage.

CHAPTER 7

Mannie and Bethi graduated in the same class as Henok, with degrees in Computer Science and Economics, respectively. Bethi's parents, Ato Dires Manyazihal and Woizero Haregeweyn Abatyihun, brought all their children to participate in the graduation ceremony.

Bethi was the third child in the family of six siblings. The oldest was her brother Gebeyaw. After migrating to Italy nine years ago, Gebeyaw had made his residence in Frascati, a suburban town near Rome. He returned to Ethiopia for the first time since then to celebrate his sister's graduation. Bethi's other older sibling was her sister Hamelmal who had also graduated from Addis Ababa University, with a degree in Electrical Engineering. She worked in the city at the Ethiopian Telecommunication Agency. Her presence in the city had been a great help for Bethi and even Mannie as they hung out at her place on weekends. Bethi's younger sister Eniyat was a second-year medical student at Gondar University. Her little brothers, Setegn and the youngest, Alazar, were high school and middle school students. The Dires family were well prepared for the ceremony, dressed in suits and holding balloons and flowers. They also arranged a decorated after-party dinner celebration at Hamelmal's residence.

As Henok and Bethi were surrounded by their families at the graduation ceremony, Mannie battled to control his emotions. He understood that his family gave little value to education and modern civilization. But he had also hoped they would understand what this day meant for him and be there to support his accomplishment. None of them showed up. The only person attending his graduation was a representative from the NGO that had raised him.

Henok made sure that his parents organized very nice presents for Mannie and stayed with him until they had to join their respective graduation halls for the ceremony. After the ceremony, Bethi begged her boyfriend to join her at the dinner party with her parents. But he did not want to steal the spotlight from her deserved celebration and insisted that he had other plans. After taking pictures with the NGO's representative and thanking him for coming, Mannie headed to a nearby restaurant for dinner with Henok, Desta and Zeineb.

Mannie and Bethi graduated, averaging GPAs among the top of their respective graduating classes. Post graduation, they were both offered opportunities to stay in the university as assistant lecturers and they did not hesitate to accept. Bethi shared residence with Hamelmal whereas Mannie and Henok rented a condominium and became roommates. Bethi continued to dedicate her spare time volunteering for the Mahbere Kidusan Association. She also spent a lot of time on the computer studying about foreign education institutions and scholarship opportunities in the United States and Europe.

Mannie started a side business helping companies build intranet systems between their office computers.[83] Mannie quickly gained recognition for his skills and professionalism. His side business rapidly grew into his main source of income. At the same time, his career as an

---

[83] It was a different time back then. Cloud computing and global data storage were not available. The internet was rarely available for public use and the network speed was very slow for file sharing. An intranet enabled office computers to communicate file updates without the need for connecting to the internet, and improved collaboration, security and operational efficiency.

assistant lecturer was off to a good start. His ability to establish positive professional relationships with people from diverse backgrounds made him a popular faculty member. His students appreciated his innocent personality.

Although his career was heading in the right direction, Mannie became troubled with his living arrangement. He loved Henok like a brother. But he was getting frustrated with him for being inconsiderate. Henok was always self-focused and a risk-taker. Mannie felt like their relationship was getting worse.

Henok was disorganized in their shared space and never liked cleaning the house. His bachelor lifestyle also discouraged Mannie from inviting Bethi to hang out with them. His teaching income was very small and his political activism was volunteer work. So Henok barely contributed to expenses other than rent.

Bethi always felt Henok was a bad influence on Mannie. She was not too excited about the two being roommates. She nagged Mannie to rent his own place. But Mannie told her that there was nothing to be concerned about. He said Henok was family and they needed to stick with each other.

Things turned from bad to worse when Henok was unable to pay his rent.[84] Henok had spent his entire month's salary in one day. When he picked up his salary, he headed straight to khat house. There he met two beautiful girls who were very friendly. He knew they were hookers, but he enjoyed their company anyway. That evening he took them out for dinner, then a couple of beers and headed to a nightclub. After the

---

[84] All public employees were paid at the end of each month, which is when they could pay their bills. This was also a time of festivity as everyone felt a little bit richer.

party, they spent the night at a pension nearby. In the morning, Henok realized that he had no money left. He had spent his entire month's salary in one night. He started to fight with the girls who were still sleeping in the hotel room, wanting them to return some of his money. But the girls were used to such customer behaviors and had hidden their money before entering the pension. Feeling poor and dirty, Henok returned home.

Mannie was waiting for him. He was disappointed when he heard about Henok's adventurous evening. In addition to rent money, Mannie had to lend Henok enough for transportation and meals. Henok promised to pay him back from next month's salary. But Mannie had had enough of this roller coaster. He told Henok to find his own place and move out within a month. Bethi was delighted to hear that Mannie had made up his mind. She commended her boyfriend for making a courageous decision.

#

When Henok and Mannie graduated, Willie still had one more year to go. But that did not bother him. For the first time in his college life, he was experiencing the greatest feeling. As a senior student he had the privilege of living in the best facility on the main campus. He was much more comfortable with his surroundings. He appreciated the progress made at the university. The number of students had increased tenfold since his freshman year. Even though the cafeteria meal had not changed much, there were multiple restaurants and cafes within a short distance.

Yet, only half of his freshman classmates were set to graduate and be able to overcome the day-to-day struggles and academic challenges.[85]

Willie promised himself to never forget those innocent students whose future was ruined by an outdated education system and unacceptable teaching practice. But he was happy as the countdown to his graduation finally started. Most importantly, for the first time in his life, his lecturer was someone who had a PhD.

People say "good things come in bunches," and it's true. As the seniors were preparing to graduate, Willie's roommate, Hasen, received a letter congratulating him for winning a DV lottery.[86]

Willie and friends were very happy for Hasen and inspired by the unusual luck. They surprised him with a private party at the Arba Minch Crocodile Ranch and prepared a barbecue of crocodile meat. In a strong show of support, the friends also joined Hasen for HIV tests which was a requirement in the visa application process.

Hasen and his potential move to the United States was the talk of the classroom. Students jealous of this unique opportunity were quoted as saying, "This world is like a hen; it lays eggs for the lucky and it poops on others." Some even suggested Hasen should leave the country immediately to avoid any risk of unexpected disaster that could cause the US to halt international flights or freeze immigration processes. But

---

[85] Fedlu was one of those victims who did not receive the necessary support from the university, fell into drug addiction and dropped out halfway into the five-year engineering program.

[86] The Diversity Visa (DV) lottery is a global immigrant visa program operated by the United States government. The program makes over 50,000 immigrant visas available every year for applicants from countries with low numbers of immigrants in the US. Tens of millions from across the globe applied for this lottery. The DV program presented great benefits for Ethiopians. Many families became dependent on money from the diaspora community. The lottery application process was also a great source of income for internet cafes across Ethiopia. It was praised as the blessing from the sky.

Hasen insisted that he needed the degree more than the visa; he owed it to all his friends who were rejected for various reasons, and he wanted to honor Yared by receiving the degree.

The relationship between Willie and Hagos had faded over the years due to the political tension surrounding the university.[87]

Despite their differences, Willie and Hagos treated each other with respect. Following the footsteps of his older brother Nati, Hagos studied mechanical engineering. Unfortunately, Hagos was not going to join Willie in graduating. He had to repeat an engineering design course for which he got an incomplete grade.[88]

On the other hand, Anteneh became very unhappy with his life. In

---

[87] Willie was never shy to criticize the country's one-party controlled government. He believed it was not sustainable. Willie believed if the political landscape was not opened for competition, it would be only a matter of time before the country resorted to military insurrection. Coming from northern Ethiopia and witnessing the horrors of civil war, Hagos was an unapologetic supporter of the current government and the progress made under their leadership. Whenever the two got the chance to have a coffee or walk around campus, they butted heads about the government's handling of racism, corruption and the law.

[88] Hagos was upset that he was graded so poorly for not completing one of the many assignments in this course. The assignment was to develop a detailed drawing of a gearbox. No practical training was provided. Most students had never even seen a gearbox. Hagos and his classmates spent weeks studying at the library about gearbox design. Then they spent days and nights in the drafting room preparing the drawing. When Hagos completed his work, it was past midnight. So he folded the document and took it with him to his dormitory. When he woke up in the morning, the document was gone. Hagos went to the class crying and told the teacher that someone stole his drawing. Unconvinced by Hagos's claim, the teacher instructed Hagod to prepare a new one. But Hagos refused to start over. He hoped the teacher would probably deduct some points. At the end of the semester, he found out that he got an "Incomplete." As a result, he could not graduate until he took the course again. Hagos was disappointed, but he had no other option. He was determined to overcome this setback.

a third-world country, life could be overwhelming unless the person was a hard worker, from a rich family, politically connected or supported by another person who lived in a wealthy country. It was even harder for a lazy person like Anteneh who was used to cutting corners and searching for easy ways out.

After getting caught stealing from passengers, Anteneh was fired from working on his uncle's truck. He felt miserable as everything he touched turned sour. So he fled out of the country and migrated toward South Africa.

Meanwhile, everything started to make sense for Willie. His graduation was an epic festival. Family and friends came from Jinka, including Dechasa, Fre, Feker, Selam and Zeineb. Henok and Mannie also returned from Addis Ababa. Seble, Yalem and Kediro also surprised him by sending him a laptop as a present.

As he and the rest of the graduating students lined up at the stage to receive their diploma, Willie could not help but wonder what they were celebrating. He asked himself, should they feel grateful for receiving the degree or should they be upbeat for defeating all the obstacles the university had thrown at them?

Willie had no answer. But he was certain of one thing, that he came out victorious. So he kept his head high with a smile, walked onto the stage waving at his family and received his recognition. He officially graduated with a Bachelor of Science degree in Hydraulics Engineering.

#

Following his graduation, Willie returned to Jinka and started his first job at the town's water authority as a project manager, hoping to make a difference.[89] He organized a team of hydraulic engineers and geologists to study groundwater capacity and survey potential excavation and distribution challenges. Based on the team's technical report, he established another team of surveyors, landscape architects and hydraulic engineers to develop conceptual designs. Using the completed documents, he worked with experienced construction estimators to analyze cost-benefit for alternative projects. He then developed multiple project proposals and made his sales pitch to his managers. They were impressed with the quality of each proposal and the level of detail presented. The proposals quickly gained political support and he received the green light to proceed to the next stage.

Willie was very excited by the progress. He became famous in his hometown. The upcoming projects and the prospect of clean water for all became a conversation at coffee shops. Residents gave him a nickname: "Engineer."

Pedestrians greeted him, "Good afternoon, Engineer."[90] Dechasa was a proud father who could not stop talking about the large amount of funding that the town administration approved for his son's projects. People praised him for choosing to return to his roots to make a difference instead of chasing better opportunities in big cities.

Willie wanted to amend the administration's procurement policy because he wanted fair and open competition between contractors.[91]

---

[89] Despite the abundant underground water resource in the area, local communities struggled with lack of water distribution. The sanitation of drinking water was also a major problem in serviced areas.

[90] Even his own friends preferred using his nickname.

[91] He hoped that would encourage general contractors to recruit small businesses and expand economic opportunities for the community. He also wanted to make sure that the contractors were paying fair wages to workers and that their hiring practices did not discriminate.

After reviewing Willie's plan, his managers were outraged and rejected it. They also spread rumors that he was condescending and egotistic. Willie took this as a wake-up call, realizing that he disturbed the wrong beehive. He refrained from pushing further.

The construction contract for his first project was opened for bids after a long delay.[92] Five construction proposals were received. It took Willie and his project team all week to review the submissions and rank the candidates.

Unusually, Willie received an invitation from his supervisor for dinner on a Saturday evening. He accepted and arrived on time at the supervisor's residence. His supervisor had already started dining with a gentleman in a suit whom Willie had interviewed in the pre-bid meeting. After dinner, the supervisor left through the back door and stayed away long enough to let the suited gentleman make an off-the-record sales pitch. Even though the person spoke hypothetically, Willie understood the message loud and clear.

Willie waited until his supervisor returned, thanked him for the meal and left nervously. A day later a bag full of money was handed to him by a kid who mentioned it was from the gentleman in a suit. Following a team meeting on Monday morning, the supervisor ordered Willie to see him in his office.

Willie knocked on the door and asked, "Sir, did you want to talk to me?"

"Come in, Willie." The supervisor seemed unusually friendly. "How

---

[92] One of the reasons for the delay was because Willie insisted on interviewing the managers of each competing contractor to ensure that the project was going to be run competently. Willie argued it was part of his risk-management strategy. The leaders caved, but he was warned that he was making enemies. He shrugged off the criticisms and focused on the task at hand.

are you doing?"

"Everything is going well. Thanks to God." Willie used a low-key approach.

"Ah come on! I heard you're doing great! You should be proud! Your hard work is paying off!" the supervisor replied.

Willie understood where the supervisor was heading. He was basically telling Willie that he knew about the money. Willie did not know what to do with the money yet.

"Thank you, sir." He kept his cool.

"You know, Willie," the supervisor got up from his seat and walked closer. "Once upon a time there was a greedy man. God blessed him with wealth. Everything he touched turned green. But he was unwilling to spread the blessings to others. His selfishness pushed away everyone he cared about. His businesses eventually went broke. Then the man went to church and begged God to visit him. God replied, 'I was with you all your life. But you pushed me out. Now you must learn what it means to be lonely.'" The supervisor held Willie's shoulder and continued. "Willie, don't be like the greedy man. Make sure to spread your blessings to your teammates."

"I understand, sir. Thank you." Willie kept his head down as he left the office. He understood that he was caught in the middle of a fraudulent network. His only options were to quit his job or adapt to the widely accepted norm.[93]

---

[93] Employees' pay was very low. Most workers supported their families on income that they received from the dark side of business. Everyone knew the practice and it was basically a "don't ask, don't tell" situation. Every official who owned a private car or an expensive house could be considered a suspect because it was obvious their regular income could not afford such properties. If the country's leaders had a genuine interest in eliminating corruption, then they would have established a minimum wage comparable to the cost of living. Instead, they let the value of the dollar increase. With inflation at an all-time high while salaries stagnated, even priests stopped receiving confession unless they got tipped.

Willie never intended to be a messiah who wanted to sacrifice himself to wash off the sins of others. Thus, he convinced himself that he could do a lot of good by staying afloat in the sea with the sharks. The construction contract was awarded to the winning bidder. The gentleman in a suit and his crew quickly mobilized the construction activities. Willie's coworkers were also adequately compensated and remained loyal to him.

The project was completed successfully. The public got fresh water and the township scored a major accomplishment. With his reputation skyrocketing, Willie's other two projects received full funding. Following similar design and bidding processes, the projects proceeded to construction. Willie and his team enjoyed the perks of leading such magnificent projects. Everything looked promising.

Halfway into the construction though, Willie experienced a major setback. The general contractor requested additional funding, claiming the construction was running out of budget. Willie ordered the construction to proceed while they negotiated on scope and cost. He campaigned for the township to provide additional funding, proposing a 50 percent budget increase. But he could not garner adequate support from the administration. With negotiations souring, the contractor froze all construction activities on both projects.

The news created public outrage. The water authority fell under immense pressure. Some in the organization called for Willie to resign. The budget deficit became a political circus. Willie urged everyone to stop finger-pointing and look for constructive solutions. But the politicians were more interested in finding out what happened to the original budget. They demanded transparency from the organization's accounting practice.

In a drastic and desperate move, the authority announced that it had conducted an internal investigation and uncovered fraudulent activities. Then the administration fired Awlachew Dechasa, effective immediately, and announced a lawsuit had been brought against him for bribery, nepotism and illegal use of government properties.

Willie complained that he was being served as the sacrificial lamb to protect others who were in a position of power. As he battled his case in court, his outspoken supporters portrayed him as a victim. Willie's sudden fall from grace was a subject of much conversation in coffee shops.[94]

Willie could not even feel sorry for himself. He was ashamed of his actions, but also frustrated that all his partners abandoned him. As if they had not enriched themselves from the dealings, some pretended to be outraged and pushed for him to be prosecuted. Finding writing to be therapeutic, he wrote poems expressing his pain, sorrow and disappointment. After penning his thoughts on paper, he would read it to himself repeatedly, pretending to have a conversation with someone else.

---

[94] It was a very difficult time for Willie. He returned home with good intentions to help solve the problems of clean water and the diseases associated with poor sanitation which he had witnessed as a child. Children regularly suffered from skin infections and intestinal parasites. Willie remembered the times when he used to poop more worms than feces. So he was delighted when he was able to complete his first clean water project, believing it worth being part of the immoral and criminal activities usual to his organization. Now he found himself in such humiliating circumstances.

Here are some of Willie's poems expressing his emotional rollercoaster (written in Amharic):

ኑሮ

እሳት ያቃጥላል ፣ ያቆስላል ይጠብሳል፤
በሰሉ ቅረበው ፣ በወጉ ለመብሰል፤
ገፍተህ እትጠጋው ፣ ማሳረርም ያውቃል።
ኑሮም እንደዚያዉ ነው ፣ ሚፋጅ እሳት አለው፤
እርር ድብን ብትል ፣ እሱ ጣጣም የለው፤
ማብሰልም ማሳረርም፣ የዘወትር ግብሩ ነዉ።

ብሶት

የበላሁት ሁሉ ቋቅ እያለኝ፤
የሚታየው ሁሉ እሰለቀሰኝ።
የወጌ ችግሩ ትዝ ቢለኝ፤
እኔስ መላ መፍጠር አቃተኝ።

ማነህ እንተ

ልብህ ትእቢተኛ ፣ አመልህ ዳተኛ፤
እፍህ ቀማሚ ነው ፣ ግብርህ ግን መናኛ።
ኒውተን እኮ ትልቅ ፣ እጅግ ብዙ እሚያውቅ፤
ግን ሌላኮ አልታጣም ፣ ከሱም ደግሞ እሚልቅ።
እና እንተ ማነህ ፣ ምጭትና ሰኬት ያልተገናኘሁ፤
ነው ወይንስ ግብዝ ነህ ፣ ከሰው እምትሻል መስሎ የሚሰማህ።

ልብህ መርሳት ይልመድ

ነገሮች እንዳላሰብከው ፣ ሊሄዱ እንደሚችሉ እውቀህ፤
ህይወት ከሰኬት ጀርባ ፣ ሽንፈትም እንዳላት አምነህ፤
ምጭትህ ሳይሰምር ቀርቶ ፣ ትንቢትህ ቅዝት ቢመሰልህ፤
የፈሰሰ ውሃ እንዳይታፈሰ ፣ መርሳትን ይልመድ ልብህ።

Nature is an imperfect phenomenon. Creatures of our universe struggle every day to overcome nature's imperfection. In fighting the daunting challenge to make the world a better place to live, people themselves transform and their way of life evolves. Those who work hard, despite a poor start, dig themselves out of the dirt and rise like a shining light. People who are resistant to change, despite coming from a position of power, become spectators and watch helplessly as others leave them behind for new adventures.

Through all the ups and downs, humans share similar desires about what they want out of life. To borrow words from the great Thomas Jefferson, "The preservation of life, liberty and the pursuit of happiness" drives everyone. It is nearly every man's dream to have a beautiful woman on his side, make children, build a family, and secure resources to provide a sustainable future for his family. A man's happiness depends on how he perceives these dreams turning into realities.

Mannie was grateful for everything that had been happening in his life. He was supposed to be out in the wild with his cousins chasing hyenas away from their cattle. Yet here he was in the nation's capital, living a dream. Best of all, Bethi said "Yes!" to his marriage proposal. They arranged a small wedding in the tradition of the Ethiopian Orthodox Church.

Mannie asked Henok to be his best man. Mannie told Henok, despite their differences, there was nobody that he would rather stand beside him at the wedding. Willie and Fetene were also among the groomsmen ushering Mannie. The surprise guest was their former high school teacher and organizer of the English Social Study (ESS) program, Molla Awtaru.

Henok somehow traced him and invited Molla to the wedding. Mannie was very excited to see his former role model joining him on this special occasion. Teacher Molla was very proud of his students and appreciated the respect and affection they showed him.

After tying the knot, Mannie and Bethi made a major announcement and caught friends and families by surprise. They had both received scholarships to start graduate studies overseas. They had already completed the process and received their travel visas. Mannie and Bethi were heading to the University of Mons-Hainaut and the Polytechnique Faculty of Mons in the city of Mons in Belgium about forty miles southwest of Brussels. Everyone was in disbelief and speechless. One scholarship would be amazing, but the two of them heading to Europe together was extraordinary. The crowd praised the new couple for their wonderful achievement. The party continued until late in the evening.

A week after their wedding, Mannie and Bethi traveled in opposite directions south and north to say their final goodbyes to their respective hometowns. Mannie's mother did not even attend his wedding out of spite that her son was mixing with a person outside his tribe.

But when she heard the news that he was going to travel to Europe, she mourned like she just lost her only son for good. She realized that her disappointment in her son for not embracing her culture prevented her from listening to what he wanted to be. She regretted failing to support him through all those years, but felt it was too late to make amends. Falling on her son's shoes she wept remorsefully, refusing to let go of his feet unless he forgave her. But Mannie had already forgiven her during his prayers.[95]

Mannie told his mother that he had never stopped loving her. He

---

[95] Besides, he understood cultural barriers were a major factor.

thanked her for never abandoning him and his sisters. Helping her to get up, the two hugged, kissed and cried. Over the next few days the family got to know each other better. It brought back some memories from the good old days.

In the end, Mannie returned to Addis Ababa surrounded by a large entourage including his mother, sisters, husbands of his sisters and some of his cousins.[96]

Bethi also arrived with her family and friends. The Hamer boys and girls got along very well with Bethi's parents. When it was finally time for the couple to fly out of Ethiopia, everyone headed to the airport. Mannie looked around and felt happy that the two families were truly enjoying each other's company. Henok and Willie also came to the airport to wish their friend bon voyage.

Pictures were taken.[97] The clock showed it was time to check in, so Mannie and Bethi said their goodbyes and went up on the escalator waving their hands proudly.

#

Work hard, play hard and live large had been Henok's motto and he was sticking with it. He published a children's book about peace, love and politics. But due to lack of adequate support from the printing

---

[96] Decorated by their traditional clothing, the Hamer boys and girls were impressive sights. Residents of Addis Ababa were inspired by their unique appearance. In every restaurant, other customers picked up the checks. When a major entertainment agency offered them a chance to join a cultural orchestra, two of Mannie's cousins were interested. Mannie led the negotiations, with the contract providing a place to stay and a regular salary. Mannie's mother learned that her son was never ashamed of his identity, he just preferred living a civilized life.

[97] Lots of pictures.

company to advertise, he was unable to sell the copies already printed. So he borrowed money from Ismael and self-funded the marketing. He personally went on tours to schools and libraries to promote his book. With help from Fetene, who was working as a news reporter following his graduation from Jimma with a degree in journalism, Henok appeared on a local FM radio program and pitched the value of educating children about politics and its role in building a peaceful and healthy relationship between citizens. He was convinced it was only a matter of time before demand for his book soared.

Meanwhile, Henok believed it was time to find a wife for himself.[98] He decided there was no better place to find a good wife than his ancestral land in Wollo. He contacted his uncles and aunts for help. They were delighted that their oldest sister's son chose to return to his roots. They quickly responded with exciting news about a beautiful girl from a religious family who was a first-year student at Gondar University. Her name was Samrawit Melese. They gave him her contact and said that she was expecting to hear from him.[99]

---

[98] He felt the women he met in the city were too fast and self-sufficient. He preferred a wife that would follow his lead and fit into his definition of a family. He considered reviewing the list he had prepared on his hometown girls during one of his summer breaks while in college. But he believed that he wanted the kind of wife that his mother was to his father.

[99] The old days of parents choosing the husband for a woman to marry were over. The new culture was that the man had to work with the woman. If she agreed to the proposal, then the man would send the elders to her parent's home for their permission. The parents would consult with their daughter and deliver their decision. It was really a formality these days as the woman was the one who was going to decide what was best for her. People were just trying to cling on to an outdated practice because they were scared of the impact a sudden change might have on the fabric of societal bonds. To put in perspective, think about the transformation of the British Monarchy. With little to no legislative, judiciary or executive role, the Queen or King would still be considered the "Head of State." But that discussion should remain for another day or another book.

Henok and Samrawit quickly hit it off during their first conversation over the phone. They talked day and night.[100] Henok felt like he could trust her and enjoyed their conversations. Samrawit was impressed with his ambition and determination to make a difference. She was convinced that he had the foundations to be a good family man.[101] They agreed to meet during her summer break.

When the time arrived, Henok traveled to Ancharo. His cousins arranged a taxi to pick him up from the bus station in Kombolcha. It had been many years since they last met and they were all surprised to see how each other had transformed. Henok was also impressed by the development in the village. The city of Kombolcha expanded a lot and its suburbs reached near the village. As they traveled up the hills toward the mountainous village, Henok observed lots of new properties.

After dinner was served, the tired Henok thanked the family and headed to the bed that was set up for him to take a rest. About two hours later, his sleep was interrupted by a noise in the house. The family was laying rugs outside and calling everyone to leave the house.

He asked one of his cousins, "What's happening?"

His cousin pulled him outside and showed him the moon, which looked orange. His cousin said, "The moon is covered in blood. It is a curse. When this happens, we cannot sleep. We have to stay out here and pray to God for mercy."

Henok tried to explain. "No, that is not a curse. I already heard earlier today that there was going to be a lunar eclipse tonight. This occurs when the earth aligns itself between the sun and the moon, and

---

[100] At the time cell phone services were activated in many Ethiopian cities and it was quickly changing from a luxurious belonging to a necessity.

[101] Even if his religious values seemed too loose.

shadows the moon."

Everyone turned toward Henok and looked at him as if he was the Satan that cursed them. His aunt rejected his explanation. "You need a prayer, Henok. I will pray for you."

Henok then realized that there was no point arguing. So he lay down on the rug and tried to get some sleep, while everyone continued their prayers. A few hours later, the family was relieved to witness that God had heard their prayers as the moon returned to its normal look. They all slept the rest of the night outside next to Henok.

Over the next two weeks, Henok spent a lot of time with Samrawit. They visited cafeterias, had dates at church gatherings and walked to picnic areas in the mountains overlooking the suburbs of Kombolcha.

Henok proposed to Samrawit. She agreed to marry him after completing her degree. Excited by the prospect, Henok wanted to make it official. He had his family send elders to her parents for permission to get married following her graduation. Her parents agreed. An engagement ceremony was held at the town's church. A few days after the engagement, Henok returned to Addis Ababa.

#

Willie decided to make use of his free time, while waiting for the court case to be decided.[102] He prepared a business proposal to incorporate a design and construction firm. Partnered with some other engineers and wealthy investors, he established Neri Construction Inc.

---

[102] His patience was inspired by a quote he remembered from a book he read in high school, "work hard every day to be the best person you can be; never feel guilty if you fall short of your goals; every sunrise offers a second chance." He realized that he could not sit and wait for the court verdict.

The firm quickly received contracts from NGOs and private institutions to drill water wells and devise stormwater retention in the rural communities. The projects quickly placed him back in the public spotlight.[103]

With public opinion shifting in his favor, the water authority dropped the lawsuit. Once a colleague of the administration, Willie now became a client. But he never forgot the betrayal and humiliation they put him through.

One day Willie was out in the field leading a geotechnical study in the grounds of Mago National Park, about thirty miles from Jinka, to design a new water diversion system across the park. He received an urgent message to return to Jinka. He knew his people always prioritized social relations over professional duties, but could not think of any urgent matter that would require him to leave work and return to town. He guessed it could be that his father was sick or one of his old friends had arrived in town. So he waited until the field work was complete, assigned another employee to take charge of the demobilization activities and returned to Jinka.

When Willie arrived home, he was handed a letter. It was from "THE UNITED STATES CITIZENSHIP AND IMMIGRATION SERVICES." Willie had seen a similar letter before and he knew what was in it. He could not believe he just won the DV Lottery. He quickly opened it and read the details. There were forms that needed to be completed and returned in three days. He did not want to waste time, so immediately completed the forms.

---

[103] In addition to providing drinking water, the potential benefits from the projects included irrigation opportunities for the local pastoralist societies, grazing water for their cattle as well as supporting afforestation initiatives. Politicians also praised the economic opportunities and the prospect of new jobs once the projects transitioned from the design stage into construction.

Willie wanted to keep the news to himself for the time being. But he soon found out that it was too late. Everyone in town had already heard about it. Everywhere he went, people congratulated him. Some offered him unwanted advice about what to expect in America or how to avoid the long wait line at the American Embassy in Addis Ababa. Others solicited him to include their daughter in the process as his wife in exchange for money or a place to stay in America.

Willie was concerned that his safety might be in danger. He understood such great news would make some people jealous.[104] There were fears that some cruel individuals out there were stabbing people using HIV-infected needles for reasons unknown. Willie became increasingly uncomfortable with his surroundings. He grew suspicious of the people around him, including close friends, aware that they might be motivated by jealousy to cause harm.[105] He decided to leave town while his DV application was being processed.

Fre was in a meeting at work when her phone rang. She was worried that her brother was calling in the middle of the day and she felt it must be urgent. At the time, Fre was working as an accountant for a bank in the town of Shashamene.[106] She asked the meeting organizer to be

---

[104] This world is full of people who do bad things to others just because they enjoy causing pain and suffering and they like seeing other people fail. There are more cynical individuals in less-educated and less-civilized parts of society.

[105] He remembered the time when a young man was poisoned and died; the rumor was that the mother of the young man's best friend fed him a poisoned meal because she could not stand watching him with a girlfriend whom she wished for her son.

[106] A major transit center, Shashamene is a very popular trade destination. Situated between several lakes, the town is a famous vacation spot for Ethiopians. Shashemene also has special meaning for the Rastafarian communities worldwide. Unfortunately, the town had a bad reputation for robbery, drug dealing and racist incidents. Surrounded by rival Sidama and Oromo tribes, the city was no stranger to conflict.

excused and ran outside to pick up the call. "Hello Williye, my prince. Is everything okay?"

"Friye, my beautiful sister! I don't mean to disturb you at work, but I just want to tell you that I have made up my mind. I am coming to live with you until I receive my US visa." Willie waited to hear his sister's response.

"Ahaha, I don't think that is a good idea. Already I don't feel safe here. Between drug addicts, gangs and political tensions, this is not a getaway place. I already submitted my request to be transferred to Hawassa." Fre poured cold water on his plan.

But Willie's mind was already made up. "Okay then, I will come to visit you for a couple of days. After that, I will go to Addis Ababa and stay there."

"That is better. Okay, I have to return to the office. I love you." Fre hung up the phone and walked back to the meeting room.

Willie quietly sold his stake in the firm to one of his partners, transferred all his money to Addis Ababa, and left town without making any noise. Only close friends and family members were aware of his plans. After staying a few days with his sister, Willie fell in love with Shashamene.

He told his sister, "Friye, this is such a vibrant town. Everyone is busy. They don't even stop to apologize when they bump into each other. You can do anything and be successful. I love the pastry markets. And the fried fish, wow, it's yummy! From what I saw in the movies, this town is like the Chinatown of New York City."

He stayed a few more days than planned. Then he took the bus to Addis Ababa where he was greeted by Henok.

"Welcome to Sheger, old friend!" Henok smiled like a happy dog who saw his caregiver.

"Hi Heni, boy am I not glad to see you!" Willie smiled back and prepared for a handshake. But Henok wrapped his arms around his friend and the two hugged.

"Follow me, a lada[107] is waiting for us." Henok led the way out of the bus station.

#

Heavy rain and hailstones were pouring on the sheet-metal roof of the building. The streets of Addis Ababa were very quiet, except for the noise from the storm. But the restaurants and bars in the Biherawi neighborhood were packed with passengers sheltering away nature. Henok and Willie were sitting at the front porch of a baklava bar. Henok and another customer got into a heated exchange over international politics.[108]

"George Bush is a dictator. How is he any different from Saddam Hussein? America is always intervening in internal matters of other countries and causing conflicts around the world in the name of spreading democracy. This world cannot be at peace unless somebody teaches America to stay in its lane," the customer argued.

But Henok disagreed, "My brother, America is a global force for good. We all need someone that we fear in order to treat each other with respect. Otherwise, this world will be chaotic while everyone fights for control. Can you imagine a world where Saddam has his hands on a

---

[107] Lada is a name commonly used for a mini taxi.

[108] The United States was at war in Afghanistan and expected another conflict with Iraq. The customer argued that America was being authoritarian by invading other countries and was concerned about the economic impact of another war in the Middle East.

nuclear weapon? If Iraq becomes a nuclear power, then all countries in the neighborhood will be scrambling to get their hands on one, Israel, Iran, Turkey and Egypt. America has to do something to bring order."

The other customer was visibly upset. "What are you talking about? Israel already has nuclear weapons.[109] Besides, this is not about nuclear, this is a question of sovereignty. America should not be allowed to have such power that it can unilaterally decide to declare war on any country that it deems a threat." The customer raised his voice as his blood boiled, "We are already struggling to make ends meet. A war with Iraq means a significant increase in oil prices. We are an agricultural nation; we import all manufactured products from other countries. The price of all imports will increase if the oil price increases. That will lead to major inflation for our people."

Always unintimidated and unafraid, Henok defended his position. "Those two are different and separate problems. Saddam Hussein is a security concern for the global community. The problem with Ethiopia's economy being sensitive to external influence is our problem to solve. We need to diversify our trade relations as well as our product portfolio. Our country has been manipulated by foreign agents throughout our history because we have been unable to admit our weaknesses and confront them. Our society resisted education for generations. We insist on preserving culture, even though it is not a unified one. For over a thousand years, our church was led by bishops assigned from Egypt, yet our fasting is longer and stricter; why is that? And don't make me bring up our tribal conflicts."

Henok's political passion was on full display. "The Westerners used

---

[109] Just because a country does not declare their nuclear weapons does not mean they do not have them. This is one of those open secrets.

to compete for colonial territories and now they compete to have a stake in the astronomic world. But we still dream about making one of our tribes more powerful than the rest. Teaching civilization to this society has been extremely difficult. We had to be forced to stop circumcising girls. Our farmers still refuse to use fertilizers and do not want to contribute to projects that would expand irrigation. My brother, if we are going to build a resilient and sustainable economy, we will need to look in the mirror and prepare to improve ourselves."

"Stop calling me brother, you traitor!" The other customer jumped off his seat and stared at Henok. "Who do you think you are? Somebody needs to teach you manners before you can criticize an entire society!"

Henok also jumped off his seat and prepared for a fight. "What? You don't like to smell your own stink?"

"Alright alright alright!" Willie quickly intervened. "You see the rain has slowed down. Let's get going before the office closes." Willie pulled his friend to the exit. Henok followed him, walking backward while engaging in a staring contest with the customer.

Willie was scheduled to pick up his US Visa-stamped passport that day. After nearly five months in Addis Ababa, he had finally completed the visa application process. They were on the way to an office in the Urael neighborhood where they were scheduled to collect the passport, when the lada driver, scared of the storm, had dropped them in front of the baklava bar.

They waited for a while on the road, worried it was getting late. Finally a taxi arrived, but it already carried more passengers than the legal limit. The driver told them to squeeze in, so they did as they were told. The taxi continued moving while the passengers pushed and shoved each other. As they approached their destination, Henok yelled for the driver to stop.

"Let's run, Heni; we're late!" Willie exited the taxi and rushed to the building. They arrived as a lady was preparing to close the office door. "Excuse me! Please don't! I need my passport." Willie begged her to let them in.

"Well, you should not have come late then." She fixed her hair back, lifted up her chin and walked past Willie. "Now if you will excuse me, I've got somewhere else to be."

"I'm sorry, sweetheart. My friend is from the countryside. He needs to learn some manners." Henok used a diplomatic approach. "He's got to catch the bus in the morning. And I will lose my mind if he stays in my house for one more day. Can you please help me get rid of him?" He gave her a box of baklava that he had picked up at the bar.

"Only because you're nice." She smiled while opening the box and let them in. "What's your name?" She stared at Willie.

Five minutes later Willie received the passport. He opened the visa page and there it was. It had his picture, personal information and phrases like "UNITED STATES OF AMERICA," "IMMIGRANT VISA" and "SERVES AS TEMPORARY I-551 EVIDENCING PERMANENT RESIDENCE FOR 1 YEAR." He read it again and again. Every time he did, his body began to shiver.

Willie and Henok nervously walked out of the building, as if somebody could attempt to steal the passport from them. They quickly entered a lada and said, "Take us to Lideta!" They did not want the driver to find out their address. So they told him to drop them off when they reached near "Dessie Hotel". Then they purchased a 200 Birr mobile card and strolled down a dirt road toward Henok's residence. For the rest of the evening, they made call after call to friends and families in

Ethiopia and abroad.

Willie's college buddy Hasen resided in Orange township in the state of New Jersey about fifteen miles outside of New York City. He was delighted to host his former roommate and help him settle in the US. Seble and Kedir also invited Willie to come to them. But Willie decided it was best for him to be with Hasen. The truth was that Willie had been fascinated by the history of NYC.[110]

Willie was proud to learn about black people's contribution in America and was encouraged by their progress over the years.[111] Willie could not wait to be a new addition to this wonderful community. He felt grateful for the sacrifices made to put him in this position.

Fre and Dechasa came to Addis Ababa as Willie prepared for his flight. As always, the father-daughter duo disagreed on everything, from which restaurant to dine in to what items Willie should plan to take with him. Willie and Henok served as mediators.

The date finally arrived. They hired a taxi and headed to the airport. The newly opened terminal was very attractive, but they were disappointed

---

[110] He had read a lot about the city that prides itself as the "city of immigrants." He remembered his high school history classes that inspired him to learn about European explorers. The competition to discover a short route to Asia and establish dominance on the spice trade brought explorers to the Americas. As some decided to settle, others continued their quest for an exit through what would become the Hudson River. The sailors realized there was no exit after reaching what would become the Great Lakes. The most impressive part was the story of Native Americans; inhabitants had already been living everywhere the explorers went.

[111] Black America's battles for equality date back to the colonial era. They had fought on both sides of the Revolutionary War. Unfortunately, their struggle for independence had to continue for another eighty-two years until slavery was officially abolished in 1865. But their quest for freedom and equality was an ongoing process. They were made to work for every victory and justify their place in society as equals. Black people achieved irreversible accomplishment in America.

by the high level of security measures at the airport.[112] Willie said his goodbyes outside, loaded his luggage on a cart and entered through the security door.

Fre had to be held back as she cried out loud and screamed, "I love you Williye! Please call me as soon as you get there!"

And then he was gone, leaving Ethiopia for the first time in his life.

---

[112] Ever since the terrorist explosion in America, the international airport in Addis Ababa had been under high alert. Only passengers were allowed to enter the terminal.

CHAPTER 8

The world was splitting in different directions.[113]

In Ethiopia, the Democratic Party announced an ambitious plan to challenge the ruling party's monopoly in national and regional elections. The election was about two years away, which was plenty of time for a campaign.[114] The party preached patience and cultivated grassroot supporters of their progressive ideology as it established offices across the country and expanded its campaign.

Henok continued to volunteer in the Democratic Party as a campaign

---

[113] After the past century filled with conflict and brutal violence, Europe was finally establishing peace. Newly formed nations in the area formerly known as Yugoslavia settled into dealing with their issues diplomatically. Several countries had joined the European Union (EU) and the Northern Atlantic Treaty Organization (NATO). Asia was still reeling from the wars in Afghanistan and Iraq. As millions of migrants fled war zones, the economy and security of the entire region were in an alarming condition. However, Africa was still dealing with an identity crisis. The effects of colonialism combined with the irresponsible and unstructured manner in which the European colonialists transferred power continued to cause civil wars and border disputes in the continent. The expansion of Al-Qaeda in the northwest, military coups in the south-central and independence wars in the east continued to shake the continent. But hope was on the horizon. The recently founded African Union (AU) was expected to improve intercontinental relations and serve as a buffer-zone to external manipulation, allowing Africans to orchestrate their own future.

[114] The goal was not to dethrone the ruling party from power; that would be an impossible battle. It was to gradually score political gains and ultimately offer the public a viable alternative in the political landscape. The party believed the will of the people and peaceful demonstration of self-rule could only be realized when multiple competing ideologies were contested in fair and secured ballot boxes. This would require patience from opposition parties and willingness from the ruling party to share power.

strategist. He was tasked with managing communication channels between the party's headquarters in Addis Ababa and campaign offices in the southern parts of the country. His involvement introduced him to key playmakers. His contribution was instrumental as the party expanded its reach to areas that were never cultivated before.[115]

In a surprise move, the party leaders nominated Henok to run for a seat in the House of Representatives from Jinka and its surroundings. Henok was ecstatic. He quickly advertised the news on all the platforms that he could afford. When his family and friends in Jinka heard that their son was running for office, they could not decide how they felt.

Current government policies excluded them from various benefits that were available for natives. All leadership positions were occupied by the sons and daughters of the native tribes. They wondered if staying too long in Addis Ababa had made Henok forgetful of this reality. But Henok was undeterred. He organized high school students to spread the word. He distributed fliers across small towns explaining how a win against the governing party was possible.

Henok called his old friends living abroad for campaign donations. Seble, Kedir, Mannie, Willie and Yalem, all were excited as Henok gave them a reason to pay attention to the upcoming election; even though none of them believed he had any realistic chance of winning against the corrupt ruling party leaders. But Anteneh was nowhere to be found; no one knew if he had made it to South Africa or got stranded somewhere in between.

---

[115] The biggest challenge was preparing competent candidates for local, regional and national representation. The organizers understood the reputation of the entire party lay on the quality of the candidates and their performance on the campaign trails. So there were many eyes on the process and the scrutiny sometimes could be overwhelming.

Kedir created a team on MySpace[116] to organize communication about the campaign. The number of team members quickly grew as he gained popularity. Using the money flowing from overseas, Henok gave public speeches at markets in every town in his electoral district. He hosted town hall meetings. In a campaign stop in a town called Omorate, Henok gave a speech that galvanized his supporters.[117]

"My brothers and sisters, fathers and mothers! Now is the moment to regain our voices. Our ancestors poured their sweat and blood on this land. This land is as much ours as it is everyone else's. We no longer accept being treated as second-class citizens!" Henok took a deep breath and waited for a cheer. But the crowd mostly stayed quiet, waiting to hear his message.

"You know, they laughed at me when they heard I was running for office. It is not because I was not qualified, my opponent is a middle school dropout. You know why? It is because they thought I was an easy target, because of my ethnic background. But they were mistaken, I mean look at us! We, the people, are proving to them we do not accept this backwardness. We preach love and unity! Unlike them, we don't have a problem with who they are as people. We believe our enemy is corrupt administration and an unjust legal system. All we want is a country that cares about its people. We want a government that serves its people and does not treat them as property.

"We want every town to designate land for public parks and recreational areas, one for every 3,000 residents or each kilometer square. Our children deserve care and protection, and a place where they can feel safe.

---

[116] A popular social networking site at the time.

[117] and outraged his opponents.

"We want a tax deduction for every dependent a person supports. It is not fair for a family man with a wife and three children to pay the same tax as a single man with no dependents.

"We want every road to be expanded to include a separate pedestrian lane and a bike lane. We live in a country where the vast majority of the population do not own vehicles, where students walk to school, and where there are more bikes and motorbikes than cars. Establishing vehicle lanes with no pedestrian and bike lanes is another example that our leaders only care about the few and the privileged, while the rest of us are being treated as property.

"We want every government office to establish a customer service agent. We are tired of waiting on the line for days just to get information.

"We want the anti-corruption agency to be completely free from any influence by the executive and judiciary bodies of government. We want the agency to be given the authority and autonomy needed in order for citizens to freely report fraud and unfair practices.

"There is only one high school in our region, yet there are tens of churches and mosques. If religious leaders care about the future of our society, then they should be expected to provide education in their facilities, for which they pay no taxes by the way!

"We want freedom of expression. The government needs to stop cracking down on journalists.

"We don't want the government to be the largest business owner in the country. We demand privatization of our service providers, which would encourage business competition which would mean better quality and more affordable services for our citizens.

"We want a national mandate to establish an annual salary increase equivalent to the annual economic inflation rate. How can we afford to live with fixed income when the government and business continue to degrade our currency and inflate prices?

"We demand term limits for all elected officials including the president, prime minister, governors, police chiefs, judges, and yes, the House of Representatives!

"My brothers and sisters, fathers and mothers! Now is the moment to regain our voices. We deserve to have a country that cares about its people, a government that serves its country and citizens that are proud of their identity. If our leaders can be stopped from inciting conflicts between citizens, racial diversity can be the beauty of our country. We can turn our differences into the source of our resilience. We can be happy with each other! Vote Henok! Elect me! And I will continue to preach love and unity! I will serve you and represent your values! Thank you! God bless you! And God bless Ethiopia!"

When Henok finished his speech, the crowd went nuts. Supporters flooded the stage and carried him over their heads. Henok's demands were branded as The Ten Commandments! People spread his words in coffee shops, churches, mosques and the markets. His campaign received lots of volunteers and monetary donations.

For the first time, the ruling party acknowledged that they had a major competitor. They tried to negotiate incentives for Henok to drop out of the race, but he refused their offers. They made threats and arrested people close to him, but that only outraged the community. Henok was determined to make a difference.

#

Mannie and Bethi loved their new home in Mons. This historic old city was mostly made up of red-brick terraced houses. They were amazed to see the large forests surrounding the city; they had never seen such green space before. The people were very friendly and considerate.

Mannie and Bethi were scared sometimes because they could not believe that humans could be so altruistic without expecting anything in return.[118]

Yes, they had to learn French to be able to interact freely and also because it was a prerequisite for their study. But they were able to navigate through the new world just fine. They also had help from other Ethiopians that they had met using the Mahbere Kidusan network.

Mannie could not help but compare this wonderful country to his homeland. He found out that, similar to Ethiopia, Belgium had a diverse history.[119] Yet Belgium ranked among the most economically advanced nations in the world. Its citizens enjoyed a high quality of life.

Mannie questioned what went wrong for Ethiopia in that its children did not have the same luck as Belgian children. He tried to research as much as he could during his spare time.[120]

---

[118] The most beautiful fact about Belgians was that they were welcoming. It was normal to see people from different backgrounds enjoying each other's company.

[119] He learned that the country was divided into predominantly Dutch-speaking, French-speaking, and German-speaking communities. The three languages served as the country's official languages. Since its secession from the Kingdom of Netherlands in 1830, Belgium had dealt with internal conflicts fueled by differences in language, culture and the unequal economic distribution between regions. It also served as the "Battlefield of Europe" during the two World Wars. But it overcame all these hurdles.

[120] What he found was, up until the end of the first millennium, Ethiopia was part of the worldwide civilization, including the expansion of Christianity and Islam. But that transformation stopped in Ethiopia, while other countries flourished. The Industrial Revolution in the 18th and 19th centuries was a major turning point for western nations as they transitioned to new manufacturing processes in textiles, steam power, machine tools and foundry. European and North American nations enjoyed sustained average income growth and improved standards of living during the Industrial Revolution. Prior to this period people relied on farming using their own strength to plow their farms or used animals like Oxen and donkeys. They used wood to warm their homes and for cooking. Everything was produced by hand and people wore clothes made from locally found materials such as cotton, animal hides and furs.

The period prior to the Industrial Revolution reminded Mannie of his family's present-day living conditions in Ethiopia. He remembered from his childhood that farming in his village was done by hand and using oxen. Growing up, he and his sisters wore clothes made locally from animal hides and from manually woven cotton. His community depended on a local blacksmith to make hand tools like knives, shovels and bow arrows. Before the first flour mills were installed by a Norwegian Christian charity, his mother used to grind corn and beans using rocks. Prior to joining the hostel where the rooms enjoyed electricity from a private generator, he used kerosene lamps as a source of light at night. The more he compared the transformations in Europe to his homeland, Mannie's appreciation for Emperor Menelik II grew significantly.[121]

Menelik built a prospering nation. Mannie was disappointed to learn about the setbacks in the post-Menelik era. Italy was at least partly to

---

[121] During the era of Zemene Mesafint (Era of the Princes), the often-volatile Ethiopian region was divided into autonomous territories with no central administration. Around the end of the 19th century, Emperor Menelik II conquered the territories that were not administered by European Colonizers and created modern-day Ethiopia. Truth be told, Menelik's army was accused of committing brutal war crimes during the battle for control against residents of the territories. Ethiopia was transformed under Emperor Menelik and rejoined modern society. He moved the nation's capital to a relatively neutral ground. Modern education was formally offered to Ethiopian children. The first modern bank was founded. His administration also introduced the nation's first modern postal system, electricity, telephone, motor cars and railroad. He outlawed slave trades, though he failed to abolish slavery completely. Menelik scored a major victory against Italian invaders in the First Italo-Ethiopian War which galvanized Ethiopia's independence and laid the groundwork for diplomatic relations on the global front as a self-governed African nation. Menelik suffered from a stroke in 1909 and could no longer lead the country. On December 12, 1913, Emperor Menelik II died. His final resting ground at the Bahta Le Mariam Monastery in Addis Ababa is a popular tourist destination.

blame.¹²² But Mannie believed that Ethiopians had to take responsibility for failing against all obstacles, and for not being able to recover quickly.¹²³

Despite Ethiopia's weaknesses, Mannie was grateful for the current administration. They had picked up the nation from extreme poverty and transformed it into a developing nation. They had been working hard in expanding education, healthcare, infrastructure, modern agriculture and manufacturing. Despite the undeniable progress made, they endured fierce criticism from the elite class over the quality and quantity of the deliverables. The administration regularly battled against cultural barriers that were resistant to development initiatives.

Mannie just hoped that they understood, in order for the country to continue to prosper, power should be relayed peacefully to the next generation.¹²⁴ He also hoped that this process would begin during the upcoming national election in which he hoped the opposition parties

---

[122] As the first European army to lose a war against an African nation during the First Italo-Ethiopian War in 1896, the Italians had to live with the humiliation of defeat which also resulted in the resignation of the then Italian Prime Minister Francesco Crispi. But the Italians were not done; they launched a second invasion in 1935 led by the fascist dictator Benito Mussolini. The five-year occupation eventually ended when the Italian army was driven out in 1941 by Ethiopian buffalo soldiers with help from the British military who were at war against the Italians during World War II. So, yeah, Italy played a detrimental role in destabilizing Ethiopia.

[123] After World War II, globalization offered opportunities for Asians, South Americans and Africans to fast-track infrastructure development and economic renaissance. As the world moved forward at pace, Ethiopia remained behind as it struggled with civil wars and political turmoil. As a result, Ethiopian children were forced to grow up under humiliating conditions where they had to beg for food, water, clothes and medicine.

[124] Mannie would agree, too, that life is full of ups and downs. There is no human who is absolute. Everyone has strengths and weaknesses. A person's life is judged by his overall achievements. Leaders are humans, too, they should be judged by their overall contribution to the next generation and their role in helping citizens improve their way of life.

would be able to gain some seats in the parliament and maintain a balance of power.

#

As his plane from Addis Ababa prepared to land at its final destination, Willie watched through the window and could not control his emotions. The bright lights magnified the heights of the sky-high towers. It is the city "that never sleeps." It is the home of the Empire State Building and the Statue of Liberty. It is the city that produced countless legendary world figures. New York! The city that speaks more languages than anywhere else in the world. It is the "land of the free and home of the brave." It is the union of diverse communities under the principle of "One Nation Under God." The United States of America! The nation the entire world looks to for hope and aspiration.

Willie was delighted to see Hasen waiting for him at the airport. Hasen loaded the luggage in the trunk and said, "Get in, bro. Let's get something to eat."

But Willie was still wandering around.

"Is this your car?" he asked with admiration. Hasen nodded his head and smiled. Willie was impressed with his friend's success. "Wow! Man, you are doing great!"

"It's not as big a deal as you might think. Cars are a necessity in this country. Pretty much everyone has a car. Trust me, you will be able to afford one within six months," Hasen explained.

The two continued talking about everything they could think of. They drove into a nearby fast-food restaurant and picked up cheeseburgers. Then Hasen took Willie to a park by the Hudson River. As they stood on a boardwalk, they could see NYC across the river. Hasen explained that they were standing in New Jersey and across the river was New York.

Then Hasen said, "Now let me show you something. It will be quick, I promise."

They walked south for about a quarter of a mile. Hasen pointed his finger and before saying a word, Willie screamed.

"The Lady of Liberty! Ohhh wow! I can't believe this!"

He could not believe such a magnificent place could be visited for free. Hasen explained to him that most tourist attractions and recreational areas in America were public facilities and easily accessible for everyone's use.

But Willie could not stand the cold any longer. "I am freezing!"

Hasen apologized for being inconsiderate and they returned to the car.

Over the next two weeks, Hasen helped Willie obtain a social security number and State ID Card. Willie started his first job as a doorman in a hotel in Manhattan. Every morning he took the bus to the city for work and returned home late in the evening. The work was not difficult. But standing outside the building in the cold was not a pleasant experience. His favorite moment was when received his paycheck every other Friday. He would look at the amount of dollars, calculate it in Ethiopian Birr and smile a big smile. Without making a sound, he would scream in his head, "I am rich, baby!"

A few months later he obtained his driver's license and started a new job at a parking lot underneath the hotel. His new job enabled him to study during slow hours. Willie recounted his life and work experiences during a phone conversation with his sister.

"Friye, everything exceeded my expectations. I do not have words to properly explain America. It is not money that makes it special; you still have to work hard to earn enough. It is not because of the beautiful buildings either; there are also many dangerous neighborhoods. I think it is the people and their tradition." Willie elaborated to his sister. "They are upbeat about the future. The kids are very mature for their ages. Old people try very hard to stay active. Americans are very generous people. If you ask for help, they will stop whatever they are doing to get you the help you need. My coworkers bring me stuff that I did not ask for, because they know I am new in the country. My only wish is to bring you here one day so you can see it for yourself."

Willie was a regular at public libraries near his residence and his workplace. He focused on improving his computer skills and studying the process for returning to school.[125]

Willie had regular phone conversations with Mannie. Since it was cheaper to call from Europe, Mannie was the one who usually called. They compared life in their respective countries and sometimes debated about which was the better side. At times, they merged calls with Seble, Yalem and Kedir and made it a group discussion.

The group was impressed with Henok's ambitious plan to compete in the upcoming Ethiopian election. They were determined to help him in the process and see it to the end.

Willie also traveled to Washington DC on a China Bus to visit Seble,

---

[125] He left no stone unturned at the library. He used MapQuest frequently to discover names of the roads and neighborhoods around him. He prepared a professional résumé and MySpace. He even completed his first tax return using forms that he found at the library. He befriended a couple of guys also regulars at the library, but he ended the friendship when he found out they were into bad habits and mostly used their computer sessions for watching pornography. Willie targeted graduate schools in the field of civil engineering. He took the Graduate Record Examination (GRE) as part of his preparation; it was a prerequisite for enrollment in most engineering programs. He submitted applications for graduate study at Rutgers University and Stony Brook University.

her husband, Walalign Zewde, and their daughter, Edilawit Zewde. He was glad to find that Seble and her family had built themselves a good life. They owned a convenience store where Seble managed the day-to-day operation.

Seble asked Willie to help her with the business. "Willie, I could use your help. It is difficult to find someone you can trust in this business. Most of the workers I hire, I either have to fire them for stealing or they quit without even giving me notice. If you can help me with this store, I promise we will open another together within a year or two."

But Willie informed her of his plans to pursue graduate study and declined the offer.

One evening when Willie returned home, he found a letter from Rutgers School of Engineering.[126] He was not sure if he believed in God anymore, but he prayed anyway before opening the letter. He was heartbroken to find out that he had not been accepted to their program. But he did not give up. He knew that one way or another, he was going to join a graduate program somewhere.

A week later, he received another letter, this time from the Graduate Admissions Office of the State University of New York at Stony Brook. They had accepted his application and referred him to enroll in the registration process and apply for financial aid.

Willie had no fear when he applied for federal loans through the Federal Student Aid (FAFSA) program to cover his tuition and living expenses. The cost of living in Long Island was almost double the cost

---

[126] Rutgers was his primary target. It was conveniently close to his current residence and work. He hoped that they would accept him. So he visited the campus in New Brunswick a lot. He made contact with faculty and student members who were also from Ethiopia. He even participated frequently in events hosted by the local Ethiopian community.

in Orange. He avoided the campus dormitory and rented a room on Craigslist from a nearby private residence.

He thanked Hasen for everything that he had done for him and moved to Long Island to begin his school year. Willie was blown away by the beauty of the university's landscaping.[127]

To his surprise, the university had a diverse student community. Chinese and Indian students probably were among the most visible out of all international students. Willie enjoyed the different cuisines in the area. There were great Italian and Latin American restaurants nearby. Willie regularly visited seafood restaurants around the marina in Port Jefferson. He loved the Soul Food restaurants near the Jamaica rail station.

To connect with his Ethiopian roots, every Sunday morning Willie attended mass at the St Mary Ethiopian Orthodox Church in Manhattan. The church eventually relocated to its new home in Yonkers. Willie loved his life as a New Yorker.

#

In Ethiopia, though, political change was not going as smoothly as Henok had hoped. In a move that would later prove to be a fatal mistake, the Democratic Party entered into a coalition with other opposition parties ahead of the national election.

The coalition party quickly gained strong support from urban communities as well as the diaspora communities living abroad. Televised

---

[127] Suffolk County is one of two counties commonly referred to as Long Island. Its north fork is decorated with chains of vineyards and wineries. The beaches at the Hamptons are popular summer colonies for the wealthy. Stony Brook University is located at the northern shore of Suffolk County. The Long Island Rail Road has a station across the campus. So traveling to the city is convenient.

debates between the ruling party members and the coalition party representatives attracted historic viewing rates. Leaders of the coalition party publicly promoted their intention to win a majority in the election and their preparedness to lead the country.

Representatives of the Democratic Party tried to tamper expectations, preached patience and urged setting a realistic long-term goal. But their views were quickly dampened by popular voices in the coalition. Without a unified objective, the coalition party approached the election date. When the voting results were announced, the coalition party won a significant number of seats for the House of Representatives and in regional assemblies across the country; but the ruling party won the majority.

Leaders of the coalition party protested the results, claiming vast election fraud and voter intimidation at the polling stations. International election observers also concurred that there was heavy election rigging. The opposition leaders boycotted the election results and called for nationwide protests. In Addis Ababa, violent protests turned into riots.

Rioters attacked businesses that were affiliated with the ruling-party members. The Democratic Party leaders were divided on whether to stick with the coalition or split from them and accept the results of the election. It was a double-edged sword. If they stuck with the coalition, then they would be abandoning their long-term goals. If they decided to split with the coalition, then they would be labeled as traitors and would never recover from the public fallout.

The government cracked down on rioters. Many people died on the streets of Addis Ababa. The coalition party leaders were arrested together with thousands of protesters. As the turmoil continued following the arrests, in a theatrical manner, the ruling party also accused the opposition of election fraud.

Despite the unrealistic nature of the claim, the ruling party filed lawsuits. Some judges resigned in protest of pressure from ranking officials. In a surprise outcome, the governing party won in the sham court ruling.

A reelection was held in many of the areas where the opposition had won in the original vote. With the opposition campaign giving up, the ruling party won back most of the seats. Some members of the Democratic Party accepted the results and served in their elected duty, but they would live long enough to realize that they could never recover their reputation. Those that did not accept the election were jailed together with the coalition leaders. The government faced persistent criticism and pressure from the Western nations to release the political prisoners.[128]

Henok was one of those candidates who had won in the original election but was forced to go through a reelection bid. He had run out of energy needed to return to the campaign trail and was drowning in frustration. It was obvious the ruling party had no intention of losing the reelection; they were prepared to make their own luck. Henok was disappointed that it had to come to this point.[129]

All the hard work, by Henok and comrades, since his college days was ruined by the one fatal decision the party made: to form a union with those who were salivating for an overnight change. As a result, the

---

[128] It took two years for the government to release the prisoners. Some fled the country. Others stayed, renewing their political pursuits by forming new parties.

[129] Henok did not enter into politics seeking fame and power. He was never interested in forcing his beliefs on others either. He wanted to make a difference. He wanted to represent what he called the "silent majority," the people with multiracial backgrounds who had been discriminated against by the constitution. He wanted to live in a country whose children could live in peace because political differences were resolved by dialogue.

nation lost a good opportunity to create a political environment where competing ideologies could be floated peacefully.

Henok's dream felt like an unrealistic fantasy. The opposition parties would probably never recover. The governing party would probably tighten its grip on power and resort to its dictatorial habits.

Heartbroken by the failure of his political ambition, Henok fled to Wollo and escaped the toxic environment in Addis Ababa. He stayed with his cousins. Samrawit recently graduated with a degree in health physics and started to work at the local clinic. Henok was very happy with his relationship with Samrawit. He planned to find a job in the area. He wanted to get married to his fiancée and settle down with her.

But Samrawit was feeling differently. She was turned off by Henok's addiction to alcohol and khat; it had gotten worse since he returned to Wollo. His continued bitterness over the failed election and his depressing view of the future rubbed her up the wrong way. She broke off their engagement. Henok was not expecting this; he thought they were having a great time. He tried to convince her that he would change to be the man she wanted. But she had already made up her mind.

Henok was humiliated by the breakup. Samrawit was the main reason why he came to Wollo. There was nothing else left there for him. So he decided to return to Addis Ababa.

Henok stayed with Ismael temporarily. He accepted his old job and returned to teaching. He also wanted to help Ismael in the business. But for the same reasons that Samrawit had broken up with Henok, Ismael did not want to involve him.[130] When Ismael banned Henok from drinking alcohol at home, Henok rented his own place and left.

---

[130] Ismael was already feeling like his brother overstayed at his home, but did not know how to tell him to find his own place.

CHAPTER 9

Mannie was disappointed by the post-election disaster in Ethiopia where the opposition gambled everything and lost, while the government was exposed for its dictatorial leadership.[131] Mannie also felt bad for Henok and sent him money to help him reestablish his life. But Mannie did not think there was anyone specifically to blame. This was the most natural outcome for Ethiopia and consistent with its history. He believed that Murphy's Law was especially true in Ethiopia.[132]

Fortunately, Mannie was pleased with the life he built with Bethi in Belgium. After graduating with her master's degree, Bethi was employed as a teacher in an elementary school. After discussing the options with his wife, Mannie extended his study in the doctorate degree program. A year later, the couple had their first child, a baby girl. They called her Sikeat Amanuel.

To help them care for their baby, the couple agreed to bring Bethi's mother, Woizero Haregeweyn, to Belgium. The grandmother adjusted to life there quickly and became the primary caregiver for baby Sikeat.

---

[131] The situation in Ethiopia also affected its diaspora communities badly. Everyone pointed fingers in different directions placing blame on others.

[132] What would have been abnormal was if the government had willingly shared power with the opposition, or if the opposition had swallowed their pride and worked with whatever was left for them. Neither side was prepared to make such difficult sacrifices for the good of the people. As a result, internal conflicts and instabilities would continue to darken the days for Ethiopian children. The most disappointing of all was that there was no lesson learned by either side, not at least one they could admit in public.

Mannie was initially concerned with the idea of living with his mother-in-law. But the two developed a very good relationship. Most of all, he was grateful to know his daughter was in good hands.

Unfortunately, Mannie was bothered by his relationship with his own family in Ethiopia. He had been sending them money since his first paycheck. In addition to regularly helping his mother and sisters, he had also sent money to his uncles, aunts, cousins, neighbors and childhood friends. But it seemed to him that the more he helped, the higher their expectation.

They had never shown appreciation for his help. Instead, they would tell him stories about the great things other people had received from relatives in America. All of a sudden he became responsible for getting them out of poverty. The worst part was that they made every problem they had an emergency. They showed disappointment that he did not help as much as they wanted.

They made him feel like an underachiever. He knew it was cultural, that no matter how much children supported their parents, the value of what parents had done for their children could never be repaid to the same level.

But Mannie had seen how Belgians raised their children, like they were the most precious part of their lives.[133] Here in Belgium, parents saved money for children to use in college and later life. Parents saved their money for their own retirement plan, too. In Ethiopia, children were their parents' retirement plans.

When Mannie's mother heard that Woizero Haregeweyn was in Belgium taking care of her grandbaby, she was furious with him. She

---

[133] Mannie thought often of the Western saying, "We do not inherit the earth from our ancestors, we borrow it from our children."

took it as disrespect that she was not the primary choice. Mannie tried to make her understand that he had to do what was best for his wife and that was to have her mother by her side to help her get through the early stages of motherhood. He promised her that she could be next, but she was not having it.

She said she had been patient with him. She said she felt embarrassed when people asked what her son had done for her. She complained that she was still living in her old house, when her neighbors moved to new houses that their children had bought for them. But choosing his stepmother over her was the last straw. She told him that he had been nothing but a disappointment all his life, just like his father. Without saying much, he apologized and hung up the phone.

Mannie knew that he owed nothing to his family. If anyone wanted to take credit for his upbringing, it should be the hostel. His last exchange with his mother was a wake-up call. At a time when he was supposed to feel successful and grateful for everything that was happening for him in Belgium, he should not be made to feel like a failure.

He was convinced that the bond with his ancestors needed to end with him. He decided to raise his child free from exposure to the culture he grew up with. He established an automatic monthly money transfer to his mother's bank account of a fixed amount. Then he shut down any and all communication with relatives in Ethiopia. He swore to himself that he would never call them again.

#

After graduating from the Law School of Emory University, Kedir got a job as a Legal Advisor for a government contractor. His job gave him the opportunity to evaluate various federal laws and regulations, and prepare legal guidance for a range of acquisition projects. Following the disastrous Ethiopian election, Kedir was touched by the news about hopeless Ethiopian migrants flocking to the Middle East, Europe and North America. These migrants risked their lives by being smuggled in dangerous conditions.[134]

In Atlanta, since there were not adequate immigration lawyers with in-depth understanding of the conditions in Ethiopia, asylum seekers had to move to Washington DC where the Ethiopian American community had established a strong presence. Kedir knew he was capable of serving his community. So he resigned from his job and opened his own firm.[135]

Kedir quickly gained popularity in the Metro-Atlanta's Ethiopian, Eritrean, Somali and Sudanese communities. His office was swamped by asylum seekers. Kedir worked day and night, and still the workload increased. He hired a paralegal to perform daily administrative duties. Then he hired a case worker who could communicate with asylees, gather facts, and develop case statements. The additional staff provided much-needed help, but the workload continued to grow.

One day, the case worker handed Kedir an asylee's draft case summary for review. While doing this, Kedir noticed some strange information. The case summary stated that this person was from Eritrea, but she was

---

[134] Many died attempting to cross the Red Sea and the Mediterranean Sea. Countless were robbed and enslaved by armed criminals in Libya, Yemen and in the Sinai Peninsula of Egypt. Those who finally arrived in their preferred destinations struggled to find legal assistance to complete immigration processing.

[135] The Law Office of Kedir Ebrahim provided affordable services, including preparing case statements for asylum seekers, helping them complete immigration forms and defending their cases in court. His firm also offered legal assistance for family-based immigration processing and translation to English of documents originally in Amharic.

born in Jinka, Ethiopia. It said she was deported to Eritrea during the war between the two countries, together with the rest of her family.

The case claimed that one of her older brothers was drafted for Eritrean military service upon their arrival there. The remaining family members were placed at a refugee camp. The family had not heard from him since. After the war ended the Eritrean government released the family from the camp. They were not given any assistance to help them integrate into their new community. Without a job or other means of income, the family became dependent on distant relatives. At the age of seventeen, the asylee was forced to run out of the country and headed to South Africa.[136]

As the situation got worse, the case said she was forced again to flee and join other migrants on a smuggling route to Mexico. She was then smuggled to Texas, but moved to Atlanta because she had people who could help there. It stated that she could not return to her birth country, which had already deported her, and the other country was led by a notorious dictator who abused his people.

Sometimes case workers were provided false information. Kedir's initial thought was that the asylee was lying to the caseworker. The asylee's name was Asmeret Fiseha. He met with her in the office. He told her that he was born and raised in Jinka but he did not recognize her. He advised her that lying to the immigration court would be a bad idea. But she insisted that she told the truth. She named her brothers, parents and other people she remembered from Jinka, including her brother's friend Willie.

Everything quickly became clear to Kedir. He realized she was

---

[136] At the time, South Africans were protesting against African migrants and extremists were attacking the migrants.

Kibrom Fiseha's baby sister. He could not believe how much she had grown. He told her that he used to play soccer with Kibrom. As he told her stories, she also remembered him. She said Kedir had changed a lot. He joked he was well aware that he was twice the size that he used to be. He promised her he would personally attend to her case. He told her that he was very sorry her family was forced out of their home and suffered so much.

As soon as she left, Kedir called Willie, "Dude, you would not believe who I just met."

"Who, Senator Barack Obama?" joked Willie.[137]

"No man. Asmeret Fiseha. You remember her brother…" Before Kedir finished explaining, Willie interrupted him.

"Are you kidding me? Is Asmeret here?" He had always wondered what happened to her family. He had felt personally guilty even though he had no power to stop the government from deporting them. He could only imagine the betrayal the family had felt. Willie thought it was the ugliest form of discrimination that he had ever witnessed.

"Yes, she is here in Atlanta. I am handling her asylum case. She had been through a lot." Kedir discussed his encounters with Asmeret.

Willie was sad to learn that Kibrom was forced to fight during the war. He had heard similar stories about Eritrean soldiers forcing refugees to pick up guns and join the battlefield. Some of them were captured by Ethiopian soldiers and became prisoners in the country that had deported them.

Willie wondered what happened to her other brother Haftom

---

[137] Ever since Kedir had opened the law firm, he had been acknowledged by local civil rights leaders for his contribution to helping migrants in the community. At the same time, the senator from Illinois was campaigning for the Democratic Party's nomination to represent the party in the presidential election.

and the rest of the family. He begged Kedir to give him her contact information, but Kedir refused to transfer a client's information without her permission. He promised to talk to her about it when they next met and give her Willie's number if she agreed.

#

Willie spent most of his free time on campus listening to campaign speeches of the then presidential candidate Barack Obama. He was inspired by the candidate's eloquent oratorical skills. Obama responded to every question from the audience, no matter how annoying or disrespectful the questions might be, with respect and using simple examples. He was always in control of his emotions. He preached love, unity and uplifting the country's middle class. Even doubters were impressed by his knowledge of American history.

Obama was direct with his views. He strongly supported the hunting down of Osama bin Laden. But he was opposed to the war in Iraq. Obama wanted to invest more in the nation's infrastructure and the development of disadvantaged communities, instead of spending a big portion of the country's budget on foreign wars. He believed that all Americans should have access to basic healthcare.

Like most Ethiopian Americans, Willie also believed, if Obama became president, the nature of the relationship between the United States and Africa would change. Willie was hopeful that Obama would help Africans to control their own destiny with less meddling from the international community.

Willie had also been searching for a way to bring his sister, Fre, to the US. When he graduated with his master's degree, prior to deciding whether to continue his study for the doctoral degree, he invited Fre to attend his graduation ceremony. But her visa application was denied at the embassy. He reached out to other Ethiopians at the church to see if anyone was interested in cross-marriage for the immigration purpose.

Willie participated in various Ethiopian American Community events to learn more about other forms of immigration that people had used before. He then heard about an event planner whose firm sponsored artists from Ethiopia for various occasions. The firm also conducted a side business of smuggling people to the country using pseudo-résumés as artists. But the price was too much for Willie to afford.

One day, Willie was invited by someone he had met at the church to a political fundraising event at Columbia University. He accepted, paid for the ticket and arrived at the conference room. This was the largest Ethiopian-American gathering that he had seen since he left his homeland.

The main guest was one of the leaders of the failed coalition party. Following his release from prison, he returned to the US. Willie heard him on YouTube discussing the need for armed rebellion against the Ethiopian government. Willie always objected to war as a solution to peace; he believed it never worked.

The guest gave a passionate speech. "We exhausted every peaceful approach. Our opponent refused to allow a democratic political process. The governing party suppressed our voters, arrested our leaders and destroyed our institutions. They increased their grip on power. At present, even judges are required to be members of the governing party. Meanwhile, our people continue to live in poverty. Our children have suffered diseases and malnutrition. Our citizens are denied basic human rights. What other choice do we have?"

Willie was disappointed hearing this guy invent a false narrative for his ultimate goal.[138] Willie supported the coalition party during the election. He was opposed to a one-party system as well. Willie was also a believer in that the constitution of Ethiopia needed to be amended. But he disagreed with the guest for suggesting there was no hope of finding a peaceful solution in Ethiopian politics.

As far as Willie was concerned, finding a peaceful avenue for opposition should be mandatory for the country. If there was no peaceful avenue, Willie would recommend politics to be left as is and citizens focus instead on education and economic development.[139] Willie felt like the politician had already made up his mind about joining armed rebellion and was simply recruiting supporters for his movement.

When the politician started taking questions from the audience, Willie raised his hand. The politician invited him to speak.

"Thank you. Uhu uhu," Willie cleared his throat. "Looking back to the time when the coalition party boycotted the election, do you still believe it was the right decision? Don't you think the country would have benefited more had the opposition accepted the results and remained competitive?"

"We had no choice at the time. No matter how much concession we made, the ruling party was not interested in democracy." The politician rubbed sweat from his bald head. "Everything we did was consistent with basic human rights and in accordance with international laws.

---

[138] Ethiopians fought each other for thousands of years. Nobody came out victorious. They just dragged each other down to the poverty line. Hunger and malnutrition had been a problem throughout Ethiopia's history. The politician was wrong to relate that to the current administration.

[139] After all, isn't bread more important than freedom? Isn't it true that some unfair traditions naturally fade away as more and more people modernize their way of life?

But the dictatorial regime murdered hundreds of peaceful protestors, arrested tens of thousands of them. Our people are still suffering in jail without the opportunity for legal representation. We did the only thing that we were capable of doing at the time—demand the government hear our voices. What they did to us and our people was uncalled for; it was inhumane." The politician looked in another direction for more questions.

But Willie was not finished. "I agree that the ruling party was everything you said. As a leader of the opposition, do you take any responsibility for the post-election riot and the follow-up massacre of innocent lives?"

The politician was visibly disturbed by Willie's insinuation. He was out of words. Two people with suits and ties approached Willie and directed him out of the room. As he exited, Willie continued his protest, yelling, "You have failed us before. How are you better than them? Why should we trust you now? Please no more war! Say no to a warmonger!"

Willie understood that he would be a public enemy in the local Ethiopian-American community. He was sure that many people were offended by his action. So he planned to avoid attending church events and other social gatherings in the short term.[140] Willie just hoped this politician got the message, that history was watching him.

As Willie was on the train back to Long Island contemplating his earlier adventure, his phone rang. He did not recognize the number, but picked it up anyway. "Hello?"

---

[140] Most people never liked talking about bad things that happened in the past; they preferred remembering the good times and pretending the journey was worth it. But Willie believed such behavior was a recipe for repeated mistakes. He believed people who were unwilling to recognize past mistakes were not prepared to correct them. He was happy that he had finally found the right way to voice his opinion.

"Hi, is this Willie? I mean, Awlachew Dechasa?" A woman was on the other end. Since she spoke to him in Amharic, he quickly guessed who it might be. Kedir had told him that Asmeret had accepted his contact information. He had been waiting to hear from her.

"Yes, this is Willie." He tried to keep his voice steady but excitement bubbled over. "Please tell me you are Asmeret!"

"Hihihi…yes I am." She laughed a little. "How did you know?"

"You were too little to remember, but I was a magician." He joked.

"Hihihi…I did not know that." She laughed again. "But I remember you were a good soccer player. Kibrish used to come home upset when he lost penalty shootouts with you."

"Hahahaha…I am surprised you have such a good memory." Willie's voice suddenly changed. "Look, before I ask about your family, I would like to apologize about how our people treated your family. I am so sorry."

"Thank you, Willie." Asmeret could not hold her tears. "I felt betrayed. Before I realized what was happening, our life quickly changed from a happy, successful family to refugees in a war zone."

She talked about some of the horrors her family endured during the war. Willie was moved as she detailed the family's journey. Her parents were currently residing at their grandmother's home in Adi Kuala. Haftom, who she referred to by his nickname Haftish, was in Egypt. He attempted multiple times to migrate to Israel, but the security forces at the border were difficult to penetrate. Thus, he settled for life in a port town on the Suez Canal. Asmeret said she had not heard from Kibrom since he was drafted for military service.

Willie and Asmeret talked over the phone for almost two hours. She appreciated his sympathy and understanding. Willie could tell from her voice how much she had missed her childhood life and her old friends in

Jinka. Despite her difficult experiences, he found her to be very positive and optimistic. He admired her strength. He wanted to make sure of one more thing before she said goodbye. "Can I call you on this number?"

"Hihihi…yes." She laughed again. "If I don't call you back first."

And the call ended.

#

Yalem became a nurse at a senior-living home in Calgary. She was a caring and loving nurse. Her patients and coworkers adored her. Since arriving in Canada, Kaleb and Yalem were roommates until he fell in love with an older woman and moved in with her. He was the closest person she had as a family in the country. He worked as a truck driver and his job regularly required him to transport goods to and from Vancouver. He was barely seen in town any longer. But whenever he had a chance, he would pick up Yalem and the two would dine in a nearby Ethiopian restaurant.

Kaleb always nagged her to ditch her on-off, long-distance relationship with Yonathan. He encouraged her to date someone from the area. He even introduced her to some of his friends. But for a reason that he could not understand, she was stuck in the past and could not move forward. During their latest dining, he raised the issue again, "Yami, you're like the sister I never had." He gave her the nickname. "I hate to see you hung up alone. Can you please open your heart to any person not named Yonathan?"

"Come on Kaleb, not again. You know how much I love Yoni. When it is true love, you fight for it and you try to make it work despite the challenges. Things are getting better. He calls me every day now."

Yalem knew that she sounded too optimistic. But it was her choice. She acknowledged that the distance had been a big hurdle in their relationship.

She visited Melbourne twice and during both visits, she could feel they had a great relationship. But when she returned home, Yonathan did not maintain the same level of enthusiasm. She often made excuses when he became emotionally distant. Yonathan recently opened a new Ethiopian Lounge in the suburb of Melbourne in a town called Footscray. He complained a lot about how much time his job needed and he could not find a reliable person to manage the day-to-day operation.

Outside of her relationship issues, life had been great for Yalem in Canada. Every day she drove to work, she looked around with happiness and praised the Lord for blessing her. The environment and its disciplined society reminded her of the time in her childhood when she used to imagine what heaven would be like.

As a child Yalem used to deal with many nightmarish dreams in which someone tried to attack her while she screamed for help. Her nightmares were usually interrupted by her parents waking her for screaming. Those dreams were no longer happening.

Yalem once returned to Ethiopia to visit her family in what turned into an emotional trip. She had left town on foot as a teenager and then returned home on a fancy helicopter. She cried as she was finally reunited with her parents, who were still alive. "Babaye, Mamaye, I missed you so much!" There were moments when she had felt this would never happen.

Her mom and dad cried with her, showing that the feeling was mutual. The family hosted a huge party celebrating her return. For the next few days, the town's beggars were served free meals in front of their house. Yalem also gathered homeless kids and gave away money to buy the equipment needed to work as shoe shiner. But the neighbors complained that she was inviting thieves and risking the safety of the neighborhood. So she gave away the remaining donation through the local church. She spent most of her time in her hometown catching up with family and friends.

Before her return to Calgary, Yalem convinced her mother to come with her to Canada for a short visit. After completing the visa process in Addis Ababa, mother and daughter flew together to Calgary. At first, her mother loved everything she was experiencing. Yalem and her mother visited a zoo, walked around the Bow River parks, shopped at the city's glamorous malls, took a ride on the train and dined at Ethiopian restaurants.

After a week, Yalem returned to work. Her mother could not cope with staying alone in the house with no one to talk to. She had no interest in staring at the TV screen when she did not even understand what they were talking about. She spent most of her time cooking Ethiopian food and sleeping on the sofa. She watched her daughter return from work and go straight to bed without having a decent conversation. At night, she could not sleep because she had napped during the day. So she monitored her daughter's sleeping habits. Yalem snored a lot. Her mother thought, "Well, at least she stopped having those nightmares."

Yalem's mother was bothered by how hard her daughter worked. She wondered how Western professional life was any different from modern slavery. Employees were expected to clock in and out at set times and perform beyond their capability. They worked hard, but they could not even afford to hire a maid to help in the house.

Most of all, she equated the private lifestyle of Canadians to a loneliness that could deprive people of the emotional satisfaction that comes from social interaction. She was shocked to learn that her daughter and neighbors did not even know each other's names; the only words they exchanged when they crossed paths in the hallway was "Hello!" or "Thank you!"

Yalem's mother asked herself, "Is this how all our children in the diaspora earn the money that they send us every month?"

She felt sorry for her daughter. She also felt ashamed for asking Yalem to buy her this and that in the past. She promised to herself that, once she returned to Ethiopia, she would never ask her daughter for a single penny again.

Yalem could not convince her mother to extend her stay. She insisted that she was worried her husband, Ato Kebede, needed her back in Jinka. The truth was, she wished she could convince Yalem to pack her stuff and move back with her to their hometown. Prior to her departure, she wanted to make sure her daughter was not going to continue to live this lonely life. She challenged Yalem to sort out her relationship with Yonathan within the next year. Otherwise, she asked Yalem to be open to an arranged marriage from Ethiopia. Yalem accepted her mother's challenge and promised to work on it.

#

The 2008 American presidential election was one of the most memorable election campaigns in history. Everyone with common sense expected that America was not ready for a black president. Some voters publicly questioned Obama's citizenship, heritage, religion and loyalty to the country and its constitution.

But in his famous acceptance speech that night in Chicago after he was declared the winner, Obama said, "And to all those who have wondered if America's beacon still burns as bright—tonight we proved once more that the true strength of our nation comes not from the might of our arms or the scale of our wealth, but from the enduring power of our ideals: democracy, liberty, opportunity and unyielding hope."[141]

Meantime, Washington DC prepared for the inauguration. Seble's family renovated their house in anticipation of hosting a large number of guests. All hotels in town were almost sold out and the remaining ones raised prices to ridiculous amounts. Seble already agreed to host Willie and Kedir. In what would be her first trip to the US, Yalem planned to join them as well. Seble's husband, Walalign, also expected some family members from the West Coast. In the days ahead of the inauguration, millions of visitors swarmed the capital to witness and celebrate this historic date.

The day of the inauguration was very cold: a blistering wind made the temperature feel like single digits. Seble's convenience store operated 24 hours. But on Tuesday, January 20, 2009, she closed the store early in the morning and gave her employees paid time off to celebrate the inauguration. Around 8:00 a.m, Seble, Walalign, their daughter Edilawit and their guests headed to a train station near their residence on Georgia Avenue. They boarded the green line train going downtown, exiting at the Archives-Navy Memorial Station and followed the crowd toward the national mall. But they found out they could not cross Pennsylvania Avenue. The road was fenced and guarded by a heavy security presence.

There were jumbo screens hanging along the street. Everyone could observe the ceremony from the staged area at the Capitol. During his inaugural address, Obama expressed his appreciation for Americans for

---

[141] This did not stop the conspiracy theories of course, but it did speak to the hearts of our immigrant friends in these pages.

"the trust that you have bestowed on me and mindful of the sacrifices borne by our ancestors." He discussed the crisis facing Americans and the world. He promised the nation that was crippled by the great economic recession to "pick ourselves up, dust ourselves off and begin again the work of remaking America."

Obama promised the Muslim world that America seeks "a new way forward based on mutual interest and mutual respect." He warned dictatorial regimes, who seek to sow conflict or blame their society's ills on the west, to "know that your people will judge you on what you can build, not what you destroy." He also warned "those who cling to power through corruption and deceit, and the silencing of dissent, know that you are on the wrong side of history." He promised that America "will extend a hand if you are willing to unclench your fist."

When Barack Hussein Obama was sworn in as the 44th President of the United States, the crowd burst into tears. Then the inaugural parade started along Pennsylvania Avenue toward the White House. As the limousine carrying President Obama and First Lady Michelle Obama approached, Seble's team joined the crowd screaming with excitement. The crowd grew even louder when the limousine stopped. The president and first lady exited the vehicle and waved left and right. The vice president and his family also followed the president walking along the parade route. The Ethiopians could not help but be swept up in this emotional journey happening across the Atlantic Ocean.

"I cannot believe this! I am standing only feet away from the most powerful person in the world, and I am not getting pushed around by police!" Kedir exclaimed. "I remember how scary it was to walk past the presidential palace in Addis Ababa. As I walked on the road, my hands used to sweat and my legs used to shake. I kept my head down, fearing

I would get shot if I looked up. The area was as quiet as a cemetery. The only people that I could see were the armed guards standing at the security posts above the tall concrete fence. What a difference!"

"Do you remember when we were kids, the time when the former Ethiopian president visited Jinka?" Seble recalled her childhood experience. "When he exited his helicopter, it looked like the lord of hell arrived. Everyone was intimidated. Security forces disturbed the crowd by beating, pushing and shoving to maintain an imaginary line. The president did not even give a speech. He quickly entered the vehicle and paraded the town. The only thing people could see were waving hands stretching out of the vehicle windows. Now look at us. We are still the same ordinary people. The only thing different is the country that we are in, its culture and the system that governs us. I wish I could share this moment with all my people back home."

"Ohhh yes, I remember. Henok and Beyina Ali were chosen to present flowers to the president." Willie nodded. "Ohhh man. Ever since that time, Henok always felt he was special. He also felt like he would one day marry Beyina. Then when we got to middle school, he found out that she was dating someone and he was devastated. He never mentioned her name ever since."

"Why are you always bringing up your childhood experience when you are having a great time?" Edilawit complained to her mother. "You should just cherish this moment."

Seble and her friends had no response to the little girl's wise observation. "You are absolutely correct, Ediliye," Seble apologized to her daughter.

Just then, a guy holding some memorabilia certificates approached and asked if they would like to buy one. It confirmed their presence in this historic inauguration. Seble read the certificate titled "A NEW BIRTH OF FREEDOM." She bought about a dozen copies and handed one to each person as a gift to remember.

CHAPTER 10

Henok struggled to cope with the challenges that life continued to throw at him. The cost of living in Addis Ababa had reached a level he could no longer afford on his teacher's salary. After paying rent, he could barely afford meals three times a day. He switched his eating habit to twice a day. He started a second job tutoring high school students, which provided some relief.[142]

One day Henok received disturbing news from Jinka. His mother was very sick and had been taken to the emergency room. The news could not have come at a worse time. It was the middle of the month and Henok had already run out of money. His next paycheck was two weeks away. But he could not wait that long. He would not be able to live with himself if she died at the hospital in Jinka.

Zeineb meant everything to Henok. She sacrificed a lot to give him and his younger siblings a better life. Because the income from their father's tailoring business used to be inconsistent and barely covered their basic needs, Zeineb had to sell Tella and Tej. It was Henok's dream to one day give his mother all the best things he knew she deserved. He

---

[142] He was not alone in this struggle; a large majority of the city's residents could not afford to keep paying their rent. The value of the dollar skyrocketed every day. Yet the average salary increase was extremely small. The city's annual inflation rate was over 50 percent. The government injected borrowed cash into the economy funding various projects. Lack of oversight on these projects allowed embezzlement. The government was the engine of the corruption machine that trapped the nation. The gap between the rich and poor was inhumanely disappointing.

wanted to see her being proud of his accomplishments.

All of that seemed impossible now. Henok felt he was out of options. He could not ask Ismael to lend him money. The two had not spoken to each other in a long time. Henok was not even able to repay money that he had borrowed from his brother in the past.

As Henok was sitting at home feeling sorry for himself, his phone rang. "Hello?" Henok picked up the call and answered quickly. It was Willie in America. Henok felt like the angel of the Lord just visited him. "Bro, my mother is at the hospital in Jinka. And I don't know what I am going to do." As Henok explained the situation, tears poured down both sides of his nose. He let out all his emotions to his childhood friend.

"I am so sorry, Heni." Willie had called to ask Henok for help with information related to a real estate financing program. But he was sad to hear of Zeineb's illness. "Heni, you know Etiye Zeineb was like a mother to me. You are not alone in this. Please calm down." He promised Henok that he would call soon and hung up the phone.

Willie quickly called all his friends and informed them of the situation. They all agreed to contribute some money. He gathered the money and sent it to Henok. Then Willie called Henok and told him about everyone's contribution. He urged Henok to bring Zeineb to Addis Ababa and get her checked in a good hospital.[143]

Willie regarded Zeineb as the best person he had known as a child. He told Henok that he would continue to assist with the medical expenses.

---

[143] The hospital in Jinka was poorly staffed. The facility's sanitation was substandard. Many people used to walk in for treatment and ended up coming out on a stretcher or, even worse, in a coffin. Many women lost their babies during delivery; some even lost their own lives due to complications. Since there was no law for protecting patients from medical negligence, victims and their families would not even get compensated for their suffering.

Henok was grateful for having such loyal friends.

The next day, Henok cashed out the money and traveled to his hometown. The same evening, he arrived in Arba Minch. He did not want to wait till morning to catch the bus. Instead, he got on the back of a loaded truck and continued the journey home by night. The wind blew dirt from the road onto the truck. Henok and the other travelers could not inhale in the dusty air. They covered their faces with light cloth to filter it. The potholes on the road made the truck dance up and down and the passengers begged the driver to slow. On one occasion, the truck's tires were slammed into a large hole; Henok almost fell off the guardrail. In the end, they arrived in Jinka around 2:00 a.m. Henok looked like he had just come out of a mine cage.

Henok asked the driver to drop him at the intersection of the road leading to the hospital. He quickly jumped off and ran toward the hospital. Its gate was already closed. Henok knocked on the metal door very hard. The gatekeeper came out of a security booth and told Henok this was not a visitation time. Henok handed some cash to the gatekeeper and the door was opened.

He hustled through the hospital hallways, searching for the room where his mother was staying. He saw his sister Feker at the other end of the hallway and rushed toward her. She looked disappointed in him. He tried to hug her, but she walked away. He had no time for family drama and just walked into the room.

Zeineb was on a ventilator. Her face looked pale and she had lost a lot of weight. Henok knew that his mother had not been feeling well for a while. But she always downplayed her pain and resisted medical treatment. So he had not taken it seriously. He was shocked to see how bad her condition was.

"How can you let this happen?" Henok directed his frustration toward his father. Desta tilted his head down and stayed quiet.

"Who are you to blame us?" Feker looked at Henok with disgust. "When was the last time you cared for this family?" The siblings started to throw insults at each other.

"Enough!" Desta screamed. "Your mother is in a life-or-death situation. All you are thinking is about your own feelings?" Desta struggled to control his anger and left the room in protest.

Henok stared down Feker and quickly followed his father outside. "I am sorry Dad," Henok apologized. "Willie sent me money. We need to take Mom to a good hospital."

Desta calmed down. The two returned to the room and discussed with the rest of the family about transferring her to a hospital in Addis Ababa. But the next scheduled flight was four days away and they could not wait that long. They decided to take her to the Arba Minch General Hospital instead. Mekit was sent to hire a minibus.

In the meantime, Henok tried to get hold of the only doctor at the hospital to get him to prepare a referral letter. But the doctor refused to write a referral because he did not believe she was in a condition to travel. After several hours of negotiations, the doctor buckled under pressure and processed her release. The family quickly moved her into the minibus and sprinted out of town.

After traveling about twenty-five miles, they approached a small town called Key Afer. Feker screamed for the bus to stop. Zeineb was struggling to breathe. They carried her out of the vehicle and laid her on the grass. Feker used her jacket to ventilate the air, hoping it would cool her mother down. But nothing they did seemed to help.

In the middle of the road, the family helplessly watched Zeineb as she took her last breath. As her heart stopped beating, Feker fell to the ground and sobbed. The family surrounded Zeineb's body and continued to cry. As the head of the family, Desta urged the family to get it together. He asked Henok to help him move her body back into the vehicle. The minibus turned around and rolled back to Jinka for the funeral.

#

The passing of Henok's mother saddened the friends in the diaspora. Willie was especially affected. In addition to being godmother to his sister, Zeineb was the mother figure from his childhood. After his mother's sudden death in the car accident, Willie did not know how he and his sister would have survived if they had not had Zeineb on their side.

Willie had tried to show his appreciation to Zeineb by sending her money on several occasions since he arrived in the US. But it now felt like he had not done enough. He wanted to return to Ethiopia, but it was a difficult time as he was finalizing his dissertation. He was getting ready to graduate in a few months.

As a onetime close friend of Henok, Mannie had many memories with Henok's family. So he also felt very bad. Kedir, Seble and Yalem did not have a close relationship with Zeineb. But they were sympathetic to the heartbreak Henok was feeling. The friends contributed more money to help out with the funeral and other expenses. They also called Henok regularly and encouraged him to remain strong and not lose hope.

Meanwhile, for the first time since his departure over a decade ago, Kedir planned to return to Ethiopia on a short trip. At the time the Ethiopian government was providing incentives for the diaspora community to invest in the homeland. Kedir arranged a deal to lease a large farmland around Jinka for a cattle production business.

As a child, Kedir used to wonder why meat was expensive, while the country was one of the largest livestock producers in the African continent. Most families in his hometown had owned at least a couple of cows, a goat and a couple of hens. But they used them more like pets than food sources. Even though there were more cattle on the roads than vehicles, beef and chicken were a once-a-week type of food for most families.

Kedir wanted to play a role in improving the supply of meat, milk and other dairy products in the market. He studied American cattle ranchers, dairy farms and the use of growth-promoting hormones. He developed a business model that he hoped would transform the traditional way of herding. Traveling to Ethiopia, he felt proud of his plans.

Upon his arrival in Addis Ababa, Kedir participated in a conference for the diaspora investors. He was encouraged by the value of his dollars; he was basically a millionaire there. Kedir was amazed by the opportunities presented.[144]

The value of money in the country made Kedir ask himself: *How come I never got a "thank you" from the people that I helped?* Friends and family members had always called him for help. After receiving the amount that they had initially asked for, they would call him back about another problem they were dealing with. That used to make him feel unappreciated and unaccomplished.

---

[144] With the nation's currency declining rapidly, the government suffered a shortage of dollar influx. They were practically giving away land for various investment opportunities. On top of that, the dollar was worth up to 50 percent more on the black market. And that was really no longer black as there were dollar exchange boutiques at every corner of the city.

In Addis Ababa, Kedir was contacted by an engineer who claimed to be working for the land management office in a district outside of the city's boundary. The engineer promised him that his office would provide over 4,000 square feet of land per person for a group of five to ten people, but the group had to agree to build a three-story building minimum. The land lease was free for ninety-nine years. The engineer and his anonymous partners demanded 50,000 Birr per lot in cash, which was equivalent to $4,000 for land in an area that was expected to be included in the city's boundary anytime. It was a bargain Kedir could not refuse.

He did not hesitate, quickly reaching out to his mother, Willie, Seble, Yalem, Mannie, Asmeret and other friends and families. He also included his grandmother in the deal. He established a group of fifteen partners and made a deal with the engineer. In less than a week, the process was complete and he acquired the land.

Kedir already knew that bribery was part of the normal business practice, but it was mind-boggling to see it happening. No administrative service was completed without delay unless a side deal was done with the officials or their representatives.

After completing his business deals, Kedir traveled with his grandmother to her birthplace in Butajira.[145] He had heard many stories about Gurage. But this was his first time visiting his ancestral home.

On the day they arrived in Butajira, they were greeted by heavy rain. Kedir smiled as the clay soil on the muddy road prevented them from walking freely. It reminded him of his childhood experience in Jinka.

---

[145] Butajira is a beautiful town in the highlands of Gurage about eighty miles south of Addis Ababa. In addition to their work ethic, the Gurage people are famous for their traditional cuisines and unique homemade beverages.

They sheltered in a nearby restaurant until the rain stopped and then ordered lunch.

Just then a little boy entered the restaurant holding a shoe shiner's kit and offered to clean up Kedir's muddied shoes. "Listro?"[146]

Knowing that they still had to walk on the mud once the rain stopped, Kedir declined his offer. "No thanks."

"Sir, you will not regret. Trust me, I do a great job." The kid was persistent. "Because you are such a nice person, I will give you a 50 percent discount."

Amused by the kid's negotiation skills, Kedir finally agreed. "Okay. But be careful to not mess up my socks."

To Kedir's surprise, the kid did a great job. Kedir tipped him much more than the price he asked.

"Thank you! Nice doing business with you!" The kid carried his kit and started calling on other customers in the restaurant. "Listro?"

Kedir smiled and told his grandmother, "This kid is amazing!"

A few minutes later, another kid appeared in front of them holding lotteries. They did not want the lottery, but they ended up buying some after the kid refused to go away. Then a third kid appeared holding home-cooked snacks. As they expected, he was ready for negotiation. They gave him some money and asked him to leave with his snacks. After finishing their lunch, while they were cleaning their hands, they saw a fourth kid entering the restaurant carrying a church donation box. They quickly paid for the lunch and hurried out.

They hopped on a horse-drawn vehicle and darted out to a nearby village where the brother of Kedir's grandmother lived.

Kedir quickly made friends with his distant relatives. One day as they

---

[146] Listro is the Amharic word for a shoe shine.

gave him a tour of the village, a house across the street caught Kedir's attention. In front of the house, there was a sign selling locally popular non-alcoholic homemade beverages there. But his eyes were attracted by a beautiful girl that was going in and out of the house.

One of his entourage told him that her name was Halimah and that she was a nurse in the clinic down the road. She also helped her mother in the house brewing the drinks. Kedir and his entourage went inside and ordered drinks. For anyone who watched them playing loudly, it would seem like the drink might be more than non-alcoholic.

As everyone was distracted by the noise, Kedir managed to introduce himself to Halimah. "Assalam Alaikum."

Seeing his appearance and outspoken personality, she already knew that he was a diaspora. "Look, just because you see me pouring drinks, it doesn't mean I'm a prostitute." She told him that she had no interest in being a fawn to a runaway fox.

"Who said I'm looking for a prostitute?" Kedir replied with a smile. He was cognizant of the widely believed stereotype about the diaspora community taking advantage of their poor homeland and disrespecting traditional values.

"Okay. I just want to set the record straight." She cooled down a little.

"My friends tell me that you're a great person. So I wanted to meet you," Kedir explained.

"How about you? What did you think when you saw me?" Halimah asked while studying his expression.

"I think you're the most beautiful woman I've ever seen." Kedir poured his heart out. "I promise you that I only have good intentions, Wollahi!"

Suddenly, a customer at the other end of the room complained that she had ignored his request for additional drinks. She apologized to the customer whom she knew by name and ran into the backroom to get drinks.

After some time, Kedir paid the bill for the entire house and left with his friends. As soon as Kedir arrived home, he announced to his grandmother and the rest of the family his intention to marry Halimah. They were all delighted. The family sent an urgent request to Halimah's parents to allow the marriage. They received a positive response. Following the tradition of Islam, a Nikah ceremony was held, and Kedir and Halimah were declared husband and wife.

A few days later, Kedir and Halimah went on honeymoon to a nearby vacation destination called Langano. Then they traveled to Addis Ababa on a shopping spree. The new couple agreed that Halimah would remain with her parents until Kedir was able to process the visa application for her to join him in Atlanta.

Kedir could not extend his stay any longer. First he returned Halimah to her hometown. With a lot accomplished and after meeting the love of his life, Kedir appreciated his homecoming experience. He flew back to the US, this time knowing that he would return again. He was already looking forward to it.

#

Willie completed writing his dissertation, which was a prerequisite for his graduation, and gave it to his graduate advisor for review. As he waited for his advisor's input, Willie started planning for a career move. He quickly realized job interviews also required lots of preparation and patience.

On one occasion, he was interviewed for a position in an oil and gas company at a career fair organized by the university. The interviewer was an African American male who openly undervalued Willie's qualification because of his slow English and the country he came from, famously known for its challenges with drought and hunger. As Willie tried to respond to one question, the interviewer impatiently interjected with more questions. The interviewer also mentioned that he had dated many Ethiopian girls in Houston and made jokes about how much Ethiopian men disliked seeing their females dating people from other ethnic backgrounds. After that, the conversation lost its direction. Willie left the interview with a clear understanding that he was not going to get the job.

Another time, Willie was invited to New Hampshire for an interview with a local engineering firm. The night before his interview, the town was hit with a severe winter storm when about three feet of snow fell. The next morning Willie expected the firm would close for a snow day, but he was informed that they were open and looking forward to interviewing him. During the interview, the hiring manager suggested that the organization needed to hire minorities to comply with affirmative action requirements.[147] Willie immediately knew that, even if they offered him the job, he was not going to accept it.

As soon as the interview was over, he took a taxi to the airport. At

---

[147] Someone once said, "The Brits fart 200 years ago, it still smells around the world." Colonial era categorization still ferments conflicts around the world. Some people still associate the lightness of a person's skin color with a better social status. Others still cannot give equal level of respect to a black person and a white person. Racism is not an American problem. It is a global issue that continues to challenge the maturity of individuals' wisdom. That said, one of the most common forms of racism in America is unconscious bias. Colored people in positions of power often found their qualifications being questioned and their status equated to affirmative action.

check-in, a white female TSA agent started asking him why he was in town only for one day and where he was heading to. He respectfully answered her questions. But she communicated on the radio and a male security personnel pulled him out of the line for further questioning. They searched his bags and checked his background on their computer. About twenty minutes later, they told him that he was free to go.

Willie also had an interview for a position at the water department of a township in northern New Jersey. The hiring manager was a female engineer originally from India. She tried hard to show Willie that she supported diversity and inclusion. Willie could not help but notice that she kept using the word "you" as she talked about the struggles of black people in America during slavery, segregation and the era of economic discrimination.

Willie could see her skin was not any lighter than his. And she already knew that he was a black immigrant. Willie asked her how Indians identified themselves. She replied that she identified herself as brown. Willie could not take it anymore. He felt disrespected.[148]

Willie did not appreciate this Indian lady pretending her ancestors did not face discrimination due to their skin color. He felt the urge to defend himself. He started by recognizing the sacrifices made by the ancestors of African Americans in order for people like the two of them to be in the position that they were at that moment. He also lectured the hiring manager about how Ethiopians resisted colonial attacks. Then he sarcastically asked what life was like in India during the 400 years as a colony. She struggled to control her anger and ended the interview

---

[148] Throughout their history, Ethiopians had battled colonial giants. They wanted the world to recognize their heroism as a self-governed nation during the era of colonialism. But they never got that recognition. So the least the world could do was to not label them wrongly and misrepresent their identity.

quickly. As he walked out of the interview room, Willie wondered if he would ever be able to control his inferiority complex and succeed in the job search.

After going through a few more iterations that ended in epic failure, Willie finally arrived at his "match-made-in-heaven" moment. He was interviewed for a faculty position at George Mason University. He was completely relaxed during the interview. He did not need to explain where he was from. All of the people who interviewed him could speak a word or two in Amharic. As he walked through the campus to find the interview location, he also came across several other Ethiopians who happened to be students, faculty members or staff employees. Following the interview, Willie was unable to sleep for several days as he anxiously waited for the results of the interview. After two weeks, he gave up hope and started looking for other opportunities.

As the job search challenged his patience, Willie also faced a difficult situation in his personal life. His relationship with Asmeret transformed into romance. They had been seeing each other here and there. He liked her a lot. But he was not sure it would turn into a serious relationship because of the distance between them. He also did not believe he was ready for a serious relationship. He wanted no distraction from his mission of bringing his sister to the US.

Asmeret also had her own mission to change her parents' living situation, help Haftom get out of Egypt and search for Kibrom. Unfortunately, she found out that she was pregnant. "Willie, I am not sure how to say this. I was feeling funny the last few days. So I took a test and it shows I am pregnant." She told him over the phone.

Willie did not know how to handle it. "Are you sure?"

"Of course I'm sure. What kind of a question is that?" She got upset.

"No, no, I didn't mean it like that." Willie refrained from asking the question he had in mind. So he took the diplomatic route. "Look, I know this is a lot to digest. But I want you to know that we're in this together and that I will support your decision." He could tell from her voice on the phone that she was relieved to hear those words.

"Thanks Willie." She exhaled. "Ewedihalehu."[149] Then she ended the call.

Sometime later, Willie successfully defended his dissertation. It was a moment that he would never forget. As far as he was concerned, that was the day of his graduation. Then he started preparation for his actual graduation ceremony.

One morning he received a phone call congratulating him for being selected for the position that he applied for at George Mason. He told the caller that he would gladly accept any offer. An hour later, he received the formal offer in an email. He immediately signed the offer sheet, prepared the requested supporting documentation and replied to the email. His professors were proud when they learned that he was Mason bound. On his graduation date, Willie felt a little emotional that he could not share the moment with his little sister. But he was grateful to be surrounded by loved ones including Asmeret, Hasen, Seble and Edilawit.

Following his graduation, Willie searched for a rental property in northern Virginia from advertisements in a local Ethiopian community magazine, *Atref*. He rented a basement of a house in the city of Alexandria. The house was only five minutes' walk from Duke Street. He could easily travel to work using public transportation.

Willie and Asmeret also agreed to move in together, but maintain a single status to focus on their personal goals. Willie wrote several emails

---

[149] "I love you" in Amharic.

expressing his gratitude to everyone who contributed to his success at Stony Brook. He visited his favorite deli one last time and enjoyed his favorite Italian hero. He traveled on the LIRR one last time. As he boarded a Washington DC-bound Amtrak from Penn Station, he promised to always call himself a New Yorker. A month after his graduation, Willie and Asmeret started their new life as a couple.

#

Yalem had been receiving marriage proposals through her parents from Jinka. But she felt like returning to her hometown to find a husband would be an embarrassment for her and her parents. She felt like society was not ready for a woman to marry a husband with inferior economic and intellectual status. Therefore, Yalem insisted she was not ready.

Yalem had already reached the conclusion that her relationship with Yonathan was going nowhere. But she was too scared to officially break it off. One Saturday morning, she sat on her porch drinking coffee while skimming through her Facebook page. She clicked the profile of Yonathan's Lounge and started reading. She was proud of his success and usually enjoyed reading and commenting on their latest posts.

Yalem knew that the lounge had hosted a guest appearance the previous night by a famous Ethiopian singer. She viewed the posted images and felt happy for Yonathan. She liked some of the pictures and also added a couple of comments. But one particular picture made her feel a certain way.

Yalem looked at it carefully. It was a couple of girls and the singer smiling at the camera. In the background she spotted Yonathan getting cozy with a girl. Yalem could feel her body shaking. She started her Facebook investigation to try to identify who the girl was. She navigated through other pictures in the lounge, Yonathan's own personal pages and the profiles of other people who made comments on the posts. She finally identified the lady and sent her a friend request.

Yalem waited for about an hour, but Yonathan's mistress did not accept her request. So Yalem started sending the mistress messages asking about the nature of her relationship with Yonathan. Since there was no response from the other end, Yalem began to lose her cool. She sent message after message insulting the lady for cheating with her boyfriend.

Finally, the lady replied with pictures of herself with Yonathan doing things only lovers were supposed to do. Yalem completely went mad! Her fingers could not type fast enough. She started sending voice recordings instead. She insulted the lady in every way possible. Then, she could not communicate anymore. She realized that she was blocked.

Yalem changed her attention to Yonathan. She ripped him apart for what he did. His only response was, "How did you find out?" She told him that she never wanted to hear from him again and hung up the phone. She erased every memory she had of him on her computer and destroyed every present that he had sent. She felt like she could never trust a man again.

Over the next few days, Yalem spent most of her time erasing anything that reminded her of Yonathan. As the burden of being in a long-distance relationship lifted, she felt like she had lost weight. She felt like a new person. Yalem never realized how much that relationship had cost her until she started living as a free woman. She was no longer reserved. She was free to go out with her friends, return home whenever she felt like it, and there was no guilty feeling.

Her friends commented that they liked the new Yalem. Her coworkers asked her if something changed because she looked younger and happier. Ever since she changed her Facebook status to "single," she had been getting messages from Ethiopian men living in Canada, America, Europe and even Ethiopia. She noticed, too, Canadian men checking her out at local coffee shops. But she did not think dating a person who was not Ethiopian would give her a happy family.

One Friday evening, Yalem went out with friends to a bar that played live traditional Ethiopian music. The place was packed. Since the dance floor was very small, people started dancing while seated. The crowd got louder when a popular Tigrinya song was played. A gentleman approached Yalem and asked her for a dance. She liked his respectful yet confident approach. So she said yes. He was a very good dancer, too. She said to herself, "He has to be from Tigray or Eritrea." When the song was over, she returned to her seat.

Minutes later, the gentleman and his friend approached again and asked if they could sit on the empty chairs at their table. The gentleman introduced himself as Arega and mentioned his friend's name was Daniel. Arega was focused on Yalem while Daniel chatted with her two other friends. After exchanging contact information with Yalem, Arega nodded to Daniel and the two returned to their original table.

Yalem and Arega exchanged text messages over the next few days and agreed to meet for dinner. When Yalem arrived at their appointment, she found Arega waiting for her with Daniel. After dinner, when Arega went to the restroom to wash his hands, Daniel shocked Yalem by shamelessly proposing that she was better off with him. He exposed Arega for being a player. Daniel told her that he was looking for something serious and that she should choose him over his friend. Very disturbed by the unexpected incident, Yalem did not know how to respond.

When Arega returned, he could tell that her mood had changed. He offered to give her a ride home and she agreed. He told Daniel to wait at the restaurant and led the way, holding her hand. When they arrived in front of Yalem's home, Arega tried to kiss her. But she slapped him with her purse. She told him that both he and his friend were losers. She quickly got out of the car and slammed the door. She warned him to never contact her again.

Yalem also tried opening herself up on other occasions, but nothing materialized. Some of the men were too focused on the politics in Ethiopia. Others had strong bias toward women. The rest were just not civilized yet. It seemed to her that they were not prepared to assimilate to the Canadian culture; they preferred to relive the lifestyle that had failed them back home. Yalem became frustrated with her dating experience.[150]

Yalem also attempted to establish friendships with men who reached out to her on Facebook. But they seemed too focused on sexting. They were so forthcoming with their requests, she wondered if there were women who would do those things for someone they had never met in person.

Despite her bad luck, Yalem never doubted that she would eventually land the right man. She was sure he was somewhere out there. But she refused to compromise on her principles and do something that she might regret later.

---

[150] The dating world is not as attractive as it might seem. If people can focus on what they can offer instead of listing what they want, then they should be able to find a good relationship. Obtaining and maintaining a serious relationship requires willingness from both sides to accept one another for who they are. It also means being able to communicate with a person from different political backgrounds, religious beliefs and so on.

CHAPTER 11

In the time since Seble emigrated from Ethiopia, she had witnessed the rapid transformation of the Washington DC Metro Area. When she first arrived, most residents in her neighborhood were predominantly black. She and her husband had lived in multiple apartment complexes in the Northwest section around Georgia Avenue. The family bought their first home near the intersection of 13th St and Kansas Avenue. They later opened their first convenience store in the neighborhood.[151]

But the demographic of the city had changed significantly in the past few years. New luxury condominiums and shopping centers, combined with increased security surveillance programs, attracted young professionals into the neighborhood. As the population's average income increased, property values also soared, which also meant significant increases in property tax. All of a sudden, residents could not afford to live in their homes, but could make significant profit if they chose to sell.

Many of Seble's Ethiopian neighbors along with the broader African American residents sold their properties and moved into suburban Maryland and Virginia.[152]

On the bright side, resilient members of the community kept their

---

[151] The Ethiopian American community contributed greatly to the city's dynamic cultural makeup. From restaurants on U Street to gas stations on all corners, night scenes in Adams Morgan to the city's taxi services, Ethiopians managed to acquire a piece of the pie. Professional Ethiopians also succeeded in both the private sector and public service.

[152] The proper word for this social evolution is known as "gentrification."

residence and actually managed to flourish in the evolving city. They witnessed improvement in educational and healthcare facilities. They also saw significant increases in their paychecks. In the meantime, they had to cope with evolving cultural norms and the way of life.

Seble hosted a big party to celebrate Edilawit's first teenage birthday. She wanted to make the day memorable. Friends and families from near and far were invited.

It turned out Edilawit also had plans to make the day memorable. At the start of her journey toward becoming an adult, she wanted to show the growth of her personality. As food and drink were served at the party, Edilawit stayed in her room with her school friends. Walalign knocked on the door and told her to come out and greet the guests; she told him that she would be there in a minute.

About thirty minutes passed. Everyone started asking about the birthday girl. Seble knocked on the door real hard and ordered her to open it. Again, Edilawit replied that she needed a few more minutes. Another thirty minutes passed and Edilawit and her friends were still inside. Her father returned to the door and gave the girls an ultimatum.

The door quickly opened and the girls started to walk toward the living room in style. They performed as if they were in a fashion show. The family did not even spot Edilawit until all the girls arrived in the living room. She had a unique haircut, all painted in rainbow colors. She wore a dress decorated with small pride flags. Seble and Walalign were disturbed by the dramatic scene.[153]

Seble had recently written a complaint letter to President Obama urging him to stop meddling in Africa's internal affairs. It was in response

---

[153] When it came to sexual freedom, Ethiopians were not as evolved as the wider American population. At the time, there were not many Ethiopians who were openly LGBTQ. Homosexuality was considered an American thing. In fact, Ethiopia had a law that criminalized homosexual practice.

to the Obama administration's warning to African nations to stop discriminating against LGBTQ individuals or face sanctions. Seble did not believe this issue was a significant concern in Africa. She also had a belief that it was a lifestyle choice people made because they wanted to try something new.[154]

The parents quickly pulled their daughter out of the scene and took her to their bedroom. "What are you thinking? Are you crazy?" Seble asked.

"It is time that you know the truth," Edilawit confidently replied. She was their only daughter. They raised her to stand out and be independent-minded. "Mom, Dad, you did not raise me to be ashamed of myself. Or to kind of feel like there was something wrong with me," she explained.

"Have you actually tried it?" Walalign asked if she ever had a sexual experience.

"No," she replied. "But I know that I am just as attracted to girls, if not more, as I am attracted to boys," she added. She also expressed her intention to experiment with both before making up her mind.

Seble was incensed by her daughter's attitude. But Walalign was more open-minded. He wanted his daughter to understand that they were blindsided by her coming out plan. He asked her to give them time to process it. He also told her that they loved her very much and their struggle was nothing against her.

Seble wanted to send her daughter to Ethiopia for spiritual therapy.[155]

---

[154] She was yet to be exposed to the community to realize how wrong she was. But all that was going to change very soon.

[155] Some Ethiopians believed holy water could heal any problem. Holy water was used to treat people with mental illness, intestinal diseases and even cancer. Many HIV/AIDS patients had forced their way out of hospital for therapy at one of the many holy water sites in the country. These holy sites were also filled with patients who wanted to be cured from a spiritual possession which they believed was haunting them.

She felt like the holy water treatment could fix her daughter's sexuality. But Walalign rejected the idea. He told her that their daughter was healthy and was just simply expressing what she wanted to do with her life. He told her that, as parents, they had to support her regardless of their personal beliefs.

Willie also advised Seble against it. He shared different stories to broaden her knowledge about the complexity of sexual identity and about how parents had dealt with similar situations in the past. He encouraged her to think progressively. He reminded her that they might be Ethiopian Americans, but Edilawit was American and she needed to be treated as one.

#

After the passing of his mother, Henok fell into a severe depression. He became distant from friends and family. His mood changed periodically. He would get angry for no reason and when he cooled down, he would suddenly become very apologetic. Henok had been known for his ultra-confident and ambitious personality, but lately he suffered from low self-esteem. He felt like everyone perceived him as weak and useless. He completely lost his hardworking mentality and became disinterested in participating in any activity.

Henok could not engage in a normal conversation with people. He struggled to concentrate on anything. If he started talking about a train, he would somehow bring up how the French used to be the best engineers, then he would talk about the beautiful stories he read about Paris, that would remind him about the time he fell in love with a girl in Addis Ababa who ended up moving to Paris. Then love would reignite his pain about how much he missed his mother.

If Henok started talking about rain, it would remind him of the time Willie and he used to dance naked outside in the rain, then he would talk about how Willie had helped his mother better than he had. Then that reminded him that he had failed his mother and he would start to cry.

Henok's siblings could not comfort their guilt-tormented brother as they were preoccupied with their own grief. And truthfully, they kind of agreed that he was partly to blame. They wanted him to suffer for it. All their life, the siblings looked up to their older brother. He was always among the most popular at home, in school, at church and in the playground. They had lived under his shadow their entire life. Their parents had big expectations for him, like they really believed he was going to change the family's fortune.

Then Henok went to college and returned a changed man. He became arrogant, a junkie, opportunist and a complete loser. Everything he tried ended up in complete failure. When their mother struggled with her illness, he could not even contribute to the medical bills. They also suspected him of wasting some of the money that he had received from America on his addiction. They barely talked to him anymore. As far as they were concerned, he was an embarrassment to the family.

It had been five months since Zeineb had died. Henok was still in Jinka, without a job or adequate income. He did not even submit a formal notice to his work when he left Addis Ababa. He was still not in a good enough mental condition to resume work, but he desperately needed money. His family denied him food in the house since he was not sharing the cost.

Unfortunately, their tough-love treatment did not work. Henok started begging other people for money. He spent any money he got on khat and cigars. So the family pushed him to return to his old job in Addis Ababa. He agreed and headed back to the capital.

On arriving, Henok immediately reported to work. The school principal was surprised to see him. The school thought Henok had been killed or something. They had tried to reach him many times by phone, mail and email, but he never returned their messages. They had filed a missing person report with the police. Because of him, the school had updated their standard operating procedure, requiring all employees and students to register their physical address and emergency contact information with the school.

The principal invited Henok to his office and closed the door. They talked about Henok's whereabouts and what he intended to do next. Henok lied completely about his experience over the last six months and told a story about how he was on a spiritual journey to a monastery to connect with his divine consciousness. He told mythical stories about his fictitious quest to purify his body, mind and soul. He declared that he was cleansed and ready to return to work.

Henok explained his plan to help students change their perspectives about life and the meaning of good citizens. As he continued to elaborate on his new revelations, the principal realized that Henok was not mentally stable. The principal also could tell that Henok had a strong addiction problem. His teeth looked like the inside of a grape. His lips were burnt from smoking. But the principal promised Henok that he would talk to the school board to get him back his old job.

Over the next few weeks, Henok returned frequently to the school to see if he could resume work. At first, the school principal told him he needed more time to convince the board. Then the principal said he could not convince the board and that there was no way Henok could return to work. But Henok kept coming and begged for help. Sometime later, the principal banned him from entering the building.

Since returning to the city, Henok had been crashing at a friend's place. Concerned by Henok's mental instability, the friend asked him to leave. Henok was practically homeless. He hung around hotels that were popular destinations for passengers from Jinka. Everyone that saw him felt sorry for how his life had turned upside down. He was a guy who once was elected to the House of Representatives.

Henok's good fortune was not over yet. He spotted a man walking to a restaurant and yelled, "Geremew Armadayso! Can you buy me dinner?"

The man did not recognize him at first. As Henok continued to talk about this and that, Geremew finally remembered this homeless person was Henok. The two had completed high school together.[156]

Geremew invited Henok to the restaurant and ordered their meals to be served on separate plates. Jinka was a small town; everybody pretty much knew each other. They also kept tabs on each other. It did not matter if a person moved out of town or even out of the country; any news about their status was a subject of discussion at coffee shops. After high school, Geremew and Henok had only seen each other a handful of times. But Geremew had heard a lot about Henok's condition. He had just not thought it'd gotten this bad.

Henok looked nothing like the handsome boy Geremew remembered from high school. Henok had lost a lot of weight. His skin looked like

---

[156] Even though Geremew did not score enough to qualify to study in a higher institution, like Henok did, Geremew was able to study in a vocational school and became a teacher. He worked his way up to becoming a principal in an elementary school in a small village town called Senegal. Senegal was about ten miles north from Jinka. It was often referred to as "Jinka's garden." It was a major producer of cabbage, kale, potato, carrot, tomato, pepper and many other vegetables.

it was pasted on his bones. Unfortunately, Henok was still in denial. He told Geremew that he was struggling financially because he had quit his job to focus on writing his second book.

As Henok discussed his great ideas, Geremew thought about how he could help Henok. He remembered the teacher shortage in his school. Under normal circumstances, he knew Henok would be overqualified for the job. But he was not sure if Henok had anything to give with his current state of mind. He tested Henok with trick questions.

To Geremew's surprise, Henok still had good recollection and his ability to analyze situations was not so bad. His biggest issue seemed to be his inability to accept reality. Henok was in denial, pretending to be in a good position. Geremew was convinced that, under strict supervision and counseling, Henok could still function as a teacher. So he decided to give Henok a second chance.

Henok was delighted with the opportunity. He promised to be a better person. After completing his business affairs, Geremew returned to Jinka with Henok at his side.

#

Kedir was on the phone with his wife Halimah when he saw Al Jazeera broadcast breaking news about the sudden death of the Ethiopian prime minister at a hospital in Brussels, where he had been secretly treated for an undisclosed illness. "Honey, I have to call you back!" Kedir abruptly ended the call and focused on the TV as he could not believe what he was hearing.

He had heard the rumors in Ethiopian news outlets that the prime minister was not in a good health condition, but there was no indication it was so critical. The prime minister had ruled the country for almost twenty years, since the fall of the former communist dictator.[157]

News of the prime minister's passing brought mixed emotions from the Ethiopian American community. Supporters of the ruling political party and those with roots from the prime minister's home of Tigray mourned the passing of their hero. He was a very controversial figure.[158]

A large proportion of the Ethiopian American community, who had left Ethiopia to escape conflict and poverty, were relieved to see the end of the ruthless authoritarian leader. A small minority of the community, though, recognized the moment as pivotal for the direction of the country.

They could only hope that his successor would understand the magnitude of challenges the country would be facing. The successor would need to find ways to address the unanswered questions without damaging the ongoing development initiatives. The country stood at the crossroads between continuous improvement or the familiar territory

---

[157] On the one hand, the prime minister was one of the most successful leaders in the history of the country. He took on one of the poorest countries in the world and transformed it into one of the fastest developing in the world. Under his leadership, the country expanded tenfold major infrastructures including schools, hospitals, banks, airports, factories, roads, electricity generators and drinking water facilities. He left a country that was among the top ten largest economies in the African continent.

[158] On the other hand, his legacy was tainted by his administration's bad record of corruption and human rights violations. Under his leadership, Ethiopia became a federation of ethnic-based regional states. The border demarcation between each state was controversial. As a result, conflicts occurred regularly between rival ethnic groups. The federal government served as mediator. The government liked this approach since they did not need to be the bad guys standing against a specific ethnic group. Unfortunately, this leadership approach destroyed the people-to-people social bond. National pride was at an all-time low as some citizens preferred to identify based on ethnic grounds. This divided loyalty also helped fuel the spread of corruption. People no longer felt ashamed, sinful or guilty for bribing anyone in need of their services. There was no accountability at any level.

of destruction.[159]

Kedir was heavily invested in businesses in Ethiopia. He had the livestock farming in Jinka and the residential properties that he was building with his partners. He also owned a construction vehicles rental business. But his business interests were not his major concern at the moment.

Kedir was more worried about the power vacuum that naturally existed when the longtime stronghold was suddenly replaced by a new leader. It could trigger another civil war. He had got used to not having to explain to his American friends about bad things that they saw in the news about his homeland. He found it demeaning to have to talk about why his people were killing each other, children were dying of hunger, or fellow Ethiopians were seeking refuge at UN camps.

Kedir never had a stake in Ethiopian politics because he felt like he had never been represented by anyone. Not until he witnessed Henok shaking the norm with his ambitious run for the House of Representatives. Following Henok's failed experiment, Kedir had shied away from politics. But this was a special situation. He felt like he needed to play a more active role supporting issues that he believed were fundamental.

As Kedir's mind continued to contemplate the fate of Ethiopian politics, Halimah called him back on Messenger. He had totally forgotten that he ended the call without saying goodbye. "I'm sorry, honey." He quickly apologized and asked if she had heard the breaking news.

"I know. I just watched the news myself. What will happen to the country now?" She was not sad at all. But she was not happy either. She

---

[159] Because of the failed leadership of the late prime minister, there was widespread division and hatred. There were many unanswered questions; some would require constitutional reform such as citizenship, rights, freedom of expression, justice and land ownership. These questions needed answers.

was just in shock. If one thing Halimah was sure of was that the country was not going to be the same again. She had little memory about her life before the former prime minister came to power.[160]

"Well, the country will exist, in one form or another. But I am not sure how stable it will be," Kedir chimed in.

"I heard his deputy will be the interim successor. He is a highly respected person. And he's from a minority tribe. Hopefully he will settle things down." She expressed her excitement about the prospect of the upcoming caretaker prime minister, who was considered a political outsider.

"Do you have an idea how I can support the country? I just don't want to get involved directly in their internal politics." Kedir asked his wife for advice.

"Why don't you find a way to play a role in supporting the construction of the Grand Ethiopian Renaissance Dam (GERD)?"[161] she suggested.

Ethiopia had been asking its diaspora community to support the project financially and diplomatically. Kedir had the ability to support both. "I think that is a great idea!" he replied with excitement. So he decided to research the issue more and find a way to help the project.

---

[160] The late prime minister was especially unpopular in Halimah's hometown as the Gurage people felt disadvantaged by many of his administration's policies.

[161] The GERD is a hydropower project under construction on Ethiopia's Blue Nile River. When completed, the 475 ft tall dam was expected to be the largest hydropower project in Africa. It was estimated to produce 15,759 GWh/yr electrical energy. In comparison, only 45 percent of Ethiopia's population had access to electricity and their total consumption was 9,060 GWh/yr. Put simply, the GERD had the potential to double the number of Ethiopians with electricity in their homes. But the project was fiercely opposed by Egypt, who were concerned that the dam would reduce the amount of water flowing downstream. Since Ethiopia announced its plan, Egypt had been utilizing its economic, military and diplomatic superiority to stop the project. But defiant Ethiopia started construction anyway.

# #

Yalem was a regular at a coffee shop in her neighborhood, even though she was not a big coffee drinker. But the atmosphere reminded her of her time in Ethiopia. So whenever she was free, she would spend a couple of hours there working on her laptop. Every time she walked into the shop, there was one barista who greeted her with a smile.

He knew her favorite order, cappuccino and chocolate cookie. They never formally introduced themselves to each other. He called her Miss Ethiopia. She called him Franc because that was the name written on his uniform. Franc always made her feel welcome. He was a tall white man. He always jokingly asked her when she would invite him for home-cooked Ethiopian food.

One particular day, Franc was very persistent. "Miss Ethiopia, I think you're a terrible cook. I mean, that's the only explanation for why you wouldn't invite me to your home." He raised the topic again as he passed her cappuccino and chocolate cookie.

"I know you're trying to trick me into inviting you to come over, but I'll pass," she replied with a smile.

But Franc wasn't smiling. "Can you at least have dinner with me in an Ethiopian restaurant of your choice?"

She stayed quiet. Franc stood in front of her and waited for a response. "Okay Franc, just one dinner," she finally agreed. But she warned him that it was not a date.

"Fantastic!" Franc joked that he was happy being single.

One Saturday afternoon, Franc showed up at Yalem's door five minutes before their appointment. "Good afternoon, Miss Ethiopia." Franc smiled as he greeted Yalem and handed her a single yellow flower.

"Franc, you shouldn't have! But thank you!" Yalem greeted him back and accepted the flower.

He did not reply. He respectfully opened the passenger door and invited her to get in. Yalem was hesitant when she agreed to the dinner date. But she did not mind the way it was going. Franc was a real gentleman. When she looked at the flower, it made her feel like she was on a real date. But she was not prepared to admit that. So she hid the flower inside her purse.

"How was your day?" Franc asked, breaking the silence.

"It was good." She smiled. "I was in the house doing laundry and cooking."

"That's nice." He kept his eyes on the road, but she saw the way his eyes crinkled when he smiled. He seemed genuinely interested. "What did you cook?"

"Vegetarian sauces." She explained, "Preparing most Ethiopian dishes takes time. So I make enough sauce to last for three days. That way, when I prepare lunch or dinner, I just have to cook the meat and mix it up with the sauce."

Minutes later, they arrived at their location. They parked the car on the side of the street and walked into the restaurant. Yalem noticed some people staring at them. She worried whether that made Franc uncomfortable. But he did not seem to pay attention to any of it. He was focused on doing his thing.

"What type of food is this?" Franc asked while pointing at the menu.

"Kitfo?" Yalem read from the menu. "Kitfo is basically a minced raw beef marinated in a blend of hot pepper, garlic, butter and some other spices. It is one of my favorite Ethiopian cuisines. But I don't like the Kitfo in this place. It's not their speciality."

A few minutes later, the waitress stopped by and asked if they were ready to order. Franc deferred to Yalem to order for him. Yalem had a long conversation in Amharic while pointing at the menu and the waitress left. She then explained to him the tradition. "Franc, Ethiopian food is traditionally shared on a plate. But please do not hesitate to tell me if you prefer yours to be served on a separate plate."

Franc wanted to tell her that he was ready to share more than food, but he held it back. "That sounds good to me. Sharing is caring." He smiled at his own joke.

"Great!" Yalem also smiled. "One more thing. We use our fingers to eat the food. So we have to wash our hands before we eat. Do you mind if I go to the restroom first?" Franc indicated that was fine by him. One at a time, they both went to the restroom to wash their hands. Then Yalem asked, "Franc, what do you know about Ethiopia?"

Franc relaxed as he explained, "Well, I know that coffee originated from Ethiopia and the country is still one of the biggest producers of the bean. Ehhh…I also know the story of Lucy, the famous human fossil." Franc took a moment to think. "Ehhh…oh yeah! I know that Ethiopians are great in track and field." He smiled and added, "Ehhh…I think that's all!"

But Yalem was very impressed. "Wow! I think we need to give you honorary citizenship!" They both laughed at the joke. Then Yalem added, "But seriously. I was expecting you to tell me about the civil war, hunger and poverty, which I am sure everyone knows about."

Franc disagreed. "Every country has had its own share of dark history. I am a proud Canadian, but I am not proud of what our settlers did to their indigenous neighbors. We also had our own struggles with disease and natural disasters throughout history. In short, no, I don't believe our bad times should define who we are as society."

As Franc continued to talk, the waitress finally returned holding a large tray. He looked at the food. It was filled with several vegetarian and meat stews of different colors served on top of injera. The spices smelled good. Following Yalem's directions, Franc took a piece of injera, immersed it in a yellow spiced lentil stew and ate it.

He liked its unique flavor, though it had a little too much garlic. Then he took a second bite, this time from a reddish stew made with split peas. His eyes suddenly filled with tears. He grabbed the glass of water in front of him and drank all of it. "That's too spicy!" he complained.

"I am so sorry! I should have told you! Please be careful! The red sauces had hot peppers."[162] Yalem felt bad. "Let me make it up to you. Please let me order you an Ethiopian beer; it will be my treat."

Franc was pleased with her gesture. They ordered beer and continued to get to know each other.

"If you don't mind, from now on, please call me JP. It's short for Jean Pierre. My name is Jean Pierre Francis," Franc formally introduced himself. "I only use Franc for business relations. But people who are close to me call me JP."

"It's nice to meet you, JP!" At that moment, Yalem felt something. "I also have a request." She smiled while keeping eye contact. "Can you please stop calling me Miss Ethiopia?" She could tell that JP was confused. "I mean, my name is Yalem Kebede. You can call me Yalem."

Then she watched JP's face relax quickly.

"It's really a pleasure to finally meet you, Yalem."

They had to practice how to pronounce each other's names properly.

---

[162] She'd forgotten to warn him that the hot pepper known as berbere in Amharic was one of the most popular spices used in Ethiopian cuisines.

As they continued to open up, JP made another announcement. "I probably gave you the wrong impression before." It was now JP's turn to monitor her reaction. He could read in her face that she was eager to know about the new revelation. "I don't just work at the coffee shop. I actually own it." JP explained that he used to work in the mining industry after graduating from college before quitting his job to start his own business.

"I am very impressed!" Yalem exclaimed.

They talked about their family, lifestyle and dreams. They joked about how little they had known about each other. Without realizing it, they lost track of time until the waitress politely informed them that the restaurant was closing in fifteen minutes. As JP prepared cash to pay the bill, Yalem insisted that she wanted to cover the beers. They paid the bill, left a generous tip and exited the restaurant.

As they drove back to her home, Yalem asked, "So JP, is there anything else that you forgot to tell me?"

"Ahh…I am afraid I like you even better than I did yesterday." He smiled. "How about you? Did you forget to tell me anything?"

"I think…" She took a deep breath and continued, "I think I am beginning to like the fact that you like me."

They both smiled and turned their eyes to the road ahead. Soon, they arrived in front of her home. JP got out of the car first and opened the door for her. After walking her to her door, JP stopped. An awkward feeling quickly surrounded them. JP knew that he had to make a careful move. He was old enough to understand that his next step was going to define the nature of their relationship.

"Uhhh…" He cleared his throat. "I had a great time!"

"I had a great time too!" Her voice softened as she looked into his eyes. It looked like she wanted him to do something.

"Can I give you a good-night kiss?" He felt relieved as the words finally dropped from his lips. But all she did was stay quiet as she continued to look into his eyes. He whispered to himself, "I guess that's a yes!" He took one step closer and slowly kissed her lips.

She closed her eyes and stayed quiet. He immediately felt like he misread the situation. "Please forgive me!" He apologized and took a step back.

She opened her eyes again. She took a step forward and kissed him back.

They held each other's shoulders and shared a long kiss. Then they let go and stepped back.

He slowly said, "I will call you tomorrow!"

Yalem nodded her head in agreement.

JP waited until she entered the house and closed the door. Then he returned to the car feeling like this was the beginning of a special relationship.

CHAPTER 12

Mannie and Bethi were blessed with a second child, a baby boy. They called him Monson Amanuel.[163] Monson was an adorable boy who was tall and strong; twenty-one inches and eight and a half pounds at birth. His sister, Sikeat, could not keep her hands off him. She loved her baby brother a lot. Her mother was worried Sikeat would try to lift her brother and accidentally drop him. She taught Sikeat to first sit down and properly hold her brother by supporting his head and shoulder. The family was very proud of the relationship that was forming between the siblings.

Woizero Haregeweyn said Sikeat reminded her of Bethi as a child. She said, "Bethi, your daughter is just like when you were a child. When Eniyat was born, you were very much in love with her. You used to cry every time she cried. You were very protective of her. You did not want even Gebeyaw and Hamelmal anywhere near her." Sikeat also loved listening to stories that her grandmother told about her mother's childhood.

The family left Belgium soon after Monson was born. They moved to Switzerland because Mannie accepted an Assistant Professor position at the University of Bern.[164] The family rented a home in the suburbs

---

[163] His name was a tribute to the city that embraced them despite their unique background, to the people that always made them feel welcome and to the nation that gave them so much.

[164] After graduating with his doctoral degree from the University of Mons, Mannie had continued to work there in a postgraduate role. That helped him gain the experience needed for the position at the University of Bern. His ability to communicate in English, French and a little bit of German also played an instrumental role in the hiring process.

of the historic city. Mannie commuted to work on a trolleybus. Bethi also started a new job as a teacher in a nearby private school. Woizero Haregeweyn continued to serve as the primary caregiver for Sikeat and Monson. Her husband, Ato Dires, frequently visited her. He spent most of his time in Europe traveling between Switzerland and Rome in Italy, where his son Gebeyaw was living.

Mannie was very surprised to learn about another European country that exercised federalism. Like his home country, Ethiopia, and his favorite country, Belgium, Switzerland was also a federation of partially self-governed regions. The country had four main regions which were constituted based on linguistic and cultural origins. There were four official national languages: German, French, Italian and Romansh. The regional administrations in Switzerland presented equal rights for all citizens, unlike Ethiopia where federalism created a strong divide between neighbors.[165]

Despite their diverse background, similar to Belgium, the Swiss people shared strong national unity. Switzerland was globally recognized as a military neutral state who prioritized humanitarian relations. It was also the birthplace of the Red Cross whose flag basically used an inverted version of the country's national flag.

Mannie's family enjoyed their life in the highland city of Bern. Unfortunately, there were very few Ethiopians there. In order to participate in a Sunday prayer at an Ethiopian Orthodox Church, the family had to travel about ninety minutes north to Zurich, or south to the Lake Geneva area. Fortunately, there were many live programs on the internet.

---

[165] In Ethiopia, regional administrations strategically indoctrinated minorities to adapt to the cultures of the majority tribes. But a minority tribe in one region was also a majority in another and vice versa. In other words, a victim tribe in one region was also an abuser in another. As a result, internal conflicts in one region usually boiled into bigger conflicts between regions. Federalism in European countries did not seem to have a similar effect.

Mannie and Bethi also continued to participate in the European Chapter of the Mahbere Kidusan Network. Bethi volunteered in the organization and served as event planner. She was responsible for organizing the planning of continental and intercontinental conferences, whereas Mannie was selected as a delegate from the European chapter to serve in an international committee tasked with establishing diplomatic relations between the Ethiopian Orthodox Tewahedo Church and its former patriarch who lived in exile in the United States.[166]

This was a very secretive mission and committee members were carefully selected following extensive background checks. When the committee announced its plan to restart negotiations between the two synods, there was little expectation that any meaningful outcome would materialize. But Mannie and others were optimistic.[167]

The committee believed that creating some form of bilateral relationship would be a major first step. They wanted to make sure that the divide would not turn into a permanent split. Should one of the two patriarchs pass away, a normalized relationship would increase the

---

[166] As the dominant religion in Ethiopia, the Orthodox Church had a direct role in the country's governance throughout history. The ability of any new leader to successfully establish a functioning government was dependent on his ability to control the hearts and minds of the religious faithful. As a result, when there was change in government, the new leaders often dictated a reform of the church's synod. That was exactly what the prime minister had done after taking over the government. He forced the church's patriarch to retire. But the patriarch fled to the US where his supporters established a rival synod on his behalf.

[167] There was a deep political divide in the diaspora community. As a result, many churches in North America and Europe severed allegiance with the official synod in Ethiopia in favor of the rival synod in exile. Later at some point, the two sides excommunicated each other. Repeated reconciliation efforts failed as the two sides stood firm in their position. The synod in exile demanded the former patriarch be returned to its rightful post, which was unacceptable for both the synod in Addis Ababa and the country's government.

opportunity to reunify the two synods. And nobody could tell what the future would bring. Ethiopian governments historically were short-lived. There was always a chance that the current government would be replaced. Which could give another opportunity for unification. In any case, the committee believed there were possibilities to make a difference and were determined to make the most of it.

#

As a naturalized American citizen who benefited greatly from his adopted country's generosity, Willie had only one wish that could not be satisfied. He wished he could help all his family and friends to emigrate from back home to the US, but this was impossible. At least he finally succeeded in bringing the person who was most important to him, his sister Fre.

It had been a month since Fre arrived at Dulles International Airport. Fre did not want to waste any time. One week after arrival, she started work as a waitress in an Ethiopian restaurant. She did not even wait until she received her social security card. At that time, Willie had bought a house in the west end of Fairfax County. The public transportation in the area was not convenient, so Willie had to give his sister a ride to and from work.

Willie's close relationship with Fre did not sit well with Asmeret. She felt like he was spending too much time at the restaurant, using Fre as an excuse. She complained to him that he had forgotten he had children at home.

By that time, Asmeret and Willie had three children. Their firstborn was a boy named Semere. A year and half later, they had twin girls, named

Rediet and Azeb. As the family quickly expanded, Willie had bought the house and moved them to the suburbs. But Asmeret was still unhappy. She was no longer satisfied with the nature of their relationship. She believed it was time for them to get married officially. She was upset that Willie was not interested in giving her the respect that she deserved as a wife.

As time passed, she felt insecure that she had no stake in Willie's finances. She monitored the equity the home had accumulated over the years and researched online to estimate his salary. She recorded the family's major expenses and had a rough idea about how much he might have in savings. The one thing she was not sure was how much money he was sending to his family in Ethiopia. She was bothered by her lack of control of the situation. To add to her insecurity, Fre came from Ethiopia and stayed with them in the house. The two women did not get along very well.

Willie could not understand why Asmeret was ungrateful with the life they were building. He covered all the major expenses in the house. Their kids had all the things American kids were supposed to have. He never asked her how she managed her finances. He tried to get her to enroll for courses at the Northern Virginia Community College, but she had no interest in studying. So he prepared a résumé and encouraged her to apply for more professional jobs that would give her opportunities for growth, but she did not want to quit her current job in a grocery store. She liked her simple job which was only walking distance from the house.

Willie felt like Asmeret was obsessed with his finances because it was the easiest way for her to add more money into her account. He argued she was the one who changed. They had had an agreement to maintain separate finances. Lately, she was trying to force him into marriage because she was worried that she would get nothing if they separated.

Willie did not understand why she had to think about separation. He began to think of marriage as a risky agreement which could cost him his hard-earned lifetime savings.

Willie was also concerned by Asmeret's attitude change. Somehow, she acted like she was always correct and he was up to no good. She did not even trust him with caring for the children. They could not have a normal conversation as they argued on every topic. As the better-educated person, Willie wanted to be heard in the house. But she made up her own mind, mostly contrary to his recommendations. He considered the growing differences as another reason to not get married. He felt like she was already bossing him around. If they got married, he believed she would try to control his entire life.

As the relationship between Willie and Asmeret became increasingly tense, Fre rented a room in northeast Washington DC and moved out. Fre wished to stay and help raise her nephew and nieces, but she did not like being in the middle of their conflict. Willie wanted his sister to stay a little longer and save enough money. But he was proud that she was already drawing her own path.

Meanwhile, the presidential election was approaching. This would be the second time he could vote. He was registered as an independent voter and voted for Obama during the president's reelection campaign. He was proud as his first vote in this great nation was to elect a black man for president. During the first inauguration of President Obama, Willie had been very sad that he could not vote because he was not yet a US citizen. He became a naturalized US citizen a couple of years into Obama's first term.

Willie became less impressed with the president's record in his second term. While assisting Fre to file her tax return, Willie became upset to find out that she would have to pay a penalty mandated by Obamacare[168] for not being enrolled in the healthcare program. Willie also believed the president could have done more to strengthen the bilateral relationship between the US and Africa. He was also critical of the president for failing to stop the expansion of the Islamic State terrorists in the Middle East and North Africa. And the deal made with Iran in regard to its nuclear program did not make any sense to Willie.

He also disagreed with the president's strategy for managing the nation's budget deficit and the alarmingly increasing national debt. Willie understood the need to change historic wrongs done to disadvantaged communities and supported increased investment to uplift lower income communities; he would just have preferred the funding to come from budget cuts to other programs. Instead, the president continued with the long-standing bad habit of borrowing more money.

And then there was the problem with the relationship between black communities and the police. Willie understood there were some police officers who abused their authorities and illegally mistreated citizens, especially black citizens. After all, it was not long ago that the American law enforcement agencies were used as tools to systematically discriminate against black people. But Willie did not believe the problem would be resolved by focusing only on police reforms.

Willie believed this was a relationship problem and there were always two sides in any relationship. The only way the relationship could improve was if there were genuine attitude changes on both sides. Since President Obama was also black, Willie believed he was best positioned to push disadvantaged communities to self-reflect and improve weaknesses in their way of life. But that never happened. The president only complained

---

[168] Formally known as the Affordable Care Act.

about police brutality when bad incidents happened.

Willie always believed that strength had to come from the inside; it was help that people should expect from outside. If the good citizens of a community organized themselves and stood against their own bad citizens, then the police would be needed only to provide additional help. If crime-infected communities were tolerant toward their bad children, but still expected the police to ensure their security, then that was a recipe for disaster. Admitting internal weaknesses and working to improve them could be painful. Sometimes it could even feel demeaning to be reminded of them. But Willie believed that was the only way those weaknesses could truly be transformed into strengths.

Willie watched on CNN some radical ideologies that Donald Trump was proposing to address some of these issues. The billionaire was a regular at the network, debating with news anchors whether his "America First!" ideology was realistic or not. Prior to watching him on the news, all Willie knew about Trump was that he hosted *The Celebrity Apprentice* and owned beauty pageants.

Some things Trump was saying did not make sense to Willie, such as questioning President Obama's citizenship and calling the Affordable Care Act socialism. Willie believed if Ethiopia provided basic healthcare for its citizens, it made no sense this great country could not do the same for its people. So Willie was a supporter of providing basic healthcare for all people in the country. Willie also disagreed with Trump's proposal for deporting illegal immigrants. He learned about Trump's business records, how he could be an opportunist and that he would have no problem sacrificing others as long as it benefited him. He considered Trump could be the type of role model that he would not want to introduce to his children.

At the same time, Willie agreed with Trump that the US needed a secured border, as any sovereign nation should. Willie also agreed that the US needed to prioritize the interests of its citizens over global cooperation. He was convinced that Trump's brash personality and fearless communication skills could be what was needed to push against establishment politicians. He could tell Trump was unafraid to take drastic action, no matter how unpopular.

When Trump announced that he was running for president, Willie became very interested and regularly followed his campaign speeches. It reminded him of the time Obama was first running for president. Despite the wide gap in their political beliefs, they were both charismatic and drew large crowds. Willie was inspired by Trump's honest perspectives on race relations, religious freedom, government bureaucracy, military priorities and international trade relations. Willie wanted America to continue to be the most generous nation in the world. But when its generosity was creating major disadvantages for its citizens, that was the right time to make changes.[169]

Willie was convinced that America needed someone like Trump to make some painful changes; someone who had thick skin to withstand the backlash. He also did not see any vision from Hilary Clinton's campaign; she was more of a continuation of the current administration. Willie became a silent supporter of Trump. He had never supported a Republican candidate before. Only his closest friends and family

---

[169] Globalization used to be mutually beneficial to both developed and underdeveloped parts of the world. Unfortunately, losing the manufacturing industry created a major crisis for many Americans. China was the major magnet who benefited most from American companies outsourcing production to countries with cheaper labor. But lately, China was becoming an aggressive rival both economically and militarily. Willie believed it was time that America made changes to its trade and military relations with China.

members were aware that he was a Trump supporter. He was already facing enough heat from his loved ones; he was worried about being discriminated against by his liberal community if they heard he was supporting a conservative candidate.

On election night, Willie voted for Trump. He watched the election results all night until Trump was announced the winner around 2:00 a.m. Before going to bed, Willie prayed for Trump to have the strength needed to endure the upcoming storm of attacks from the media and the resistance from establishment politicians and diplomats. He also prayed for American politics to have enough ductility to survive the upcoming turmoil and Trump's necessary but divisive agendas.

#

Two key ingredients for building a good relationship are internal readiness and a good first impression. The two individuals coming into a relationship have to be mentally prepared for it. There is no convincing needed when two individuals already have the desire to form a good partnership. These individuals do not have anything to hide about their future ambitions. They are willing to compromise on their core principles. That is when the second ingredient, a good first impression, is needed.

When two people meet for the first time, their minds quickly develop an image of each other. That image is based on their observations of each other's physical appearance, demeanor, opinion and empathy. Both individuals ask themselves if the image they created for the other person is someone that attracts their soul. That first impression determines if the individuals can make themselves available to each other. So if they are both mentally ready and have created a good impression of one another, then that relationship is destined to produce many good memories and last for a very long time.

Yalem and JP's romance flourished quickly. They had been spending a lot of time together. Yalem was captivated by his work ethic and politeness. JP had always been attracted to her beauty; he liked watching her walk around. As he got to know her better, he developed a feeling that was difficult to express in words. All he knew was that her presence in his life gave him stability. What seemed like an unlikely relationship started after both sides developed a good impression of one another and at a time when they were both prepared for serious commitment.

They had already got to know each other for quite some time before they had to define the nature of their relationship. In her late thirties, Yalem was fully prepared for true love regardless of where it was coming from. She was willing to make compromises. JP had also had all the adventures a man needed in his life before settling with one woman. He was pursuing his passion as an entrepreneur. In his previous life, he had endured dangerous living conditions as a mine worker in the northern Manitoba province. Yalem and JP were in a beautiful relationship. They looked very good together.

A few months in, Yalem learned that she was pregnant. Her first reaction was fear. She was not sure it was the right time in the relationship for her to have a child. She also was not sure how JP would react to the news. More importantly, she had heard a lot of stories about some women in their late thirties who had difficulty maintaining pregnancy.

She consulted with Seble about what to do. Seble advised her to tell JP straight away and make a decision together. As Yalem continued to contemplate her next steps, the pregnancy transitioned into the second trimester. During one of her radiology sessions, the nurse revealed that the ultrasound images showed she was having twins. Yalem was not sure how to take the news. She never heard of any twins in her family's history. She was not sure if it was good or bad. It was then that she realized she could not keep this secret from JP anymore. If he wanted to be a part of the process, great. If not, at least she would know that she was on her own to decide what was best for the future.

JP was ecstatic when he heard the pregnancy news. He told Yalem that it was the best news he had ever received. She felt relieved with his response. A few days later, JP asked if Yalem would like to meet his parents. Yalem agreed. She had never heard JP mentioning his parents before.

JP told her that his father's name was Sedfeld Francis and his mother's was Margeret Francis. Francis Senior[170] was a military veteran who was deployed to Central Africa for two years serving in a United Nations Peacekeeping Mission during the Congo civil war. Mrs. Francis[171] was a retired psychologist who used to work in correctional centers assisting inmates to overcome their deepest fears.

Maggie and Sed met at a local recovery center where she used to volunteer and he used to attend a program to help him recover from post-traumatic stress disorder. Their relationship started in friendship. About two years later, they got married. Maggie and Sed had three children: Alfred, Madeline and JP.

Alfred had made a home in Alaska and not returned in several years. He got married to a Native Alaskan and had two children. Maggie and Sed had traveled to Alaska twice to visit their grandchildren. Madeline

---

[170] He used the nickname 'Sed'.

[171] She preferred to be called Maggie.

lived with her husband and three children in Edmonton. JP was the youngest of the three.

JP and Yalem drove about forty-five minutes south from the city to his parents' home. As they pulled into a long driveway in front of a colonial-style home, Maggie was already waiting for them at the door. Maggie was a big woman with an even bigger smile. She hugged Yalem so tight that Yalem had to hold her breath.

The rest of the family also greeted them as they entered the house. Sed gave Yalem a warm welcome. Madeline and her husband were present for the special occasion. The family made Yalem very comfortable. Sed had already started drinking before they arrived.

"You remind me of a young girl I met in Congo," Sed told Yalem.

"Dad! That is not polite!" Madeline quickly interrupted her father. "Please excuse him. Sometimes my father can be annoying," she apologized on his behalf. "Have you been back to Ethiopia?" She asked Yalem.

"It's been a while, but yes." Yalem looked sad. "I'd like to visit more often but it's hard." She explained why she was unable to return to her homeland.

"But your mother came to Canada to visit you." JP shifted the conversation to a more exciting direction and told a funny story that he had heard about her mother's experience in Canada.

Then everyone shared their awkward stories about their first trip to a new environment. Sed told a story about how he used to be treated like a celebrity at a bar near his command post in Congo; he used to buy beers for everyone at the bar and it would cost him less than ten dollars. Madeline again cut him off and complained he was being insensitive. But Yalem actually liked Sed's personality.

After dinner, JP and Yalem prepared to return to the city. Maggie begged them to stay the night in one of the guest rooms. JP explained that they had other plans in the morning. Maggie warned Yalem that she would be checking up on her regularly and told her that she would like to help as needed during Yalem's pregnancy. Yalem said Maggie was welcome to call her anytime.

Madeline offered Yalem baby furniture and toys that she had in her storage. Yalem chose her words carefully to not come across as rude. She told Madeline it was too early to think about that yet.

Sed joked about how life was boring before Yalem arrived at his home. He warned her not to be a stranger anymore. After saying goodbye to everyone, JP and Yalem drove away to Calgary. While on the road, JP asked Yalem if his family disappointed her.

"No, I loved them, especially Sed," she told him.

"Is it the right time for you to introduce me to your parents?" JP asked.

"I don't know; are we ready to get married?" she replied jokingly. "But seriously, my parents would immediately assume that we are getting married."

"Why don't we just do it then? Let's get married!" Just like that, JP proposed. He slowed down the car and turned his head to Yalem.

"Well, in that case, you will need to make a formal request to my parents." She smiled. "I have to warn you; when they find out that you are white, their reaction may offend you."

"Don't worry about that; they will love me like a son," he replied.

Over the next couple of weeks following this memorable ride, JP practiced reading his proposal in Amharic and prepared a video record. He contacted Yalem's younger brother, Zeryihun, on Messenger. The two collaborated to set up a live video meeting with Yalem's parents. JP surprised them by proposing in Amharic. The rest of the communication was by using Zeryihun as a translator.

The parents approved the proposal under one condition; the wedding had to take place in Ethiopia.[172]

JP felt that was a great idea. Since Yalem's pregnancy was in its third trimester, he asked for the marriage to be scheduled after the baby was born. Everyone agreed with the plan. Yalem was very happy to hear that her wedding was going to be celebrated in her hometown.

#

Henok quickly became a popular teacher in Senegal Elementary School. Geremew was praised as a model leader for his role in helping Henok turn his life around.[173]

Henok's teaching style was interactive and every student participated in demonstrative exercises. He wanted his students not to just learn theory; he also wanted them to understand its application using real-world examples. He spent most of his free time preparing for his classes. Unfortunately, he could not quit chewing khat and smoking cigarettes. But he was able to manage his consumption.

Geremew was a devoted evangelical.[174] He had strict discipline for

---

[172] Well, either the culture evolved fast, or Yalem had very progressive parents.

[173] He did not just give Henok a position at the school. He also arranged a rental place for Henok to live near the school. He monitored Henok's daily routines and spending habits. Henok was not fond of micro-management, but he understood that was the condition for his continued employment.

[174] The Evangelical Church was just beginning to expand in the region. Using strong backing from international sponsors, the church assisted residents with medical bills, offered marriage counseling, sponsored summer camps for children and provided skills training. The church presented itself as a modern and less restrictive alternative to the major religions in the area. While other religions focused on educating their followers about life after death, the evangelicals showed the public how religion could help improve life on earth. Many people converted. The church became an integral part of the community.

which he credited his religious upbringing. He felt responsible for making sure Henok's rehabilitation became successful and encouraged Henok to join him in church events. Henok initially was not happy about it. As they participated in group prayers and gospel sessions, Henok's attitude toward the religion slowly changed. He found it more interesting and convenient compared with standing for four hours at Sunday Mass at the Orthodox Church.

Henok proposed to the church's leadership a new project that could help the local community. One of the major problems in the area at the time was sanitation.[175]

Henok argued the church could help change this habit. He wanted to build public shower and toilet rooms in highly populated areas. The church approved the plan and appointed Henok as the program manager. Henok worked with volunteer engineers to design the plan. He also worked with local authorities for land acquisition and obtaining permits. Then the construction of the first public restroom started. In less than two months, the restroom was completed and opened for public use.

Henok and the church initially received praise from all sides. They were encouraged by the outpouring of support and started planning a second location. But an unanticipated problem occurred.

The new restroom quickly became dirty. None of the locals took the initiative to clean it. Henok and the church quickly faced backlash. With the focus having been on constructing the facility, they did not

---

[175] Traditionally, bathrooms were never a priority for the local community. As most families spent a large portion of their day on their farms, they just cleaned themselves in the woods. This habit continued even as the area became urbanized. Families used to build brand-new homes with no plans for bathrooms. These were always an afterthought. As a result, most families dug holes in their backyards and used them as toilets. They then showered at nearby rivers where they also used to wash their clothes.

make any plans for its operation. The local authorities refused to accept the responsibility for regular cleaning and maintenance of the facility. The church was forced to accept the responsibility for its daily operation.

Henok was instructed to freeze the plan for the second location until they found a middle ground with local authorities on operational issues. Instead, he was tasked with planning smaller restrooms. The church decided to shift attention to constructing individual restrooms for families who would be willing to maintain them. Many families registered for the individual restroom construction program.

As Henok and the evangelical church scrambled to improve the living conditions of poor residents, the community was in turmoil, once again, by political tensions.[176]

One day, a minibus was traveling from Jinka on its way to a village town called Hana. It carried twenty-six passengers. Most were small business owners who traveled regularly to the village for trading at a farmer's market that opened only once a week. There were eight women on the bus and two infants. Halfway along the road, the bus was forced to stop by armed gang members from one of the local tribes.

The tribes were protesting the regional administration's "favoritism" toward a rival tribe. At first, the passengers assumed it was a robbery. They begged the gang members to spare their valuables. The armed men

---

[176] The area around Jinka was home to over ten indigenous tribes who always competed for dominance. Then there were the multiracial residents who settled in the urbanized areas; they were referred to as Amhara simply because their main language was Amharic. Whenever the tribes had conflict with the government, the so-called Amharas were the prime targets. The tribes complained urbanization was destroying their culture and languages. They refused to accept change as a natural human evolution. If the government could not do anything about it, they were determined to force their agenda by trying to eradicate everyone who did not look or speak like the locals.

questioned everyone about their identity and the nature of their business.

These evil maniacs started executing passengers while they were seated. The passengers begged for their lives. But the armed men had already made up their minds. They murdered everyone on the bus except for the two infants, two men who proved they were from the same tribe, and the driver. They saved the driver because they needed him to take back their message to Jinka.

The minibus massacre horrified residents of Jinka.[177]

Such terrifying incidents had happened numerous times in different parts of the region. The government could not stop such targeted attacks as the villagers were protective of the identities of the gang members. In addition, the government had disarmed all urban residents when they came to power. But the tribes were allowed to maintain their weapons. That meant residents of the towns could not even protect themselves from their heavily armed counterparts.

One of the victims of the massacre was Henok's father, Ato Desta Agegnehu. Desta was on his way to deliver school uniforms that he tailored for students who had ordered them during his trip the previous week. Since demand for tailoring was shrinking in Jinka, thanks to jeans and other manufactured clothes, Desta had been taking his business on road trips to nearby villages. He could not have imagined the risk

---

[177] The fight to conserve cultures, languages and religions from transformation was not just happening in southern Ethiopia, it was all over the country. Ever since federalism became the law of the land, the government could not satisfy the growing demands from the empowered local administrations. Many of the country's regional states battled for greater autonomy. Also, each regional state had their own problems from ethnic groups who wanted to secede and form new states. For an outsider, it could look like none of these people wanted to live side by side. And then there were those who wanted to abolish the ethnic-based federalism and replace it with a unified central government. There were many questions and no solutions.

could be fatal.

The news of Desta's murder devastated the family. Before the family could send a messenger to Senegal, Henok received the news accidentally from strangers who babbled about the minibus massacre and the identities of the victims. Henok could not control his balance. He fell down on the ground of the coffee shop where he was playing with some friends and cried out loud. His friends tried to calm him. But Henok ran out of the coffee shop and bolted down the hill toward Jinka.

Henok did not even want to wait for a ride. An hour later, he arrived at his parents' home in Jinka. He could hear crowds sobbing while he was still a few blocks away from his home. When the crowd saw him reach the front door, the voices went louder. Even people who had not known Desta personally became emotional watching the pain on the faces of the family. Henok and his siblings were still recovering from the death of their mother. Everyone worried they may never recover from this tragic incident.

CHAPTER 13

Mannie and other members of the international committee worked tirelessly to restart negotiations between the two synods of the Ethiopian Orthodox Tewahedo Church. They started with informal discussions with representatives of each synod privately, which helped them establish legitimacy. Then the committee facilitated communication between the two sides. Both remained firm in their positions and did not look ready to make compromises.

The committee had to prioritize their objectives because the synods refused to meet each other directly for negotiation. They did not want it to appear to the public as if they acknowledged each other. But they agreed to recognize the committee as the official and only communication channel for continued dialogue. A memorandum of understanding was signed by each side. The committee promoted the signed agreement as a first step toward normalizing the relationship. The public could finally hope that unification was a realistic possibility.

Shortly after, shocking news was announced from Addis Ababa. The patriarch of the official synod of the Ethiopian Orthodox Tewahedo Church passed away from an undisclosed illness. There was no indication that the patriarch was dealing with a serious health issue and many Ethiopians were distraught by his death.[178]

---

[178] He was a very influential patriarch who modernized the church and expanded its influence. Despite the controversies surrounding his close relationship to the country's ruling party, the vast majority of Ethiopians had respected his holiness.

Various speculations swirled around his potential successors. Most people in the diaspora community pushed for the exiled patriarch to be reinstated and unify the two synods. But that proposal could not gain enough momentum from inside Ethiopia. The synod in Addis Ababa surprised the world by electing a relatively unknown figure to become the next patriarch of the church. The decision outraged supporters of the synod in exile. All ties between the two sides fell apart once more. All the hard work of Mannie and his colleagues was ruined.

Mannie felt like a fool for hoping to make a difference. Living in Europe, he learned what positivity and forward thinking could do to help communities resolve their differences diplomatically. His desire to share what he learned with his countrymen, his dream of one day seeing Ethiopia look like a European nation, made him forget the honest truth.[179]

Frustrated by the disappointing ending of the committee, Mannie shifted his undivided attention to his family. He watched Sikeat getting on the school bus in the morning and returning in the afternoon. He could tell that she was happy and stress-free, like any child should be. He took Monson to playgrounds and watched him trying to catch flies. Monson was so innocent and adorable. Mannie thought about his wife, Bethi. She was settled with her work and life in Bern. Woizero Haregeweyn never felt lonely in a foreign land, having been surrounded by grandchildren and with Ato Dires visiting every now and then. Mannie felt grateful

---

[179] That good systems are not built by accident and bad systems do not exist by mistake. The choices people make for generations determines the overall outcome of their collective work. Successful communities are those who make unselfish decisions under difficult circumstances and sacrifice their comforts to help one another. Unsuccessful communities are those who do not learn from past mistakes and continue to live with old habits. Sure, there are external factors, but the community's destiny is completely dependent on the actions they take to overcome them.

for the life they were able to build.

But the family was still dealing with a problem that had been troubling them for a while. Alazar, Ato Dires and Woizero Haregeweyn's youngest child, became a migrant in Libya and was stationed at a UN refugee camp near a town called Waddan. Alazar fled Ethiopia because he was unable to find a job, even though he had a degree in accounting. That's when he decided to travel to Italy by any means necessary and live with his brother Gebeyaw.

The family was worried for his safety as the security crisis in Libya was very bad. Even if he managed to get on a boat to Italy, there was no guarantee of making it alive. To avoid getting caught, the smuggling boats often risked crossing the Mediterranean Sea during the storm season. There were many migrant boats that went missing at sea.

Alazar's journey began when he fled Ethiopia on foot. After crossing the border with Sudan, he traveled to Khartoum and stayed there until he figured out his next move. Then he found smugglers who had a trafficking network from Sudan to Chad and all the way to Libya's capital, Tripoli. They informed him that they also had an agreement with another trafficking agency in Libya who could help him cross the Mediterranean Sea and drop him off somewhere on the Italian peninsula. They told him that he would be on his own after that. Alazar was not worried about what would happen once he reached Italy.

The cost for being smuggled from Khartoum to Tripoli was set at three thousand dollars. Bethi and Gebeyaw paid through MoneyGram. Alazar followed the smugglers along with fifteen other refugees from Ethiopia, Eritrea and Somalia. When they reached Sudan's border, they were transferred to another vehicle which was operated by a different group of smugglers.

The trip north across the Sahara Desert was the most inhumane experience one could have. There were no formal roads; the smugglers drove on the dusty plain where there was nothing in sight. The migrants were frightened. They could not speak the smugglers' language. Also, the smugglers exchanged the passengers at multiple trafficking stations. Some of the smugglers robbed the passengers; others committed unthinkable acts.

Alazar promised to himself that if he made it out of all this, he would never talk about the evil things that were done to him. After a month-long nightmarish journey, the smugglers evacuated the migrants in front of the UN refugee camp in Waddan and gave them the contact information for the traffickers who could transport them across the Mediterranean.

Alazar was afraid to leave the refugee camp. Following the civil war that took the life of former leader Muammar Gaddafi, armed militias controlled different parts of the country. To make matters worse, the Islamic militants known as ISIS used the power vacuum, making the country its recruiting and training ground.

Some migrants were bored with sitting in the camp all day and night. They asked to be allowed to work in the town. The camp managers made an arrangement with local companies who needed help. The companies promised to provide secure transportation and employment. The migrants were picked up and dropped off at a predetermined time.

Alazar was tempted to join the labor force. Then he learned that the workers were not being paid. The companies warned them against complaining to the camp managers. So Alazar decided to stay put. He stayed at the camp for over a year.

The camp had an asylum process to give the migrants a chance to be transferred to generous nations. As the refugee situation was bad, the asylum process was extremely slow. Frustrated with the processing delay, Alazar left the camp and headed to the city of Misrata on the Mediterranean coast. He and six other migrants rented a small room there. They could not find a job as residents refused to allow migrants to work. There was no safe place for migrants in Libya.[180]

Alazar and friends relied on money that was sent to them from family members in Europe and America. They avoided going outside, fearing for their safety. ISIS members had recently abducted Ethiopian migrants from their hideout and beheaded them on live video streaming. Though there was contradicting information, the terrorists claimed the victims were targeted because they were Christians. The migrants scrambled to escape the horror.

The cost for boarding a migrant boat to cross the sea to Europe was four thousand dollars. Three of Alazar's friends paid the fee and were picked up by traffickers from their room. It was several months before Alazar and the remaining three other migrants found out the status of their friends. The friends sent a Facebook message with a picture from the city of Bari in Italy.

Motivated by the news, two more migrants decided to take the trip, leaving Alazar and one other friend in the room. But their boat was chased by Italian and Maltese Patrols, forced to change course and docked on the coast of Tunisia. They stayed on the coast for a few days as the smugglers demanded additional payment. After reaching a compromise, the boat sailed again and arrived in Sicily.

When Alazar and his last remaining friend received the news that

---

[180] The crisis in Libya damaged the country's once prosperous economy. Inflation skyrocketed and unemployment soared. Angry Libyans joined armed struggles. Anti-migrant attacks were at an alarming rate.

the second group also made it to Italy, they were convinced that there was nothing left for them in Libya. They made arrangements to get on the next migrant boat. At around midnight, the boat sailed toward their dream destination.

There was some rain and mild wind. As well as about a dozen people, the boat was loaded with illegal substances. Midway into the sea, a storm became stronger, whipping the water into huge waves. The overloaded boat was pitched and tossed by the waves. The smugglers completely lost control of it. The migrants screamed helplessly as they watched the boat sinking. The waves carried the boat into darkness.

Three days later the Maltese coast guard spotted a partially submerged boat floating near the island. They found three dead bodies inside. A search and rescue team was quickly deployed. They found an additional five dead bodies. Television reporters showed horrific images of the dead migrants. Humanitarian agencies scrambled to investigate the identities of the victims.

#

Kedir made a significant contribution to the construction of the GERD project. He established a strong relationship with the project's fundraising committee and got permission to visit the project site. He also made a significant personal investment and served as the regional organizer for selling bonds to the diaspora community. Using his political connections, Kedir helped raise awareness about the ongoing issue with the project. He wrote letters regularly to his local congressional representative asking for political support.[181]

Kedir also lobbied fellow diaspora members to do the same. The need for international support became more important than ever when Ethiopia's caretaker prime minister abruptly announced that he would resign from his position.[182]

Meanwhile, Kedir expanded his business empire in Ethiopia. He partnered with other diaspora entrepreneurs on international trade. The partnership exported alcoholic beverages from Ethiopia to the US and imported medicines back to Ethiopia. Kedir hired his second cousin to manage the daily operation of his businesses in Ethiopia. Kedir was known to be a frequent traveler.

He purchased a large villa for Halimah in Meki, a town about fifty miles east from Butajira. By then, Halimah was a mother of four children. Her oldest son, Nusredin, and the second, Jamal, were born only fifteen months apart. Then the family welcomed their third child, a daughter named Hamlet. Kedir felt like they had enough children and wanted Halimah to use birth control. But she refused to do it for

---

[181] Diplomatic influence was critical as Ethiopia continued to rebuff pressure from Egypt. Ethiopia considered the Nile River as its most untapped treasure. Egypt, who had relied on the river for a freshwater supply since the days of Joseph and Potiphar, considered their water share from the river a matter of national security. There was no easy solution.

[182] He was fed up with the exhausting tension from all sides. Political elites who supported the former prime minister did not allow the caretaker to establish control. Externally, Western nations pressured Ethiopia to reach a deal with Egypt on the GERD. The arrest of an influential Saudi-Ethiopian billionaire, an important figure in Ethiopia, by the kingdom's new crown prince on charges related to corruption created another problem. The country's once flourishing economy started to stagnate. To make matters worse, hundreds of protesters died when a peaceful demonstration turned violent. The prime minister's resignation increased the political tension. As negotiations were underway to elect the next prime minister, every ethnic group wanted the successor to be from their side.

religious reasons. The couple were given counseling from religious elders who convinced Kedir to appreciate God's blessings. Two years later, the family welcomed a second daughter, whom they named Meriam.

Halimah was happy with the life she built with Kedir and living close to her parents. She had everything she needed. She had visited the US on multiple occasions. But she had no interest in permanently leaving her country. As a devout Muslim woman, she preferred a simpler life. She had a husband she could count on and that was good enough.

The Ethiopian ruling party finally elected a new prime minister.[183]

At first, everyone was delighted by the election of the new prime minister and the prospect of a better future. He was presented by the media as one of the most decent human beings. Citizens with nationalist ideologies strongly supported the prime minister who seemed to be supportive of integration. Federalists were also optimistic that they would be allowed to continue to reshape their regions with an image and identity that reflected the ethnic group with the majority population.

The prime minister seemed to be talking with two mouths. When he met with multiracial communities, he said Ethiopianism was a spiritual bond that could not be broken and that he was supportive of constitutional reforms to give equal rights to all citizens. On the other side, his speech to federalism supporters showed that he had no problem with their desire for greater autonomy in their region. These were two

---

[183] In a rare moment of unity, the Oromia and Amhara regions made a secret deal and used their majority vote to elect a relatively unknown figure from the Oromo ethnic group. The newly elected prime minister had the traits needed at a time the nation frowned from racial turmoil. He was young, charismatic, educated, a veteran and had a humble upbringing. He grew up speaking both Amharic and Oromo languages and learned to speak good Tigrinya and English. He was also a great orator; he connected with citizens from every corner. He preached patience as the government instilled reform measures.

completely contradicting positions.

In order for federalists to develop greater autonomy, they needed to suppress nationalist business, religious and social practices. They could only achieve their objectives if they could continue to marginalize ethnic minorities in their regions, eviscerate new settlers from their legally acquired homes and control inter-regional exchanges. It was not clear how the prime minister intended to represent both ideologies.

The international community, on the other hand, fell in love with the Ethiopian leader. His announcement to privatize major economic sectors in the country gained huge diplomatic support. The prime minister also announced that his government intended to honor the terms of the international ruling on the territorial conflict with Eritrea and cede land to its northern neighbor.

He became the first Ethiopian official since the bloody border war to visit Eritrea's capital. Eritrean televisions showed the love affair in Asmara between the leaders of the two countries as they hugged and kissed each other. The two sides made a peace deal which officially ended the nearly two decades of cold war between the two countries. The African Union and the UN commended the new direction.[184]

The sudden affection with Eritrea was a difficult scenario to watch for families who had lost a lot due to the war. There were many skeptics that could not visualize how the federal government could peacefully

---

[184] The prime minister later won the Nobel Peace Prize for his peace effort in the region. Organizations that were once labeled terrorists returned to the country. The Eritrean president visited Addis Ababa where he was celebrated as the lost brother returning home; it seemed as if the hundreds of thousands of lives lost because of the war this guy started had been forgotten. Regardless, the administration was clearly doing an impressive job normalizing relationships with key stakeholders. But no action was taken yet to reform the constitution. So it was still not clear which direction the administration was leaning.

cede a land from one region without the approval of the regional administration. Ethiopia's northern region of Tigray had no appetite for the peace deal.[185]

The prime minister also traveled to the US for dialogue with the Ethiopian diaspora communities. He magically brought together politicians from completely opposite ideologies to hold hands in public. He declared certain political activists, who had been wanted in Ethiopia on terrorism charges, were free to return to their homeland.

Perhaps his most magical accomplishment was his work in uniting the two opposing synods of the Orthodox Church. Before departing for the US, he had already persuaded the Ethiopian patriarch to reconcile. While in the US he met with the patriarch of the exiled synod. Soon after, he announced that an agreement was reached between the two synods to reunite.

The agreement allowed the exiled patriarch to return to his country to serve as spiritual leader with authority equal to the current patriarch who would continue to govern the church's administrative affairs. The agreement basically ended the exiled synod and all churches in the diaspora became united. After years of failed negotiations, including the one led by Mannie and company, the prime minister somehow managed to peacefully resolve the conflict with just a couple of meetings.[186]

Meanwhile, Kedir and his family could sense that a new dynamic was brewing. They could feel that violence against minorities and new settlers was spreading fast in different parts of the country. Kedir was

---

[185] From the get-go, leaders of Tigray were not on board with the prime minister. Their relationship got worse when the government arrested former officials, who were mostly from the Tigray region, on corruption-related charges. The arrests directly or indirectly marginalized the people of Tigray.

[186] One could only wonder what he had said to them.

convinced his family could no longer live there peacefully. So he made a plan to permanently relocate his wife and children to the US, where their liberty would be protected and society allowed cultural diversification.

#

Willie did not believe that he was the only conservative in the Ethiopian American community. The community's culture was founded on strong religious and family values. They prioritized group freedom over individual rights. Their bad experience with socialism in Ethiopia meant they did not come all the way to America looking for a handout. They had a short history as immigrants in the country, but they worked hard and built strong reputations in every city where they settled. Children were raised to embrace their heritage. So the community clearly had a conservative lifestyle.

However, to the contrary, the community was an unapologetic supporter of the Democratic Party. They did not feel their vote welcomed by the Republican Party. There was a belief within the community that Republicans were not open to diversity and their party was influenced more by identity politics than fundamental conservative values. These were voters the party could have used in some key battleground suburbs like in Northern Virginia, central Maryland and the twin cities of Minnesota.

Willie considered himself as one of those conservatives who always voted for Democrats because they never felt represented by Republican candidates. However, Willie had regrets as his community was missing the opportunity of being represented by both political parties. He knew participation in both parties would help influence the direction of the political movement in each.

It was this belief that led Willie to gravitate toward Donald Trump's unorthodox campaign for presidency. Willie voted for Trump because he was a political outsider and had a long résumé working with diverse groups of individuals.

Sadly, Willie's love affair with Trump proved to be short-lived. As pressure mounted from different directions, the president needed reliable and influential allies. So he sided with the right-wing sector of the political spectrum. The president's alignment with extremists angered rational conservatives like Willie. Willie was offended by Trump's unfair positions on various high-profile topics.

Willie considered Trump's executive order to ban visitors from Muslim countries a cheap and politically motivated attack against minorities. Willie could not understand how Trump would be totally opposed to law enforcement reforms; it was no secret that these agencies had been weaponized throughout American history to discriminate against people of color. During the controversies surrounding Confederate statues, Willie was disappointed that the president sided with white nationalists who neglected the fact that those statues reflected the darkest moments of American history and the people who stood on the wrong side of the civil war. To make matters worse, Trump was not just unfair with his treatment of illegal immigrants, he also wanted to limit family-based legal immigration. Trump also wanted to stop the Diversity Visa (DV) lottery program. As an immigrant who benefited from both of these legal immigration programs, Willie was strongly opposed to the administration's effort to slow down legal immigration.

Perhaps the most irreparable damage to Willie's relationship with the Trump administration was when the US attempted to force Ethiopia to reach a deal on the GERD project on terms favorable to the Egyptians.[187]

A US delegation led by the Treasury Secretary started mediating the negotiations between the Northeastern African countries. At the beginning everything looked promising. At some point, President Trump even boasted that he deserved a Nobel Peace Prize for his efforts. As negotiations made good progress, the president met with foreign ministers of both countries in the White House.

During the president's authoritative and pressing negotiation tactics, the Ethiopian delegation sensed that the US was siding with Egypt and was no longer a neutral mediator. The delegation respected the presidency and patiently participated in the meeting and a press briefing at the end. But after returning to their hotel and discussing with authorities in Addis Ababa, Ethiopia announced that it was withdrawing from the negotiations mediated by the US. It asked the African Union to take over as mediator.[188]

Shortly after, the Trump administration announced plans to halt foreign-aid money allocated to Ethiopia. At that point, it was no secret that the president was tipping the scale to favor Egypt at the expense of Ethiopia. Fearing imminent threat, the Ethiopian Ministry of Defense

---

[187] At that point, Ethiopia had already started its first stage of filling the reservoir behind the hydraulic dam. Once it became obvious the construction of GERD could not be stopped, Egypt shifted its attention to slowing down the water-filling process. Had Ethiopia had agreed to Egypt's demand, it would have taken almost two decades to fill the dam. When it was announced that Ethiopia had begun filling the reservoir, it created an outrage in Cairo. Ethiopia refused to cave to the pressure from its northern neighbor. It was at that moment that President Trump placed the US at the center of the most contentious negotiations in Africa. But his bullying approach quickly spilled more fuel on the fire.

[188] The Trump administration thought a deal had been reached before Ethiopia dropped out of the negotiation. Trump berated Ethiopia for making "a big mistake" by not agreeing to his offer. He even suggested that Egypt could "blow up the dam."

mobilized its forces to protect the dam. For the first time in the long-running dispute, a military conflict seemed a possibility.[189]

The Ethiopian American community was shocked by the actions of the Trump administration. No one wanted to see another war. This was especially personal for Willie who voted for Trump. He had hoped a Trump presidency would mean the US would take its hands off issues in other countries and put the focus on rebuilding the American economy. He was upset by the administration making a bad situation even worse. Willie started a nationwide petition online to condemn the actions by the Trump administration.[190]

Willie also published open letters calling on all Ethiopian Americans to vote against Trump in the upcoming national election. Willie's newfound activism reignited his relationship with his childhood friend Kedir.[191]

Willie and Kedir worked with other activists to campaign in battleground states like Georgia, Virginia and Minnesota under the slogan "A Vote for Biden is A Vote Against Trump!" and "Ethiopians Against Trump!"

Meanwhile, Yalem and JP's wedding date was approaching. Willie started a travel plan for his family to participate in the wedding in Ethiopia. This would become the family's first homecoming visit. Asmeret,

---

[189] The escalating tension between the two American allies marked the biggest diplomatic failure of Trump's administration in Africa.

[190] Willie wasn't the only one. Ethiopian Americans gathered in Washington DC to protest the administration's continued pressure against Ethiopia. The GERD was financed by selling bonds to Ethiopians across the globe since it could not secure loans from international banks. Thus, the diaspora community was directly invested.

[191] Like Willie, Kedir was worried that a Trump reelection would mean war between the Northeastern African nations.

who had a painful memory from her last moments in Jinka, did not know how she could handle her emotions on this trip.

Willie encouraged Asmeret to face her fear and anger. She was still recovering from the trauma of her family's deportation during the war between Ethiopia and Eritrea. She was convinced to use the trip as therapy. Besides, it would not hurt to reconnect with some old friends.

Willie and Asmeret also obtained passports for Semere, Rediet and Azeb. The children were in elementary school already. They had a good idea of what to expect from life in their parents' birthplace. As a result, they were not excited about the trip. But they were happy to have an excuse to miss school for two weeks. Fre did not have much of a relationship with Yalem. So she was not planning to join the homecoming trip.

#

Seble and Walalign's family enjoyed many successes over the years. Edilawit grew into a wonderful young adult. She completed pre-med at the University of the District of Columbia and was accepted to Howard University's College of Medicine. The family's size also expanded as Walalign's mother and father relocated from Ethiopia and became permanent residents in Washington DC. Seble and Walalign had a rental property in the Southeastern district. The grandparents occupied the ground floor there and served as the supervisors on site.

Edilawit had a very good relationship with her grandparents and often visited them for a sleepover. Seble's little sister, Hermela, also lived nearby as she joined the University of Maryland College Park Campus on full scholarship to study her PhD in biochemistry. The family were living their American dream before an evil enemy by the name of COVID-19 attacked everyone without discrimination.[192]

Small business owners like Seble and Walalign were among the most affected by the pandemic. When the pandemic was first declared, little was known about the virus and there was a lot of confusing direction from the local and federal governments.

At the beginning, Seble's family were forced to close their convenience store. Then they were allowed to reopen under strict requirements for masking, social distancing and sanitation. Shortly afterwards, they were forced to close again due to a sudden spike in infection rates. Then, yet again, they could open but under similar restrictions.[193]

To make matters worse for small business owners, the population of Washington DC reduced dramatically as government institutions and

---

[192] COVID-19 is a disease caused by a virus called Severe Acute Respiratory Syndrome CoronaVirus 2 (SARS-CoV-2). The novel virus was first detected in the Chinese city of Wuhan and in just two months became a worldwide pandemic. All attempts to contain its spread failed dramatically. COVID-19 typically spreads from one person to another when inhaling contaminated air. Infected individuals are typically contagious for two weeks. The symptoms can be confused with some of the common seasonal illnesses such as fever, dry cough, fatigue, sore throat, stomachache and diarrhea. Severe illness is more likely in elderly patients and those with certain underlying medical conditions.

[193] The economic and social impact of the pandemic was felt all around the world. Countries closed their borders and international activities halted. Global shipping and logistics delays created a shortage of supplies. In the US, the federal government declared the pandemic as a national public health emergency. Local jurisdictions ordered people to stay in place. Sporting games were canceled. Schools closed their doors. Mask mandates and social distancing requirements created stressful conditions as families scrambled for clarification. Despite the restrictions and sacrifices, the infection rate continued to climb and the death toll multiplied. Isolation from social activities created a serious mental health crisis. Misinformation circulated through social media and exacerbated the already intense political divisions.

many large companies required their employees to work from home. This allowed many people to move out to the suburbs for better social distancing as well as to save on living costs. In addition, the remaining residents had very restricted social movement which was an existential threat for retail businesses such as convenience stores.

Furthermore, the pandemic forced consumers to change their shopping patterns. More consumers shopped online and stocked large supplies in their homes. All these factors dramatically reduced the demand for convenience stores. The interruptions in supply chains also caused shortages and escalated business operation and maintenance costs.

Many businesses closed permanently. And those that survived had to make painful changes. Seble and Walalign's store had been losing money since the virus started its terror. They had received very good offers to sell the property from developers who planned to demolish the building and construct a fast-food restaurant.

Many residents in Washington DC relocated to safer remote areas. Seble and Walalign also began to consider getting away from the depressing condition of living in isolation. They owned a home in the southern Ethiopian city of Hawassa and heard good reviews from other people that had moved to Ethiopia to escape the pandemic.[194]

Seble and Walalign could not find a reason to stay. They had barely

---

[194] The impact of the COVID-19 pandemic in Ethiopia was dramatically different. Ethiopia was also among the early victims. It declared a state of emergency shortly after the US. But Ethiopia refrained from shutting down its economy. Ethiopian Airlines was one of the few international airlines that continued services. Despite travel restrictions in most countries, Ethiopia refused to enforce travel bans. Instead, it mandated passengers quarantine upon arrival in the country. The pandemic was considered a myth in many parts of the country as residents were yet to witness any infected people. Many Ethiopian Americans returned to the homeland to stay away from the chaotic situation in the US.

seen their daughter during the pandemic. And when she visited, there was no hugging and everyone had to wear masks and maintain social distance. The family had not seen the grandparents in person for months because they did not want to risk exposing them as they had been dealing with other medical conditions.

Grocery shopping became a horrifying experience. They had to shop alone because walking in pairs was not allowed. When they returned from the store, they had to quickly change and wash the clothes they had worn. What used to be normal human interaction became the most frightening experiences.

Despite all the precautions they had taken, the family encountered their worst nightmare. Both grandparents tested positive for COVID-19 and were taken to St. Elizabeth's Hospital. Their grandfather worsened and was put on a ventilator just a week after entering the hospital. Their grandmother was seriously ill as well. Family members were not allowed to enter the hospital. Walalign's family received updates on the conditions of the grandparents over the phone. It was an agonizing experience to not know what to do. They felt helpless.

Then came the worst news one could expect in that condition. Walalign received a call from the hospital informing him of the passing of his father. The family mourned the tragic event. But they were forced to wait for a funeral service as the hospital's clearance procedure took several days to approve the collection of the coffin.

Three days later, Walalign received another call from the hospital. He quickly answered the phone hoping it was to inform them that they could hold the funeral. Walalign looked like he was having a panic attack. Seble jumped off her seat and helped her husband to sit down. She asked the person on the other end of the phone what was happening.

She was distraught to hear that her mother-in-law also died while in hospital care. The medical report said the grandmother died from a heart attack after hearing the passing of her husband. The family was devastated. A joint funeral was held and the grandparents were buried together in the same grave.

Seble and Walalign were convinced that they needed to get away from the horrific scenes in Washington DC. They had their house in Hawassa renovated prior to their departure and arranged a real estate management firm to rent their home. They made a deal with one of the developers to sell their store. And they informed their daughter of their plan to move back to Ethiopia. They were not sure if it was temporary or if they were leaving for good. All they knew was that they needed an escape.

They felt like they were losing their minds. Edilawit understood the situation and supported their plan. After all, she had her own life and knowing that they were safe would give her comfort. Seble and Walalign were very upset by the Trump administration's handling of the pandemic. They would have liked to wait until the upcoming election to make their voices heard. But their desire to save themselves outweighed their dislike of the president.

They purchased the earliest available ticket on Ethiopian Airlines and departed from Dulles Airport. Edilawit was not sure what the future would bring. But she waved goodbye as the Ethiopian flag bearer lifted off the ground and climbed to the sky.

CHAPTER 14

It was a cold and breezy Saturday morning in Jinka. Henok was on his way to the Neri River to take a bath.

Lately, he made it his daily routine to wake up early, walk the mile to the river and take a bath. He could not wait till he escaped the busy streets in his neighborhood and entered the wilderness. He no longer enjoyed running into people who wanted to engage in long conversations.

Henok had changed a lot since his father's murder. He was no longer a socially active person. He preferred spending most of his time alone in the woods or chewing khat in his backyard. The walk to the river through the grass field made him feel disconnected from his demons. He giggled alone when the frosts on the grass touched his legs and tickled.

He usually sat on the riverside, observing the surrounding view and listening to the birds singing and water flowing through the valley. He would imagine living in a different world. He would take off all his clothes and jump into the middle of the river. As he dipped inside the cold water, he could feel all his stress washing from his head.

He wished he did not have to get out of the water. As the morning air began to warm from the rising sun, Henok knew that more and more people would flock to the river. So he always timed his exit before the crowd started to get noisy.

Anyway, on that particular Saturday morning, Henok was walking down the busy street crossing the town's market to the river. He heard his brother, Mekit, calling him.

"Hi, Heni! Heni!" Mekit was washing his hands in front of a Kurit House.

Henok tried to ignore his brother, pretended he did not hear him and kept going. Henok had not been on good terms with his siblings for a while. The siblings had been dealing with different family dramas.

Henok had not returned to his job in Senegal since their father was murdered by the gang attack. He had not been mentally stable. He talked a lot to himself. Kids in the neighborhood mocked him for not taking care of himself. They called him names like "Kizhibi" and "Thestata." The closest meaning for these words in English would be "confused" or "challenged."

Mekit, on the other hand, coerced the family to sell their father's tailoring business and bought a refurbished truck. He used the truck to work as a contractor, supplying aggregate rocks and sand to construction sites. Unfortunately, the truck broke down regularly and it had been costing more money for repair than it was generating. But Mekit was unfazed by the challenges and continued to work hard.

Feker opened a hair salon in the living room of the family's house. She had a two-year-old daughter whose father was unknown.

Selam worked as a nurse in a clinic in Gazer. She was married with three children. Under constant pressure from her husband, Selam had asked the siblings to sell their parents' home and split their inheritance.

The other siblings were offended that she would make such a selfish request and refused to agree. Selam threatened to sue them in court to get her inheritance share.

The family drama caused a rift between the siblings. They barely talked to each other anymore. At home, they did everything they could to avoid talking to one another.

Henok assumed that Mekit was calling him to make fun of him or to complain about something. But Mekit continued yelling his name. So Henok turned to Mekit and yelled back, "What do you want?"

"You got nothing that I want, you Kizhibi!" Mekit replied angrily. "Come over here; Mannie is inside! Your friend Mannie!"

"I don't know anyone by that name! I don't have a friend called Mannie!" Henok shrugged him off. He thought his brother was making a joke. It was also his way of expressing his dissatisfaction with his old friend for not maintaining contact.

"I'm not joking. He's here." Mekit was serious.

Henok then realized that maybe his brother was telling the truth. He followed Mekit into the restaurant. There were about a dozen people circling around a large tray filled with a variety of raw meats and Tej glasses. With his shiny hair and unique dressing style, despite the long time-lapse, it was not difficult to identify the European.

Henok quickly spotted his old college roommate. "Woow! Dr. Amanuel Lemeta! My brother from another mother!" Henok forgot his disappointment; he was genuinely excited.

The two greeted each other with big hugs. Mannie asked everyone to create space and pulled in a chair for Henok to sit next to him.

Mannie tried to hide his sadness at seeing Henok in such bad shape. Henok could not concentrate on one topic. He would ask a question and as Mannie was giving a response, he would change the topic of conversation.

Mannie patiently answered Henok's questions. He told Henok that he brought his family to attend Yalem's wedding. Mannie's family had stayed a few days with his mother in Hamer before arriving in Jinka. He told some funny stories about his kids' first encounter with their grandmother and aunts. Then Mannie asked, "How have you been, Heni?"

"Everything is going well," Henok pretended. "I am taking a sabbatical from my teaching job and currently pursuing some other interests."

"That's great, Heni." Mannie knew it was a lie. But he did not want his old friend to feel down.

"Yeah. In fact, I think you can help. I am very interested in traveling abroad for graduate study. I have been applying to various universities in Europe and America." It did not take long for Henok to ask for another favor.

Mannie remembered some of the confusing emails that he had received from Henok asking for sponsorship. Before the conversation took an unpleasant turn, Mannie knew he needed to steer it in a different direction. He took sunglasses out of his pocket and asked, "Heni, I brought you these. Do you like them?"

Henok quickly put on the glasses and looked at himself in a mirror inside the restaurant. "I love them!" He smiled.

After the feast, Mannie took Henok to the hotel to introduce him to his family who were staying at Hotel Jinka. The hotel was fully reserved for two weeks serving the wedding attendees from North America and Europe. It was a modern hotel built to cater for tourists and senior government officials. Even the menu at the hotel's cafe was filled with foreign-style choices like omelet, burger and sandwiches. Mannie was surprised to see such an elegant hotel in Jinka. He noticed a lot had changed over the past two decades. But he could also see that most people were still struggling financially.

Seble and Walalign were the first to arrive from Hawassa. They had been organizing the wedding, set for the following Saturday. Willie and his family were already on the way from Addis Ababa and expected to arrive on Sunday. Yalem, JP and their family were expected to arrive in Jinka on Tuesday ahead of the wedding date.

Kedir was already in the country with his family in Meki. Since Kedir's grandmother had already left Jinka to live in her new home in Addis Ababa, he no longer had any other family members in the town. So he planned to make a short trip with his family on Friday, just in time for the wedding on the following day.

Sikeat and Monson were playing in the hotel garden when they saw their father coming in. "Papa! Papa!" they shouted with excitement as they ran toward Mannie and jumped on his shoulders.

Mannie lifted them up and gave them kisses. He turned around with a big smile and introduced them to Henok. Before Mannie could finish explaining who Henok was, Sikeat interrupted and said, "Je te connais. Tu es Henok; celui qui lisait la Bible pour papa!"

Even though they were taught to speak Amharic at home, the kids were more comfortable communicating in French.

Henok did not understand what was said.

Mannie laughed at his daughter's memory and replied, "Oui! Vous avez raison ma fille. C'est Henok." Then Mannie explained to Henok that Sikeat remembered him teaching the Bible to her father. Sikeat loved listening to her father's childhood stories and memorized the names of some of her favorite characters.

"Bonjour! Bonjour!" Henok tried to connect with the kids using the only French word he knew.[195]

Using her broken Amharic, Sikeat asked Henok many questions about what her father was like back in the day, why Henok always seemed to find himself in sticky situations and if he could introduce

---

[195] Mannie told his kids to talk in Amharic.

her to Merigeta Estezia. Monson quietly watched Henok's expression. Just then, Bethi came out of the cafe.

"Henok? Is that you? How are you?" Bethi greeted Henok.

Henok gave her a mild response. The two were never each other's fans. Henok blamed her for breaking up his friendship with Mannie. And Bethi always considered Henok as a bad influence that was preventing Mannie from growing.

Mannie and his kids led the way into the hotel's cafe and ordered drinks for everyone. They talked about the old days and about some of their thrilling experiences.

The next day, Dechasa and his new wife, Amelewerk, were at the town's airport waiting for Willie and his family. Dechasa and Amelewerk watched the plane descend in the sky, then a few minutes later, the kids were the first to exit and ran toward their grandfather. Thanks to Viber, Whatsapp and Imo, the kids regularly video chatted with their grandfather.

Dechasa had a better relationship with Asmeret and the grandkids than with his own son and daughter. Willie and Fre could not let go of the past. To make matters worse, Dechasa always presented himself as a great father and took pride in the sacrifices he made to raise his children. But Willie and Fre never wanted to give him credit, so it angered them to hear his stories.

After the meet and greet, the family headed to the taxi station. The only rides available were motorbikes and two-person sized minicars called "Bajaji." The drivers quickly surrounded the family and lobbied to be picked. One driver was the loudest, calling Willie by name.

"Anteneh?" Willie asked. "What are you doing here? I thought you were in South Africa." The two greeted each other.

The family needed five Bajajis. Willie arranged for Azeb to sit with

Amelewerk on one, Semere and Rediet got on the second, and the third was for luggage. Then Willie secretly plotted with Dechasa, who spoke privately with the remaining two drivers and got on the fourth vehicle alone.

Willie and Asmeret traveled in the final vehicle with Anteneh in the back. Talkative as usual, Anteneh told stories about how he returned to Jinka. Apparently he was doing well in Johannesburg until his store was burned down by anti-migrant protesters. That was when he decided to return home and start from scratch.

"Where are you taking us?" Asmeret screamed after noticing that they were separated from the first three vehicles. Willie smiled and explained that Anteneh was just doing what he was told. He asked her to trust him and be patient.

Many of the roads and buildings had been restructured. Since Asmeret left town at a young age, except for some common parts, she could not recognize the area. But as soon as she saw the police station, she figured out where they were taking her. Her childhood home was only a block away from the police station.

The Bajajis stopped when they reached a gated house which was very familiar to Asmeret. Dechasa and Willie quickly walked to the gate and knocked on the door. A gentleman who looked like he was in his fifties opened the door. Dechasa explained the situation and asked for permission to tour the house. The man hesitantly agreed and let them in.

Except for the painting on the outside, the house had not been upgraded at all. Asmeret remembered the stories behind some features of the house, like the extra latches on the back of the main entrance door which their father installed after the family had received death threats.

Asmeret entered a room that was once a bedroom for her and her brothers. She could not control her emotions as she replayed those normal childhood memories and everything that had happened after the war. She asked to be left alone in the room for a little while. They left her and went to the living room.

"Are you the owner?" Willie asked.

"Yes. My wife and I bought it from its previous owner five years ago. My wife passed away a year ago." The man answered.

Willie could tell the man was still grieving. "I am sorry for your loss," Willie consoled him. "I don't mean to be rude. But as you can see, this house means a lot to my wife. So I have to ask, have you considered selling it?"

"Well eh…" the man contemplated. "Since my wife passed, I have been considering returning to my hometown in Gidole."

"Please, name a price that can make your wish come true." Henok offered to buy the house.

"I have spent a lot of money in the backyard. And ahhh, I recently replaced the roof." The man started to increase his price. "Eight hundred thousand birr[196] would be reasonable," he said.

"What?" Dechasa and Anteneh screamed in protest. "That is twice the market value. Look at the roof; it doesn't look like much work was done on it."

But Willie smiled and outstretched his hand to make a deal. The man could not believe it. He quickly shook Willie's hand in agreement.

Minutes later, Asmeret came out to the living room. She was surprised to find everyone in a good mood. Willie broke the news, "You're now the owner of this house, baby!"

"Thank you, Honey! Thank you! Thank you! Thank you!" She jumped

---

[196] Roughly eighteen thousand US dollars at that time.

and climbed up on his neck. She hugged him tight and told him slowly, "This is the best present you have ever given me." Asmeret was touched by her husband's heartfelt present.

"What about our children?" he joked. He already knew her response would be something like, "The kids are my gift to you!"

They thanked the man for his willingness and drove to Dechasa's home. They found their kids playing outside with new friends they just made in the neighborhood.

Inside, Amelewerk was preparing dinner. Asmeret wanted to change first, but she was told that all luggage was sent straight to the hotel. Some things never change; Asmeret had to walk all the way to the backyard to use the bathroom, and she had to carry a jar of water because there was no plumbing in the bathroom.

Willie washed his children's hands at the water fountain in the backyard. Then everyone sat around a big rectangular dining table. The food smelled delicious. There was chicken stew, beef stews with red sauce and curry sauce, homemade yogurt and multiple vegetable dishes as well.

"What should I make for the children? Maybe they can eat the vegetables with bread?" Amelewerk was worried that the hot sauces in the meat stews could be too much for the foreigners. But Willie told her not to worry.

"These kids grew up eating injera. They love spicy food." Willie explained how strong the Ethiopian community was in the Washington DC metro area and that they had access to many products from back home. "It is basically like living in a fantasy Ethiopia, where you still get to keep your identity, but you work and live in a highly developed society."

Asmeret supported her husband's claim and added that she even baked her own injera at home.

"But you have Donald Trump!" Dechasa poked his son's pain.

"Only for one more month! And then, he is gone!" Willie proudly remembered his contribution to ensuring Trump's loss. In all the battleground states where he campaigned by appearing in churches and writing articles on local Amharic news outlets, Trump received a lower percentage of the vote than in his first election. According to Willie, Ethiopian Americans had something to do with handing the presidency to Joe Biden.

"What if he refuses to accept the election result? Isn't he complaining about election fraud?" Dechasa reminded his son that the election might not be over yet.

"It doesn't matter what he says. The rule of law applies to everyone. This is the United States of America we are talking about. There are checks and balances at every authority level," Willie responded confidently.[197]

"I heard you voted for him the first time! Why?" Dechasa did not seem to back down either.

Asmeret realized why the father-son duo usually did not get along. She could sense that the conversation was heading downhill. The adults were drinking Tella. Asmeret felt Willie and Dechasa might have had a little too much to drink.

Dinner was over by then and the kids went back to playing with their new friends outside. The neighborhood kids were entertained by the Americans' unique accent and how they unintentionally mixed English words while speaking in Amharic.

"We need to go to the hotel. I need to take a shower and the kids need to rest." Asmeret got off her chair and started helping Amelewerk

---

[197] Ah, if we only had all this confidence now…

pick up the dishes.

But Amelewerk refused to accept Asmeret's help, out of respect of course, and suggested getting the kids ready instead. Asmeret thanked Amelewerk for the lovely dinner and went outside to call the kids.

Willie asked his wife to give him ten minutes and went with Anteneh to the house across the street. They knocked on the door, but no one answered. They went into the backyard asking, "Hello? Is anybody home?"

A woman was in the kitchen baking injera. She had already heard that Willie was in the neighborhood. She was delighted to see he remembered her family and came in person to say hello. It did not take long for Willie to realize this woman was Feker.

They were friends on Facebook where she had been regularly posting pictures. After a brief conversation, Willie gave Feker some cash, told her that he would visit again and returned across the street.

Asmeret and her kids were already in their Bajajis, waiting for Willie and Anteneh.

Dechasa and his wife watched from their door as the Bajajis drove away.

On their way back, Willie saw Anteneh muttering over the phone. Willie had also noticed him getting agitated by texts he had received frequently during dinner. When the phone hung up, Willie curiously asked, "Trouble in paradise?"

"Ohhh no, no!" Anteneh whispered nervously. He did not realize Willie was paying attention. "It's just my roommate. He was only asking if I would be there for dinner."

Anteneh did not want to go into details. Willie understood the situation. He told Anteneh that he would tip him well for all his troubles.

When they reached the hotel, Willie did not want to detain the drivers any longer. He paid them very generously and wished Anteneh the best of luck with his roommate. Anteneh and the other drivers were delighted by the pay and went on their way.

When Willie and his family entered the hotel's cafe, their friends greeted them shouting, "Surprise!"

Seble, Walalign, Mannie, Bethi and Henok were awaiting their arrival. Everyone hid behind curtains when Willie and his family arrived at the hotel, and greeted them by spraying the room with champagne.

Semere, Rediet and Azeb were the most excited by the reunion. Seble was their "favorite auntie" and they were very happy to see her for the first time in several months. A few minutes later, Asmeret took her kids to bed. The friends ordered more drinks and continued to play.

Willie was a little bothered by Henok continually calling him "Professor Awlachew." But he did not want to embarrass Henok, so he decided to tolerate it. The party continued all night.

Meanwhile, Yalem and JP arrived in Addis Ababa on Sunday evening. They stayed in a really nice international hotel near the airport. The family ordered room service for dinner. But their two children, Andrew (his mother called him Andu) and Michelle (her mother called her Mitu), did not like the taste and refused to eat.

They were accompanied by JP's parents, Sed and Maggie; his big sister, Madeline; and her husband, Greg. Greg suggested they should go out to the city and find a restaurant the kids might like.

All eyes turned to Yalem for guidance, but she was not in a position to help. She had only been in the city once before and the city had changed a lot since then.

They called the hotel's front desk to arrange a taxi and someone to guide them to the city. The taxi driver took the family to a McDonald's-inspired burger joint in a very crowded neighborhood. The kids loved the burger, but they did not touch the fries as "it's nothing like McDonald's fries!"

The next day, the family toured the city. The ladies enjoyed a wonderful spa therapy for a very low price they could not believe. They all saw that the city was as modern as any other technologically advanced and socially diverse city in the world. They were able to communicate in English with no difficulty in every place they visited.

On Tuesday afternoon, their plane arrived at Jinka airport.[198]

As they exited the plane, they could see Seble and some other people outside a wire fence waving and talking to them.

"Now, this is what I remember from Africa!" Sed exclaimed as he stretched his legs and looked around the airport. "Fresh air, clean sky and green environment!"

After a brief meet and greet, they took Bajajis to the hotel. Everyone had different reactions to the scenes they were observing as they drove through the town.

Madeline felt sad for the cats, dogs and other domestic animals when she watched them eating dirt from the ground.

Maggie was disturbed to see some women walking barefoot while carrying firewood on their backs.

Greg and JP were amused by kids chasing their Bajajis; they handed out chocolate bars which attracted more kids to join the chase.

But Yalem was filled with emotions.

Sed was joyful as he relived his memories on the battlefield.

---

[198] In stark contrast to the airport in Addis Ababa, this airport was very small. Theirs was the only plane. Except for the plane's landing and the paved walkway to a small terminal building, the area was undeveloped land.

As was the tradition, the bride's family did not want to interact with the bridegroom before the wedding day. So JP and his family stayed in the hotel. Yalem took her children to visit her parents.

Ato Kebede was busy outside his house building tents for the wedding party. He was filled with joy as watched his daughter getting off a Bajaji. "Kulibi Gabriel, thank you! Thank you for bringing me my grandchildren! Elililililili!" Ato Kebede praised his favorite saint as he kissed his grandkids turn by turn.

Andu and Mitu tried to protect their cheeks as their grandfather's beard rubbed on them.

"Elililililili! Elililililili! Kidane Mihiret, mother of my Lord! May your name be praised forever! Elililililili! Elililililili!" Yalem's mother came out of her house giving praise to the Holy Mary. Her face was sweating and her hands were covered with dust from the work she had been doing in the kitchen. But that did not stop her from hugging and kissing her daughter and her grandchildren. "Andiye! Mituye! Come to your grandma!" She lifted the kids from the ground.

There were at least fifteen women in the back who had been volunteering to prepare the ingredients needed for the wedding party food. "Abeba Ayesh Woyi, Abeba Ayesh Woyi; Balenjeroche Gibu Kebete." The ladies sang a traditional song in Amharic to greet the guests. When translated to English, the song meant, "Look at these flowers; please come inside our precious guests."

"Ho Bilen Metan, Ho Bilen; Emama Alu Bilen!" The men who had been helping Ato Kebede with building the tents responded with their own song. The English translation is, "We came home excited; Looking for our mother."

Confused by what was happening, Andu and Mitu started crying and stared at their mother to save them. But she had her hands full greeting the men and women that surrounded her. Attracted by the noise, the neighborhood kids flocked to Ato Kebede's house.[199]

At the hotel, Maggie and Madeline dressed in traditional clothing and blended in with the locals. They toured nearby markets shopping for antiques. The men were mostly wasted from drinking Tella and Tej. Sed switched to a locally made tequila-like drink called "Areke."

Normally secluded to provide privacy for guests, Hotel Jinka became the go-to place for strangers who wanted free drinks and others who were looking to sell their handmade products.

On the wedding day, the party started early. A large crowd gathered at the hotel. The crowd paraded uptown on foot to the bride's home. JP was in the middle, surrounded by family and friends. They danced and sang as they headed to the wedding venue.

When they approached the tents, they were met by a much louder, mostly girls, crowd coming out of the tents. It was a beautiful scene to watch. Then the bride's family greeted the guests and invited them to enter the tents. There was a staged area already arranged for everyone to sit. The wedding vow was administered by a priest. Then lunch was served and the bride's and the groom's families got to know each other.

"I have to be honest about one thing," Sed complained as everyone started preparing to return to the hotel. "I cannot walk any longer. Please leave me here with Kebede."

"No worries, Sed. I got limousines arranged." Seble assured him.

Outside of the tents, there were three limousines covered with flowers.

---

[199] Over the next few days, the house became the destination for children and young adults who wanted to party in what would become the biggest wedding the town had ever hosted. If you weren't there, you felt jealous you missed out, even if you had a good reason not to have gone.

"Now we're talking!" Sed exclaimed.

As soon as the limousines entered the hotel, Seble ordered the gates to be closed so the guests could have some privacy. The children continued to play in the garden. JP, Greg and Sed wanted to rest and left for their rooms. Maggie and Madeline also followed them. The remaining adults sat at the cafe looking out to the garden.

"It feels great to be back home with friends and family," Willie said, looking around contentedly. "I wish we could all remain here forever. Look at our children; they are at peace."

"My friend, don't let the party cloud your judgment." Kedir spilled reality on Willie's fantasy. "It's still the same old Ethiopia. It's a great place to visit, but life is too uncertain for residents. That's why I am moving my family to Atlanta at the end of the school year."

"I wish I could convince my parents to come with me to Canada. My dad refuses to leave Ethiopia." Yalem imagined how great it would be to have her entire family around her.

"Bethi and I have news." Mannie announced. "We are going to build shelter homes for orphans in Hamer."

"Woow! That is great news!" Seble cheered. "Congratulations Bethi and Mannie!"

"Guys, what about me?" Henok moaned. He had been so quiet, they almost forgot that he was still with them. "I need you to help me."

"What do you have in mind, Heni?" Willie asked.

"I would like to join a graduate school. Can you please help me?" Henok begged.

"Well, if you're serious, Heni, the president of Hawassa University is a good friend of mine. I can make a call to see what we can do." Mannie offered to help.

"That would be amazing. Please my friend, I need your help."

"Mannie, if you can take care of admission, then I will get him a place to live." Seble thought that Henok could live in one of the rooms of a ranch that she built behind her main residence in Hawassa.

The other friends also pledged to cover the tuition and cost of living. Henok was grateful and expressed his appreciation by kissing the ground in front of his friends.

"Come on Heni, that's not necessary," Seble exclaimed. "Just make sure to focus on the school and never let us down."

Henok promised to make them proud.

"Look at us!" Yalem said proudly. "Nobody expected us to be where we are today! I am proud of all of you!"

"I think we should write a book!" Mannie suggested. "Our life experience can be a valuable resource for our future generation. What do you think?"

Everyone loved the idea.[200] They brainstormed what story everyone would be willing to share, whether they should write a memoir or a reality-based fictitious story, and who would be willing to write it. The friends also agreed to plan an annual reunion and encourage their children to establish better relationships with one another.

---

[200] This is a reminder that at some point, they all loved the idea. The author takes fictitious liberty after that.

CHAPTER 15

Most people misunderstand how democracy should work. Democracy only works when everyone gets fair and equal treatment. Democracy is power, and as Uncle Ben advised Peter Parker, "With great power comes great responsibility."

When an established system disadvantages a sector of society, everyone needs to be willing to correct it. Otherwise, that system will not be sustainable. But it feels like most people are only focused on making sure that the system that governs them addresses their rights and gives them freedom and opportunity to prosper. They do not care how the same system treats others. As a result, people who tend to benefit from a system support it, while those who are negatively affected oppose it.

Because of this selfishness, the opposition will suffer until it generates enough momentum to overthrow the system and replace it with another that favors them. Then the roles reverse. The former victims turn into abusers and the used-to-be conservatives become freedom fighters.

It is human nature to take sides, favor one over another and harm those that stand on the opposite spectrum. Though this societal divide is a bigger problem in underdeveloped parts of the world, it is a major struggle in the developed nations as well.

For example in the US, up until the desegregation movement, the democratic party supported white supremacy and defended states' rights to enslave black people. As a result, the southern American states overwhelmingly supported the party. Then the party changed its ideology and decided to be a champion for the individual freedom of all people. Upset southern voters shifted their allegiance to the Republican Party.[201]

Ethiopia suffered from similar problems throughout its history. Its citizens always struggled for freedom and equality. Unfortunately, one community's struggle for freedom and equality was also motivated by hatred and jealousy toward a rival community. Every ethnic group struggled to preserve their identity and no one was interested in integrating with each other to form a new identity.

Each ethnic group understood that their ability to preserve their identity was also dependent on the inability of another group to maintain theirs. There was never a freedom movement that was truly inclusive. Every government established in that land had been racially divisive. As a result, every new regime had to demolish and reconstruct the country's entire government systems and functions. One would have to count back to ancient times to find the last time an Ethiopian government stayed in power for half a century.

So that was what made the recent leadership transitions in the country very special. Ethiopia was able to transition power peacefully on two consecutive occasions. Despite the late prime minister's overwhelming favoritism to Tigray, often alienating the Oromo and Amhara ethnic groups, power was still peacefully transferred to the caretaker prime minister who was from the Wolayita ethnic group. Subsequently, the government was able to elect the new prime minister, who was from

---

[201] The founders of this great nation understood the reality of human nature. They designed the constitution to allow flexibility and introduced checks and balances that can tip the scale toward fairness. Over the years, many sectors of the public had dealt with systemic discrimination and violent attacks. But these issues were often resolved diplomatically and the victimized communities usually received fair judgment. That continued progress toward fairness and equity is what makes America the beacon of democracy for the entire world.

Oromia, garnering strong support from a wide range of ethnic groups. Such continuity of governance created a hope that the old cycle had been broken and that the country was heading to a new era where political differences could be resolved without resorting to violence.

It had been a few weeks since Yalem's wedding in Jinka and everyone returned to their regular life. Seble was back home in Hawassa, browsing on her phone through TikTok videos while sitting on her living room sofa. She loved catching up with life in America and followed many influencers from the DC metro area. She laughed at funny videos that made stereotypical jokes about people who took the first COVID vaccine and their reactions when they were told that they would need a booster.

Then she came across an angry video of a woman that she had known from a church in Silver Spring. The woman was very upset about a war in her home region of Tigray and accused the Ethiopian government of targeting her people. Seble was aware that the federal government and the Tigray regional administration had been challenging each other and escalating tension in the country. But this was breaking news for her.

Apparently, the woman had been posting updates about a new war beginning in the region and sending divisive messages to fellow Ethiopians. It was not surprising that Seble was hearing major Ethiopian news on social media. There was always a lack of free press in Ethiopia and most breaking news reached the global audience before it got released on domestic news outlets.

The next day, the Ethiopian government confirmed that a special military operation was underway in response to an attack by the regional militia forces against federal military bases in the Tigray region. The two sides had been at an impasse regarding the political direction in the country and made a sequence of controversial moves to retaliate against each other. The unsuccessful attack was a plot by the regional administration to take control of the bases. Unfortunately, the incident forced the federal government to take immediate military action.[202]

Over the next days and weeks, the war devastated a once prosperous region and boiled over into neighboring states. Seble felt let down once again by leaders who were supposed to find ways to maintain peace and security. She had lived through two major wars and several other tribal conflicts during her childhood. When she decided to return from the US, she thought those days were gone. But she was being forced to witness another civil war between people whose differences she was not even sure she understood.

Seble cursed the leaders and everyone who supported the warring sides.[203]

She had no side in this war and refused to have anything to do with it. She was heartbroken and felt helpless watching the victims and their stories on social media.

Seble decided to move back to her old life in Washington DC.

---

[202] There is nothing more demeaning than war. People get murdered, children lose parents, women get assaulted, men die from hunger, seniors suffer from lack of medicines, plants get destroyed and animals die from drought. Everyone suffers during war. But people seem to forget this reality when everything is going well. They tend to forget that ideological differences are not worth fighting for. Some begin to crave war to defeat others with different beliefs. Once the war starts, everyone scrambles to find shelter and begs for it to stop. But they find it to be too little too late. The war will consume everything the land has produced until there is nothing left.

[203] Images from the war in northern Ethiopia showed the sad realities of civil war. There is nothing fair about war and there is no good side. Everyone who plays a role in leading people to engage in armed conflict will forever have their hands stained from the blood of the victims. Their hands will never be cleansed in this life and thereafter.

#

Almost a year after Yalem's wedding, Willie was in his Virginia home setting up his TV with wireless speakers, a PlayStation box, portable cameras and a computer. He was preparing a videoconferencing system to participate in the first annual reunion. A virtual reunion event was planned as different variants of COVID-19 continued to be a problem.

Those in the Washington DC Metro Area planned to gather in Willie's house.

Yalem's family were preparing for virtual attendance from Calgary.

Mannie's family were back in Bern getting ready as well.

Kedir had decided to postpone his plan to move his family to Atlanta, to avoid enrolling his children in a virtual school. Most public schools in America continued to operate virtually. Kedir felt virtual learning would be too complicated for his children who would also have to make many adjustments to get used to a new culture. But the family were still preparing to attend the reunion event virtually from Meki.

Henok was also excited to continue to rebuild his network with his friends. He was in Meki as Kedir invited him to celebrate the reunion with the family. Henok had been studying a master's degree program at Hawassa University. Though his addiction recovery continued to be an ongoing struggle, he was in a much better state of mind. When Seble and Walalign moved to DC, they gave him the authority to look after their property and to manage the rents and related activities.

Willie and Mannie had been collaborating for weeks on the reunion plan. They wanted to make sure the event was interactive and that there were plenty of activities for the adults and children.

"Memo! Memo is here!" Semere yelled, watching through the window as Fre stepped out of a car.

Seble also exited from the passenger side, and slammed the door. She looked mad. She and Walalign argued the entire trip about his driving skills. Thanks to the pandemic, there wasn't much traffic on the road. But Seble was uncomfortable and blamed her husband for driving like a maniac. Walalign felt like she was just complaining for no reason, like she always did. He parked the car in the driveway and stayed a few steps behind his wife.

"Auntie Seble!" Rediet and Azeb greeted her. "Did you bring us a present?"

Seble grinned. "Check the trunk!"

The kids screamed with excitement as they found a Ryan's World Treasure Box. Semere was a big DC United fan and was very happy as Fre got him a Wayne Rooney jersey.

Asmeret and Willie came out of the house and greeted the guests. It was not a bad day for the season, but the wind made it feel colder than it actually was. The adults complained it was cold and went inside. But the children did not seem to be bothered by it.

Willie warned the guests that they were being streamed live. There were cameras and speakers in the living room and kitchen. On the television, Sikeat and Monson were live showing off their piano skills. Mannie and Bethi wore cultural clothes.

"Oh my gosh! Bethi, I love your dress! Where did you get it?" Seble asked.

"You like it? My sister sent it to me from Addis Ababa," Bethi explained. Just then, Yalem logged in.

"Hello? Do you hear me? I can hear you guys." Yalem needed help to unmute herself and turn on the camera. With help from Mannie, she finally appeared on camera with Andrew and Michelle seated on her left and right. She explained that JP would be a little late for the party as he was needed at the coffee shop.

Rediet and Azeb showed off their new presents to their virtual friends. Andrew and Michelle also showcased their toy collections.

Just then, Kedir's family joined the conference. Nusredin, Jamal, Hamlet and Meriam were jealous of the toys they were watching on camera. They also presented to the screen the toys that their father recently brought them from America.

The children competed against each other to describe their toys. The adults could barely talk to each other and urged the kids to calm down.

Edilawit was the last one, arriving late. If it wasn't for her mother's nagging, she would have preferred to stay away from her parents' friends and family members. They always had something to say about her appearance, hairstyle or something like that. She had also heard some of them gossiping about her personal choices. The gossip was always focused on the things that made her different from the rest, and nothing about the great things that she had achieved, as if they were trying to make her feel like there was something wrong with her.

Mannie muted all other attendees and announced, "Okay, my dear friends and family! I know you're not done catching up with each other and I apologize. I will be brief and you will return to making noise… hahaha. I just want to announce the program. I know there is plenty of food at all of our gatherings. We will begin by serving lunch while everyone continues to mingle. Then we will have a math competition for the kids. Next, a family trivia challenge. As you know, our life story is now written down. I know you all read the manuscript and we will discuss our reviews and feedback. Finally, we will play music and let everyone drop off as they wish. Thank you for your patience, and now, back to making noise!" When the microphones were unmuted, the conference quickly got loud.

"Hi Semere, can you do this?" Nusredin yelled. He held his nose with his left hand while trying to insert the elbow of his right hand inside the opening between his left arm and chest. In turn, Semere showed off his floss dance moves. All the other kids followed with demonstrations of their talent. They continued to play while lunch was served.

Unfortunately, the internet connection at Kedir's party kept dropping out every once in a while. So they were forced to turn off their video, which helped the audio to function much better.

After lunch, Mannie and Willie took turns calling numbers in Amharic and asking the kids to repeat it in English. The children were fully engaged. Mannie and Willie switched the questions to addition and subtraction, and still the kids remained active. Then the questions moved to multiplication and division, which bored most of the children, especially the younger ones.

The adults realized they needed to change the game for the kids to stay interested in the event. The crowd asked for the trivia challenge to begin. Mannie watched the clock and explained it was a little too early according to the agenda. But he lost the argument and agreed to start the trivia.

He described the ground rules, "Okay, I would like everyone to mute their microphones. Each party house will be working on the questions as a team. Each question will have multiple choices. Please write down the answers and do not reveal yours until I finish announcing all questions. At the end, we will review the answers together." Mannie asked if everyone was ready, then he announced, "Let the game begin!"

Here are some of the trivia questions from the first Annual Reunion of The Children of Jinka.[204]

---

[204] A note from the author on these pages: these facts are current to 2021. One should update the facts if using this game after publication of this book. Besides, you should all know better. Things change all the time!

The Children of Jinka 1st Annual Reunion Trivia Questions	
What is the population of Ethiopia? = **105 million**	What is the GDP of Ethiopia? = **$111 billion**
What is the population of the US? = **330 million**	What is the GDP of the US? = **$23,315 billion**
What is the population of Canada? = **37 million**	What is the GDP of Canada? = **$1,988 billion**
What is the population of Switzerland? = **9 million**	What is the GDP of Switzerland? = **$807 billion**
How many colleges are there in Ethiopia? = **60**	How many hospitals are there in Ethiopia? = **411**
How many colleges are there in the US? = **3,982**	How many hospitals are there in the US? = **6,093**
How many colleges are there in Canada? = **436**	How many hospitals are there in Canada? = **1,300**
How many colleges are there in Switzerland? = **40**	How many hospitals are there in Switzerland? = **276**
When were diplomatic relations established between the US and Ethiopia? = **1903**	
When were diplomatic relations established between Canada and Ethiopia? = **1956**	
When were diplomatic relations established between Switzerland and Ethiopia? = **1878**	

The trivia challenge proved to be very interactive. Both the adults and children fully took part in discussions. When the results were announced, Bethi and her children won first place. The other teams accused Mannie of preparing questions from sources that his family were more familiar with.

He asked himself whether the accusations were valid, thought about it and said, "Ahhhaa! My friends, I think you guys have a point. My kids love global history and geography. I promise you that we will improve for next year."

Then he suggested that they all should collaborate in preparing the questions in the future. They also discussed ways to make future trivia challenges more entertaining, and many ideas were proposed. A fifteen-minute break was announced and everyone scrambled to use the restrooms.

When they returned from break, Mannie and Willie arranged soccer games on PlayStation online. The children in the two houses competed. Andrew and Michelle were too young to play and Kedir did not purchase the game for his children because it was too expensive in Ethiopia and required an upgrade of the home internet system. So Kedir's and Yalem's children observed.

The last item on the agenda was the discussion about the draft fictitious book that was written based on their life story.[205]

Everyone had plenty of criticism, especially of the characters representing them and the personalities that they were portrayed as having. Since the kids still occupied the videoconference, the adults took their discussion to a group chat on Viber.

One participant complained their character was portrayed as a loser when it should have been viewed as an ambitious optimist.

Another person was upset that there were too many embarrassing details about their family.

---

[205] The fact that you are holding it in your hands presumes that all concerns were properly addressed—or the author did not think they were legitimate concerns.

A third person argued the book told too many inaccurate stories about Ethiopia and portrayed it as a bad place to be born.

There were also those who felt like the book focused a little too much on the negatives, did not dig deeper into happy times and missed opportunities to expand on romantic adventures.

One particular person questioned the motive behind writing the book and whether it achieved its objective.

A person who had been listening quietly asked how the title of the book was chosen.

The author explained that the characters were intentionally modified to give them their own personalities. Some historical facts could be subject to debate, the same way every historian writes their version of events; the details usually were inconsistent, but all the stories included in this book were based on historical sources and personal experiences.

The author argued that telling the truth, even though the truth could be painful, was one of the main objectives of the book. This being a novel, of course there were fictitious events that were added to make it interesting. But the author rejected suggestions to sugar-coat reality just because reality could make some people uncomfortable.

It would be up to the readers[206] to confront weaknesses, and if the intention is to push society in a better direction and build stronger communities, take measures to make improvements.

The author asked everyone to look around and identify what they all had in common. The author reminded them that, despite their continued attempt to assimilate to the culture and identity of their new worlds, they were still strangers to their surrounding communities. Their experiences in their home country were no different; they had been

---

[206] That's you.

treated as intruders by the society that had raised them.

Everyone finally agreed with the author that their stories should be told fully by including the good and bad. The author also took notes and promised to address some of their concerns.[207]

Lastly, the author encouraged everyone to be proud of their book and the fact that their stories will live forever. After all, this was the story of *The Foreigners*.

---

[207] Let the record show that the author did as promised.

THE END